T0194111

UNCOMMON COLLECTABLES

LISA DEWAR

iUniverse, Inc.
Bloomington

UNCOMMON COLLECTABLES

iUniverse books may be ordered through booksellers or by contacting:

iUniverse
1663 Liberty Drive
Bloomington, IN 47403
www.iuniverse.com
1-800-Authors (1-800-288-4677)

ISBN: 978-1-4759-7780-6 (sc)
ISBN: 978-1-4759-7781-3 (hc)
ISBN: 978-1-4759-7782-0 (e)

Library of Congress Control Number: 2013903366

Printed in the United States of America

iUniverse rev. date: 3/7/2013

For Tania
And in memory of Jeff Noble

Thumbing your way to Vegas, dirty
And dreaming like you're outta control
Save your tears and laughter
Because this is the ride
And this is the show
Pretty Vegas, INXS

JANUARY

"How much do you think a human life is worth? You know — in dollars and cents," Scarlett asked. She was taking her time getting dressed. While her official business transaction was complete, she had one more item on the agenda. Today, instead of leaving the casino and going shopping, she needed to ask some key questions. If the man sprawled naked on the couch answered them correctly, her whole life was about to change.

"I guess it would depend on who it is. You, for instance, are worth millions. The asshole that continually parks his piece of shit Audi too close to my Bentley; I give him a value of fifty cents, tops." The man took a mouthful of sparkling wine, and his face showed that he immediately regretted it.

Scarlett remembered the days of sipping Dom Perignon after their sessions. Mionetto was no substitution. But, she knew that with his current financial situation — and if he wanted to keep using her special services — he had to make cuts somewhere. All of a sudden, the Mionetto didn't seem so harsh.

"Be serious. How much is a human life worth?" She was looking directly into his eyes.

"Okay, seriously. I remember back when I was in LA; you could get someone killed for a couple grand — maybe less if they pissed off the wrong person. In the gangs, people will do it for free to boost their street cred. In corporate America, you're probably worth whatever your life insurance policy says plus some extra, based on your sentimental value to family and friends. Where you going with this?"

"What if I could solve your problem, but there were a few casualties along the way?"

The man thought for a few minutes, alternately taking a long pull off of his smoke, and a gulp of wine. Scarlett knew that he was in a bind and would do almost anything to get his ass out of the fire; but killing people to do it? Over the five years that he had been using her services, they had become friends, of a sort. He knew that what he told her was confidential. Five thousand dollars a visit ensured it. She knew about the failing casino. She knew about the savage people that he owed money to. And, she knew that the days of five thousand dollar an hour dalliances were coming to an end. Sobering thoughts on so many levels.

"You serious? Who's going to die, and who's doing the killing?"

Scarlett told him about her plan. It was fairly simple, and there was very little risk to him. His upside was twenty million — maybe more. She knew he would be hard-pressed to find the downside. It wouldn't solve his problem completely, but it would buy him some valuable time. He didn't know the victims, and wouldn't care if they lived or died. The plan had a decent chance of success and best of all, Scarlett didn't want to get paid unless she delivered on her promises.

He took another drink, and with his free hand, grabbed a handful of breast. "You have a wicked mind. I like that in a woman. Count me in."

Scarlett leaned in to his touch and for the first time, she enjoyed his cold, clammy fingers on her skin. The man who paid handsomely for the use of her body was the final piece in the puzzle. For the past five years she had been obsessed with two things — revenge, and money. She was about to get both.

MARCH

SUNDAY

One

THE COLLECTOR, WHO SAT at a slot machine close to one of the Aria's stairwell exits, tried to look surprised as a screaming girl burst through the door onto the gaming floor. *Wow, that was fast,* he thought. He glanced at his watch. It had only been ten minutes. He hadn't expected anyone to find the dead woman for at least another twenty.

With their attention diverted for a second, or two at best, he watched as the gamblers resumed the pressing of buttons and swishing of cards on the tables. No one wanted to lose their momentum. It looked like the Aria's patrons dismissed the excitement as someone who had just beat the odds and won a big jackpot; but he knew better. The warm package held tightly under his left arm only made a slight bump under his jacket, but was a big, red flag — had anyone cared to look closely. So far, no one had bothered.

He knew that for the plan to succeed, he would have to leave the hotel as quickly as possible without being obvious; but he wanted to savor the moment just a little longer. *It was really happening.* A rush of tingling adrenaline coursed through his veins as he thought of what the warm lump under his arm promised. He felt his arousal starting, as his brain fast-forwarded to the end of the week — that was when the real fun would begin.

The Collector looked down at his finger as it pressed the play button, and noticed an eraser-head-sized drop of blood on his hand. He pulled a tissue from his right pocket and wiped the spot away. He had covered himself in the equivalent of a large lobster bib during the act. The thin plastic sheeting had then doubled as the bag that held his prize. He tried to look discrete as he checked himself for other spatter. Luckily, there was none. His clothes were clean and his jacket was full. Life was good.

Or at least it would be once he got out of the casino without being arrested.

He took the risk of lifting his head from the slot machine and scanned the area. Everyone in sight was focused on getting their next big win. The screaming woman was already long forgotten.

It still seemed like a crazy dream. Fantasy was finally becoming reality. He had the first of many perfect collectables. This one was by far the easiest, and had held the least risk that he would get caught. From this point forward, the tasks would be significantly harder. He would no longer have an assistant like he did today. He was officially on his own. However, in contrast, the payoff would be bigger…much bigger. Just another gamble in an endless string of Las Vegas wagers he had made over the years.

One more spin on the machine. Seven. Seven. Cherry. Not a winner.

He hit the cash out button and walked toward the cashier's cage — twenty in, thirty out. The money was a nice bonus, but the commemorative piece tucked away in his coat was the real reason for the grin on his face. No one was looking at him — no one cared. He looked like every other gambler in the Aria; glazed eyes from too much booze and too many hours at the slots.

He couldn't wait to leave the hotel so that he could take a good look at his prize. He was going to take more than his fair share from the casinos over the next week; but it wasn't going to be cash, like the other 99% of patrons wanted.

From this spot, it was exactly six hundred and three steps to his next victim.

Two

BY THE TIME DEVON Cartwright and his partner Holland Grant arrived on the scene, there was a full-fledged panic attack happening in the staff-only area of the casino. The two Las Vegas PD detectives were secreted into the Aria from a back entrance as soon as they arrived. In a city built on fantasy, murder wasn't considered a selling feature.

"One of our housekeeping staff found her. We left the body just as we found it, but the cleaner and a security guard walked into the stairwell and stepped in the blood. I hope that didn't contaminate the crime scene." The squirrely little man with slicked-back hair had identified himself as the on-duty manager of the hotel — nothing more, just his title — but his business card showed his name to be Mitchell Sanders.

"Hopefully not," Devon replied, as they walked through back passageways to the stairwell's entrance. He was momentarily grateful that there were so many CSI-type TV shows, even though most were a twisted version of real homicide work.

"We're going to need you to keep all of your staff out of the area while we do our initial search. We'll need to speak to the security guard and the housekeeper. There will be others joining us shortly. Please just direct them to us, and we'll take care of the rest." Devon unraveled some yellow crime scene tape and cordoned off a large section of the interior hall.

"Sorry, but this is one of the main arteries of the hotel. I can't have you blocking the staff from doing their jobs. Is that tape really necessary?" the manager asked.

Devon noticed how his tone and demeanor changed once Mitchell Sanders realized that a homicide investigation might hinder the flow of business. "Yeah, it's necessary. We'll have to do this at each and every entrance to this stairwell. We'll try to be out of your way as soon as possible; but I assume that you want us to do our job properly and catch the killer." He matched his tone to that of the manager; polite, but with an edge of annoyance, and was pleased when the man nodded and walked away.

With over a hundred murder cases under his belt, Devon expected to process the scene with his usual professionalism; wanting to respect the person who lay dead in front of him.

All of that went out the window as he caught sight of the dead woman.

"Fuck me; what the hell happened?" Devon almost gasped the words. This wasn't like anything he had seen before. He had witnessed his share of party-girls who met the wrong John, drug peddlers who cut each other up over territory, and gamblers who ended their lives once the money ran out; that was normal — this was something else entirely.

The first word that came to Devon's mind was *gruesome*, followed shortly behind by *brutal*. The woman's body looked normal, but her head....*holy shit*...the pastrami sandwich he had eaten earlier rose up in his throat. He managed to swallow hard to keep it in place. He took a few moments to compose himself before he got started on the job at hand.

Devon spoke quietly into his cell phone's voice recorder, "Female victim found lying face down in the interior service stairway at the Aria. Found wearing a black, strapless dress and black heels. Victim looks to be about five foot eight, thirty years old, and has had her entire scalp removed." As Devon spoke, Holland took pictures of the woman and the surrounding stairs, walls and ceiling from as many angles as possible.

"Someone she knows maybe? It feels personal to me. Why take her hair?" Devon asked.

Holland continued snapping pictures, knowing that he wasn't

looking for an immediate reply. "I'm going to flip her over — see if there's a purse underneath her, some kind of ID." As he moved the woman's body onto its side, the sticky pool of beet-red blood grew a little in size. Her throat had been slashed, deep and long, all the way to her spine. And where her hair should have been was reduced to a smooth, blood-covered skull.

Holland tugged at a small clutch under the body and at the same time found something even more curious. "Check this out," he said. As he spoke, he removed a small, folded paper from between the woman's breasts and unfolded it into an 8 ½ by 11 inch page. "Holy shit. This can't be good. You see that? *Divinity's Desire?* What does that mean?" Holland asked, as he passed the paper to Devon.

Nothing in Devon's homicide training or experience had prepared him for what he saw. The image on the page was a grotesque collection of body parts, painstakingly pasted together into the picture of one woman. *Divinity's Desire* was printed in Times New Roman at the bottom of the page. Devon held the paper up as Holland snapped a few shots of the image and the clutch. "Check the purse."

The blood-soaked purse contained an Aria staff ID which stated that their victim's name was Stacy Bailey. Other items included a pack of breath mints, a lipstick, a hundred dollars cash, a set of keys, and a small cell phone. Everything was bagged for transportation to the crime lab.

Holland clicked another dozen pictures and let out a long sigh. "What kind of sick bastard did this? And, what's with the picture?"

"Don't know, but it looks to me like this won't be our last vic," Devon said.

"CSU and the ME should be here soon. Let's go talk to the manager and see if he can identify our girl. I'm thinking that this is going to be a long night."

Three

WITHIN TEN MINUTES OF securing the scene and getting the crime scene unit in place, Devon and Holland had the answer that they were looking for. The victim was, as her ID had told them, an Aria cocktail waitress named Stacy Bailey, age thirty-two. She was on a two-day weekend and was scheduled to work the late shift the following day.

Devon spoke to the Aria's on-duty manager, who by this point in time was back into his regular routine of barking out orders to his staff. "Did Stacy have a husband or boyfriend that we can talk to?"

Sanders, who was still looking irritated with the whole situation, squared himself up with Devon's face as he replied, "I have no idea. I'm going to have to direct you to HR. All I can tell you is that our staff and their families have been security-checked and screened."

"We'll need to get her address and family contact information. Did she have any close friends here that we can talk to? Any regular customers that she served?"

"I'll talk to the girls and see who she was friends with," the manager replied. No mention of the customers.

Devon noticed a waitress glance nervously at the men as she walked by. The manager gave her a 'get-back-to-work' glare as he added, "Look; we're the new kid on the block. There were *billions* of dollars invested into the City Centre project, and more specifically, this hotel and casino. We really can't afford any negative publicity.

I assume that you will conduct your investigation without involving our patrons?"

This was the side of Las Vegas that Devon hated more than anything — the city was built on a façade, a sparkling, multi-colored façade of lights, sex, and indulgence. The only reason for its existence was to take money from people who believed that maybe they could beat the odds —hoping to be the rare winner in a sea of losers. Not that long ago, he had been one of them. He quickly pushed the memory from his mind. There was no point in living in the past. It was the equivalent of driving your car by looking only through the rearview mirror.

"We'll do our best not to involve anyone that doesn't need to be involved. However, I assume that you don't mind if we get your security tapes from the past twenty-four hours, and a guest list. This *is* a homicide investigation." This girl's death didn't matter one iota as long as the drinks were flowing and the cash was rolling in. Devon found it challenging to hold back his anger, but luckily the manager's face changed — he had gotten his point across.

Mitchell Sanders seemed to realize his lack of sympathy and replied in a hushed voice, "I'm sorry. I hope you understand my concerns. Of course we will assist your team in every way possible."

Four

DEVON MARCHED OFF TO talk to the Aria's Human Resource department while Holland talked to the head of hotel security to gain access to the video surveillance footage. According to HR, Stacy was single, no family in the city, and lived in an apartment on the west side. Her personnel file photo showed a woman who looked vibrant, with a full head of long, dark hair. She had been with the Aria for six months and was a model employee. The HR Manager noted that the hotel had a strict hiring policy, and Stacy's background check had nothing noteworthy, or she wouldn't have gotten the job. She had given her landlord's name as her emergency contact number.

By the time the two detectives came back to the hotel's manager, he had rounded up three women who were friends of the dead girl. They all huddled together in their black, low cut-dresses, with tears leaving trails of mascara snaking down their perfectly-powdered faces. Devon noted that the hotel was obviously selective on more than just their staff's security status. All three women were well-endowed, were stunningly beautiful, and had legs that went on forever. The more the casino dazzled its customers, the higher-end clientele that frequented their gaming floor. Devon was impressed — these girls were pretty spectacular. The talent level at his neighborhood casino was nothing in comparison. Mind you, no one at his local casino dropped more than a couple hundred in a sitting— not even a drop in the bucket to what was spent here.

Devon fell into his typical hardnosed cop routine. "I know this is difficult, but I need to ask you a few questions. Was Stacy dating anyone? Was she having any issues with any of the customers? Anything you can tell us would be helpful."

The only blond in the group spoke softly in between sobs, "She wasn't dating anyone, which was crazy, 'cuz she was such a nice girl. She used to waitress at Harrah's in Laughlin. I know that she had a messy breakup with an ex-boyfriend a few years ago, and that's why she came to Vegas. She caught the guy with another woman."

One of the brunettes spoke next. "I just saw her on Friday. I just can't believe she's gone. It doesn't make sense that someone would do this to her. I wish I would've given her a big hug the last time I saw her. I was super-swamped Friday night. I can't even remember if I said goodbye." She broke down in a torrent of tears.

"Did she mention any customers who were giving her a hard time? Was the ex back again?" Devon felt for the women, but needed to get information as quickly as possible.

The second brunette, who seemed to be in the best emotional and mental shape of all three, glanced at the two other women before she spoke. "I probably knew Stacy the best; we were pretty close. We aren't supposed to date the customers — definitely not on the property — but I think she met a guy. She called me on Saturday night and asked me if I could get her an access card."

The blond, who only a moment before was a puddle of gooey sorrow, shot her an angry look as she interrupted, "Don't do this, Cindy."

The brunette shook her head. "She was our friend. Someone killed her. You want the guy to get away with this? They're the cops, Shelley. They need to know."

The blond backed off, and the brunette continued, "Some of the staff know about a dead area where the security cameras can't see you. You can get into the service hallway and up to the guest rooms. If you "borrow" an access card from one of the housekeeping staff, you can go into one of the suites and have some fun. The only thing you have to do is clean up afterwards. Look, I know that it's not above-board, but it doesn't happen very often — just if you're really trying to impress someone."

So now they knew why she was in the hallway; next step was to find out with whom. "Did she tell you who she was trying to impress? Who she was taking to the suite?"

"She didn't say. All I know is that she went out on a date with the guy in the afternoon, and she wanted to get to know him a little better. He must have been pretty hot for her to bring him here. Otherwise she would have taken the guy back to her apartment. It's small, but it's clean. Nothing to be ashamed of."

The blond was shredding a Kleenex as she spoke, "Are you going to tell our boss about the camera thing? He already rides us all like ponies. I can't imagine what would happen if he found out that we use the suites. I really need this job. I have a kid at home."

Devon looked at the woman and weighed his options. She was just a working-class girl who would probably never be able to afford the type of luxury that the hotel's invited guests were offered. All three were probably so scared that they would be on the straight and narrow for quite a while. And word would spread among the other staff. "It will come out at some point. But, I doubt that I'll need to mention any specific names." All three women looked relieved.

Devon wrote down their names, gave each of them a business card, and listened to promises that if they thought of anything, they would call him. It was standard procedure; but he knew that the cards would be thrown away the second he walked away, and chances were, he would never hear from any of them again. *Too bad,* he thought to himself, *the talkative brunette was a hottie.*

Regrouping in the back hallway, Devon and Holland did a quick debrief. It was obvious that the Aria had some issues with in-house security; but that told them little else about who killed their victim. The ME had finally arrived, and the crime scene team was busy dusting for prints at each of the many access doors to the interior hallway, and gathering trace evidence. The pieces of the puzzle were being collected, and now it was up to Devon and Holland to put them into place. They needed a lead. There wouldn't be any sleep for the next forty-eight hours; maybe only twenty-four if they caught a break.

As they left the hotel lobby, they both grabbed barrel-sized cups of black coffee for brain fuel, compliments of Mitchell Sanders. First stop: the dead woman's apartment.

Five

"THE CHICK WAS A real knockout. Had these crazy, pale eyes. Gonna miss seeing her in the hallway." Stubby, the building manager, talked nervously as he smoothed down his greasy salt and pepper hair.

Devon turned to face him, and felt irritated having to change his focus to look at his five foot four pudgy frame and pale skin. In all the years in homicide, he had visited hundreds, maybe even thousands of apartment buildings; and almost all of them were run by a man or woman that fit Stubby's description. Each and every time, it was the same old thing — Devon's head was screaming, *Get out of my face and let me work!* But somehow, his mouth managed to say something on the polite side. Today his reply consisted of, "Thanks, but we can handle it from here. You can just shut the door behind you. We'll let you know when we're done."

Stubby looked hurt, but did as he was told.

Stacy Bailey's apartment was just as the brunette has described; tiny, but neat and clean. It was no more than six hundred square feet, but felt homey and warm.

"You take the bedroom, and I'll check out here," Holland said.

Devon was about to object, but his partner was already rooting around in the dead woman's tiny kitchen. He hated nothing more than going through victim's bedrooms. It felt like you were betraying a trust somehow by touching their most personal items without them present. He hated it, but for the past two weeks Holland was off in his own world. It wasn't worth starting a fight.

Devon spoke into his recorder, "Queen sized mattress, doesn't look like it's been slept in. Bedside table has a reading lamp, a book on Chinese dialects, and a Bible. Strange bedtime stories for a waitress. Drawer is empty. No pictures or photographs. Feels like a hospital room."

He then moved to the closet, pushing clothes from side to side, looking for any hints about their victim. "Woman was a neat freak. Work clothes hung on the right side of the closet, personal on the left. Lots of black dresses. Same as Aria waitresses. Personal side is run-of-the- mill jeans and T-shirts."

Devon moved the personal stack over, and something caught his eye at the back of the closet. He tugged at the hanger, and pulled out a Louis Vuitton handbag. It still had a forty-two hundred dollar tag on it from the designer's shop in Caesar's Palace. It looked to be more expensive than all of the rest of the closet put together. How could a waitress afford a four thousand dollar purse? The rest of her wardrobe, shoes and accessories, were fitting of a waitress' salary; but a Louis Vuitton? Was it a gift? Why hadn't she used it? Did the waitress have sticky fingers? It was bagged and tagged for future investigation, along with the Chinese dialect book.

Finally, Devon looked through the dresser drawers. He always left this part for last, as it made him the most uncomfortable. Touching someone's underwear without their permission, and without them being in it, just felt wrong; even if he was trying to solve their murder. The dresser had seven separate drawers, and each one was just as organized as the closet. He removed the perfectly-folded articles of clothing and placed them back after checking each space. "Socks, bras, panties all present. No Victoria Secret or Fredericks. Probably no sugar-daddy."

Just as Devon entered the bathroom to continue the search, Holland yelled, "Could we be so lucky? Glad this girl was organized. Check this out, partner."

Devon walked into the front room and was handed a piece of paper, handwritten with three distinct columns. At the top of each was a heading: Prince, Pauper, and Preacher. Each column was further divided into a Pro list and a Con list.

"This girl was trying to decide who to go on a date with. I betcha one of these guys is our killer." Holland was excited.

"Hate to burst your bubble, but there's no name for each of those guys, just headings. It sure as hell doesn't tell us who the Prince is, or who the Pauper and Preacher are. It also doesn't tell us who she chose as her play date."

"I get it; but at least we know who to target."

"You find a laptop anywhere?" Devon asked.

"Nope; seems strange, but maybe our girl wasn't a technology whiz. Let's canvass the neighbors to see if anyone saw who she left with on Saturday. I can feel it; we'll have this thing solved in the next twenty-four, and I'll be back home getting a foot rub from my wife. You should get married, buddy; those foot rubs sure are nice when you solve a case." Holland had been trying to get Devon married off since the day that they met each other. After seven years, the topic still found its way into the conversation at least once every two weeks.

"Hey, I'm glad that you're so optimistic; and forgive me for being a glass-half-empty kinda guy, but I wouldn't be telling Maggie to warm her hands up quite yet." The two of them laughed and split up to do the door-to-door canvass of the building.

Six

THERE WERE A TOTAL of twelve apartments on the same floor as Stacy's. Holland started at the next door to the left, and Devon went to the right. With Holland's first two attempts, he had no response. Either the inhabitants were out, or just weren't interested in opening the door to strangers. His experience after years of doing door-to-doors was that usually it was fifty-fifty. At apartment number three he heard rustling, and then the door moved open slightly, but was still held in place with a chain lock. He wanted to tell whoever was behind the door that the damn chain locks did nothing to help you if someone wanted to come in. Most were flimsy and wouldn't hold up against a teenage boy.

"What do you want?" a small voice said from behind the chain.

"Ma'am, I am Detective Grant." He held his badge up to the crack in the doorway. "Can I talk to you about one of your neighbors, Stacy Bailey?"

"I don't know her," the voice replied. Based on the height and tone of the sound, the apartment's occupant was a five foot tall woman.

"I'm just wondering if you saw her with anyone on Saturday. Maybe leaving the building together?" Holland wished that he could see who he was talking to. Her voice sounded like it had been ravaged by a lifetime of hard living and cigarettes.

"I don't like to leave the house, so I don't see much. Plus, I keep out of other people's business. If you want to get information on people, go talk to that busy-body Glenna. She lives across the hall in five-twenty-two. If you hurry, you can find her at Sam's Town. She'll be at the Fifty Lion slot machine under the Penny Way sign." She watched through the slit in the door, waiting for the detective to finish taking notes before she continued, "She won't be hard to find. She's there every day in her sparkly visor. If she's winning, she won't be home until daybreak. If she's losing, you might catch her here about two. And if you see her, tell her she still owes me six eggs from last month. I'm not made of money like she is."

"Thanks Ma'am. I'll try to remember to do that." *She's not a busy body*, he thought.

With that, the door closed tightly, and Holland heard the snap of the deadbolt. At least she had a secondary lock. He felt a little less guilty that he hadn't had the chain-lock security conversation with her.

The canvas of the building went on for another half hour, but according to those who *did* open their doors, no one had seen anything. From all accounts, Stacy had been almost invisible in the building since the day she moved in. She didn't have guests, didn't play loud music, and didn't cook anything exotic to "stink up the hallway"— in other words, she was a perfect tenant and neighbor.

Holland wondered how the neighbors had continually missed the pretty brunette in their travels. The majority of the other occupants were significantly older than the dead waitress. She should have turned a few heads over the last six months, if only with the males in the building. Something didn't seem right.

Seven

GLENNA KING WAS EASY to find on the Sam's Town casino floor. Stacy's neighbor had described her location perfectly. The slight woman, about seventy years old, was perched at a penny slot and didn't even look up when the detectives introduced themselves. They found themselves forced to talk to the light that was reflected off of her golfing visor which was covered in pink rhinestones. She continued to pound on the spin button as quickly as possible, at fifty cents a spin.

"Damn lions. You see that Frank? I lost more of your money. If you weren't so busy up there screwing Betty, I wouldn't be down here losing your hard-earned dollars. Are you happy now?" the old woman barked at the ceiling.

"Uh, Ma'am, we need to talk to you about your neighbor, Stacy Bailey." Devon didn't even know how to address the other comment that the woman had made.

"What about her?" she snapped. Still no eye contact.

"We heard from your friend in apartment five-twenty-five that you were friends with Ms. Bailey. Did you know her well?"

The reels were coming to a halt and Glenna was distracted. "See Frank? Another fifty cents down the drain. Are you happy now, you cheating jerk?"

Devon sat beside the woman at another slot game and tried to grab her attention. "Mrs. King, is there a problem here? Do you need our help with your husband? Is he in the hotel with another woman?"

Finally she turned her head away from the spinning screen and looked at the detective directly. "Don't be silly young man. Unless you have some special powers, you can't do anything. Frank isn't upstairs in the hotel; he's up in heaven...probably down in hell, actually." She turned her head to the sky again, "Right Frank? He died just so he could have sex with that floozy who lived downstairs from us. He always had a thing for her. She used to wink at him when she spoke — what kind of person does that with another woman's husband? My mother taught me that you kept that kind of thing for the bedroom. Betty died, then *KABAM,* he dies. Coincidence? I don't think so. He always wanted to have relations with her, but he couldn't do it when we were married. So he had to die to live out his little fantasy. He left me alone, and now I'm getting my revenge. I get to spend his money in here. He was a cheap Scotsman. That's why we lived in that tiny apartment. Now *I* have our savings and *his* life insurance money. I'm getting the last laugh...aren't I Frank?"

Devon looked up at Holland and had to stifle a laugh. That was a story that he was going to be telling in the squad room for the next week. It didn't help the investigation, but it was worth the drive to the off-strip casino just to hear this nut-bar of a woman speak. It was a bit sad, but a woman thinking that her husband was up in heaven, *or maybe hell*, screwing a dead neighbor...that was priceless. "I'm sorry to hear about your husband Mrs. King; but we really need to know anything you can tell us about Stacy Bailey."

Glenna held her wrinkled finger against the spin button and hit it on a regular basis while she spoke. "She works shift work at that new hotel on the strip; so I don't know her that well. We talked a few times because she likes cats and I have a big old tomboy named Walter. He's all I have left now that Frank is gone. She's a nice girl— pets Walter's head and brings over a can of tuna sometimes. Why are you asking about her?"

"She was murdered. Did you see her on the weekend? Maybe leaving her apartment with someone?"

Glenna's finger hovered over the spin button but she didn't push it down. Devon was secretly pleased that the murder had stopped the gambling rampage, if only for a moment. "Murdered? But she was such a nice girl. Walter will miss her. I saw her on Saturday. She was leaving at the same time as I was leaving for here. She was wearing a black, slinky dress. I remember because it wasn't her regular work clothes, and I asked her where she was going."

"Where did she say she was going to, Mrs. King? What time did you see her?"

"It was five o'clock for sure. That's when the cab driver picks me up every day, because I hate to be alone in the apartment at night. It's not good for a lady of my age. The casino is a much safer place for me to be after dark. They have security. Stacy told me that she was going to meet a new gentleman caller. Didn't say his name — just that she was excited, and he was her ticket out of waitressing. She even gave me a hug." She paused for a moment. "Come to think of it, that part was a bit odd — she never hugged me. Just at Christmas that one time."

"No name? Any description of the guy? Did she tell you that he was tall? Handsome? Thin? Fat? Hair color?" Devon thought back to the Pros and Cons list they had found. It was looking more and more like the best lead they had. Who was it that their victim would have picked as husband material out of the three? They needed to take a long look at the list of suitors.

Glenna didn't seem to know anything of substance, and after a few more questions, Devon and Holland thanked her, and headed back to their office to review the security tapes and get an update from the ME and CSU team. Devon took a glance back at the old woman as they left the casino floor and shook his head — she was already back to her conversation with Frank.

MONDAY

Eight

THE COLLECTOR WALTZED THROUGH the strip-side entrance of the Monte Carlo hotel with a confident swagger. The perfumed air coated his sinuses as he walked past the lobby bar toward the back of the casino. He had reviewed today's plan prior to leaving his house, and knew that it was bullet-proof. He had access to information about the casino that very few people knew about. That knowledge made him invisible, and invincible. Plus, yesterday he was a blond and clean shaven, and today he had black hair and a goatee. All part of the plan. The security cameras could record him all they wanted.

The news of his last encounter hadn't even hit the radar yet — the Aria had done well in downplaying the specifics of the suspicious death in their hallway, just as he had hoped. After today, things would change. One murder on the strip was disconcerting; but two? That was going to cause more of a panic. By the end of the week, the customers would be afraid, and the staff would be petrified. Perfect.

From this point forward, he would have to do everything by the book. No fuck-ups. The opportunity that he had been given wasn't to be taken lightly. It was like being asked to throw out the first pitch at the World Series, or being allowed to golf a round with Phil Mickelson. You can't pay for the privilege; it's offered, and you accept it graciously. As he walked through the Monte Carlo, he was filled with gratitude and excitement.

He glanced at a couple at the blackjack table. The man, in his early thirties, was playing twenty-five dollars a hand, and had a mile-high stack of chips. The woman at his side had a nice smile, but the rest of her body was a swampy mess. Nothing of interest. He wandered around for another five minutes, and then exited the casino the same way that he had entered.

His next victim could be found just outside of the back service bays of the hotel. Tons of food and liquor were transported through the doors on a daily basis; but at this time of night, there was very little traffic. The delivery crews were at home with their families, and the night shift stayed inside, except when they needed to dump garbage or have a smoke.

Five minutes later, the third door from the left opened, and the Collector watched the woman exit the building. She wasn't the most statuesque of the girls on the hotel's staff. But this time, it wasn't her body he was looking for. He watched as she brushed her long, blond hair back from her face as she looked for her ride. As soon as she spotted him, her eyes lit up. Perfect.

He leaned out of the driver's side window. "Going somewhere, pretty lady?"

"Just looking for a handsome prince to whisk me away," she replied.

The Collector got out of his car and pulled her close to him, nuzzling his face in her hair.

"Mmmmm…I missed you too." She pulled him close. It was all of a second later when she felt the prick of a needle going into her neck. Within moments, Kenalynn Markerson was laying on the ground, unable to move.

The Collector grabbed a pistol that was tucked into the back of his belt and put the silenced muzzle directly against the young woman's chest. A quiet pop was all that filled the desert air. He waited a few more seconds for her heart to stop pumping, and then got busy with the hacksaw. *Get the blade in between the first and second cervical vertebrae, and move back and forth quickly, with even pressure on the saw.* He had been given the specifics on where to cut ahead of time, and found it relatively easy to complete the task without attracting attention. It took just under a minute to remove the girl's head from the rest of her body. He grabbed a green garbage bag from his front seat, and deposited the head inside. The rest of the body was left beside the dumpster at the back of the hotel.

This time he hadn't waited around to hear the screams when the kitchen staff found her body. With Stacy it had been easy to hide her hair in a plastic bag in his coat. It was a little tougher to hide a full-sized human head.

Despite the fact that there was still a glimmer of light in the sky and there were quite a few people around on the strip, not one of them paid any attention to the man driving away from the back of the Monte Carlo. He had been told just the right time and place where he would never be caught — just a regular part of the scenery in behind the busy hotel.

His next victim was a mere three hundred steps away; but first he had to store his latest prize and work on joining the two pieces of his beautiful doll together. Tomorrow was another day, and another piece of the puzzle.

Nine

DEVON AND HOLLAND HAD spent all of Sunday night and Monday looking through the security tapes from the Aria, but didn't see anything or anyone that looked suspicious. The thousands of people who walked through the doors of the casino each and every day all started to look the same to Devon, who was fueled by a bucket-load of black coffee and a dozen sugary pastries. The Aria's hotel manager had confirmed that a guest room on the sixth floor had been accessed out of sequence with a housekeeping room card.

"Okay, what have we got?" Holland asked.

"The ME confirmed that Stacy Bailey died from the knife wound to her throat, and was killed in the hotel staircase. She had a mixture of red wine and tranquilizers in her system. She was scalped after she was dead — thank God for small miracles." Devon was reviewing the autopsy report. "CSU is running hundreds of fingerprints from the stairwell and the hotel room. It's gonna take a while before they come back with anything solid."

"According to this," Holland pointed to an email on his screen, "Three Louis Vuitton purses of the same style as the one found in Stacy's closet were purchased in the prior six-month period. Two were out-of-state residents who haven't been back to the Nevada area since, and one was sold to the owner of the Hard Rock Hotel. I got one of the admin staff to try to set up a meeting but they haven't called back yet."

Devon was reading his email as well. "CSU went through Stacy's cell records. The last call was to the waitress who set up the room access for Stacy and her unknown guest. No other calls in a month. And they say that the patchwork picture was printed from a standard inkjet printer on photo-grade paper. Nothing unusual about the paper or the ink, and there were partial fingerprints, but no match so far in the system."

"The note is cryptic, but it's the best lead we have," Holland said. He tacked it up on his whiteboard so that Devon could get a better look.

Prince		Pauper		Preacher	
Pros	Cons	Pros	Cons	Pros	Cons
Money	Player?	Handsome in a boyish way	Money	Wants to settle down	Money?
Good looking	Probably short term	Respectful	GUND	Would never cheat	Mom issues?
Private plane	No spark	Diamond in the rough?	Height	Adventurous	Workaholic
Generous	Accent	Funny Spiritual		Trustworthy	Scandal

Devon rewrote the columns on a whiteboard so that they could make notes beside each item. They both stared at Stacy's personal thought inventory, and tried to get inside the mind of the thirty-two year-old woman.

"So, which one would you pick if you were single? The good-looking guy with all the cash, the guy who's broke but makes you laugh and might be a diamond in the rough, or a preacher who wants a wife and who will never cheat on you like your last SOB boyfriend?" Devon asked.

Holland growled out his response. "Why are you asking me? I have no idea how women think. I've been married for close to six years and I *still* have no idea why someone as wonderful as my wife would ever pick a middle-aged homicide detective, who has now been out of the house for more than twenty-four hours while she's at home with our three-year-old daughter." He took a deep breath, a slug of his coffee and after a minute, apologized. "Sorry; I'm tired." After another swig he stood up and walked toward the board. "Something doesn't make sense to me on this one. Why put the word spiritual under the Pauper, when that word *should* fit under the Preacher?"

Devon ignored the outburst and moved on. "Maybe it's a given that the Preacher is spiritual? I'm wondering how the Prince is good-looking, but they have no spark?"

"No idea. And what is GUND?"

"Geographically undesirable. He lives far from her." Devon caught his partner's sideways glance. "Don't look at me like that. Who wants to date someone who lives at the other end of the city? It makes for a lot of excess driving. More convenient to find someone who lives close by."

"Okay, so we're looking for a good-looking guy who has a private plane. I assume that if the guy is rich, he wouldn't be a GUND no matter where he lived. He has an accent and acts like a playboy, or maybe has a gambling issue — the word 'player' could go either way. Bachelor number two is probably a blue-collar worker who lives at the other end of the city, has a sense of humor and is short — that one will be hard."

"Hang on a second. She didn't say that he was too short; maybe too tall? And what about if he lives in another city — not the other *end* of the city?"

"Good point. And finally, bachelor number three is a preacher who is, or was, involved in a scandal and has mommy issues? Good Lord; we are going to be here for the rest of our lives figuring that out. There are a whole lotta churches that are involved in scandal. But I kinda like this angle, because it ties in to the picture...Divinity's Desire could have a religious connection to it."

"I ran a search on Divinity's Desire but nothing comes up. The word divinity tends to have religious meanings, but the desire? Maybe a guy with a God complex?"

"Where does the book on Chinese dialects play in? One of the guys is Chinese? Or did she just have an interest in languages?"

"Wish I knew."

There wasn't an obvious connection between a prince, a pauper or a preacher and anyone who entered the hotel lobby or the casino gaming floor from Saturday at noon to Sunday at 5p.m. They were on their way out the door to once again interview Cindy, the brunette waitress who worked with their victim, when Devon's desk phone rang. He listened for a total of three seconds before he spoke.

"Oh shit."

Holland saw the look on his partner's face and immediately grabbed his jacket — they had another dead woman. "Fill me in on the way. Where are we going?"

"The Monte Carlo. They just found a girl in the back alley, shot, same computer printout in her cleavage; and this one is missing her head."

"Who *is* this guy?" Holland asked.

"I told you not to count on that foot rub," Devon replied.

Ten

THE CELL PHONE ON Sammy "Griz" Hanson's hip buzzed twice, then stopped. It was the signal that it was time for him to check in with the big boss. He excused himself from the table covered in seafood at RM's in Mandalay Bay, and left his dinner guests for the privacy of the promenade of the hotel. It was only a moment after he dialed the local number that his call was picked up.

"I heard another woman died tonight on the strip. Call Scarlett and remind her that we need press coverage on this one. We want the exploits of our guy front and center on the news starting ASAP."

Griz was pleased. Things were starting to fall into place perfectly. "Consider it done."

"How's Chet holding up? Is he ready for the fight? " the man on the other end of the line asked.

"Better than ever. You don't have to worry about anything."

"Have you told him the news yet? Does he know what he has to do?"

"Not yet. Leave Chet up to me. I can handle him."

"You'd better. This is going to make us a shitload if everything works out as planned. Don't let me down."

Griz was nodding, not that the caller on the other end of the line could see, and was about to promise that Chet *wouldn't* let him down when the line went dead. For a moment he wondered if the elaborate plan would actually pay off. There were a lot of moving parts, and so much could go wrong. Two murders was a step in the right direction. His next call was to Scarlett.

"What?" Her standard answer to his calls.

"The boss wanted me to call you to make sure that you had the press going to the Monte Carlo tonight."

"Already done. Don't bother to call me every night. You just worry about your end of the deal and leave the press coverage to me. Understand?"

"Just following orders." Griz was pissed off with her abrupt tone, but knew that she was a key component to the success of the plan. If her portion failed, then the whole house of cards would come crumbling down, and there would be casualties along the way. Maybe even his own neck in a noose. He ended with, "Call me if you need me," knowing that the woman would never need his help. In the old days, women like her were called ball-breakers, and for good reason. He ended the call and walked calmly back to the restaurant to finish his meal with the businessmen who were in Vegas to protect their own investments. They were enjoying the final bites of their meal, and were looking for Griz to make some pretty lofty promises.

He had a moment before he crossed over from the promenade to the bustling restaurant where he wondered which was more of a risk — pissing off the man who he had just talked to, or upsetting the businessmen who were stuffing their faces with seafood. In a couple of days he was going to have to let one or the other down. It was all about calculated risk. If he made the man on the phone happy, he could be an instant millionaire; if he made the businessmen happy, he would have a long and fruitful career in boxing — if he played his cards right and Chet pulled through. The second option was a higher-risk bet.

The title fight was a dream of major proportions for both Chet and Griz. After ten years of working with the young boxer, he was finally ready. So many long hours at the gym, and so much bullshit that the trainer had dealt with, as he groomed the street fighting thug into a world-class fighter. But Griz was a practical man, and he knew what the future was going to hold...it wasn't pretty. Chet was going up against Laz Butte, and the guy was good. He was one of the few men who had the charisma of Ali combined with the speed and finesse of Floyd Patterson. Chet could win this fight, but he would never be offered the big bucks from advertisers. His very colorful past would keep him just this side of the big money.

Griz' personality didn't include a big "patience" quotient. At fifty he wasn't getting any younger; and while the long-term boxing career was a safer choice, he had already sold his soul to the other man for the quick hit of immediate wealth. He was going to have to keep his promises and hope that he could get out of town before the businessmen at the table had a chance to catch up. Decision made, at least for the moment, he reminded himself that the wild card in the deck was Chet. He would have to pull through exactly as promised or the whole plan was going to disintegrate. He returned to the table, where the men were in the process of ordering a round of thirty-year-old Scotch. "Sorry for the interruption gentlemen — where were we?"

One of the men, who could only be described as a giant block of cement, with his balding head and broad shoulders, smiled at the trainer, exposing two gold eye teeth. He looked like a black modern-day Dracula, with his bloodshot eyes. "I think you were about to pick up the tab."

To most anyone, that comment wouldn't have come across as anything more than a suggestion, or maybe even a joke; but Griz knew that it was meant to show who held the dominant position in the relationship. In canine terms, the huge man had just dry-humped the trainer, and there was nothing that he could do about it. Griz was starting to second-guess his original decision on who he was going to side with, when the fight happened.

Eleven

THE SCENE AT THE Monte Carlo was considerably different than the stairwell in the Aria the day before. This time, it was a circus of gigantic proportions. The press was everywhere. Newspapers, TV and radio newscasters greeted Holland and Devon with flashes of cameras and a dozen microphones stuck in their faces.

Devon spouted the standard comment to the horde of media who were yelling questions from all angles. "Nothing to report right now." Then he heard something that stopped him in his tracks and made him turn to face the crowd.

"Is it true that this is the second dead cocktail waitress in as many days?"

The woman was asking the right question. To the best of his knowledge, the death at the Aria the night before was still under wraps. How did she know that this was victim number two?

"Where did you hear that?" he asked, with a tilt of his head.

"Is it true?" she asked.

"We are in the middle of an investigation, and we aren't in a position to discuss the details of the case right now. Miss...?"

"Mehgan Bowman, Las Vegas Sun." She held out her hand, but Devon didn't oblige her with his.

"No comment, Miss Bowman."

Devon turned away, ducking under the yellow police tape, then went directly to the Medical Examiner, who was already on site. Maureen Lamont was unbelievably good at her job; but when she was engaged with a body, there were no pleasantries exchanged — it was all business from the first second that she saw the detectives.

"She's only been dead about an hour. Gunshot wound directly to the heart. Then I'm guessing he cut through her neck with a serrated knife, but I'll have to give you the specifics once I get her on the slab and get a chance to look closely at the wound. Was she drugged like the last girl? I don't know; but I'll call once we get the tox screen back. CSU is collecting what they can, but this is a high-traffic area, so don't get your hopes up. One thing's for sure — it's the same guy. The printout in her cleavage is the same."

"Any idea who she is?" Devon asked.

"Without a head, she's going to be hard to identify; but the ID in the purse we found beside the body says her name is Kenalynn Markerson. Used to be a pretty girl, if you look at her driver's license. Twenty-seven years old and according to the staff here, she's a cocktail waitress who just got off shift about the same time that she died. Looks like our guy met her in the back of the hotel and got down to business immediately." Maureen was taking pictures, and never even looked up.

"Okay, let us know what you find. We're going inside to talk to the staff."

"I'll call as soon as I can. This guy is getting brave. It was still daylight when he killed her. How no one saw him I will never know." Maureen Lamont walked away — end of discussion.

Twelve

THE COLLECTOR WAS SAFELY at home by the time the ME and the two detectives were chatting about his handiwork. He quickly moved the severed head to the refrigerator to keep it as fresh as possible. He made himself some dinner, and prepared his work surface for the coupling of the two parts. It occurred to him as he took the roast beef, bread and mayonnaise from the top shelf, that the dismembering of the parts might be easier than the reassembly. His mother had never taught him how to sew when he was a child, and he hadn't taken Home Ec. classes in school. Worst of all, it wasn't the kind of thing that you could Google – How to sew body parts together. He wondered what the search engine would come back with if he typed it in — *'Did you mean — How to sew a dress bodice together?'* The thought made him laugh out loud.

He wanted to talk to Scarlett, but he knew that was impossible now. She had given him the recipe for success, but he could no longer ask her any questions. She said that if he followed the instructions *exactly*, he would get the prize — and oh what a prize it was! His father had told him once to dream the biggest dream possible, because dreaming was free. This one was a whopper. Once he achieved his goal, no one could ever take the success away... it would be forever imprinted on his brain.

He swiped the crumbs of sandwich from his face, and wiped the kitchen counter clean. His host was providing a very nice house for him to complete his work, and he wanted to show appreciation by keeping it as neat and tidy as possible. Some might judge him as a maniac, but he never wanted to be considered an animal — clean as you go.

With a sewing kit in hand and the counter covered in a thick, black plastic sheet, he removed the head and the hair from the fridge. He carefully removed the blond hair from the severed head with a scalpel. The woman's face was now even more visible. It was perfect. She had a perfect nose, perfect cheekbones, and a perfectly proportioned mouth.

The scalped hair, which had been in the cooler overnight, was not as pliable as he had hoped it would be. He placed the long, brown locks on top of the other girl's bare skull and almost wept with joy. It was exactly as he had imagined it would look.

The next step was to sew it into place. He threaded clear fishing line into the eye of the needle, and began to secure the hair to the remaining flesh of the second woman's head. He hummed happily to himself as he worked, and twenty minutes later he had completed the task.

He turned the head around so that he could see the woman's face, fluffed her bangs with his fingers, and decided that he was proud of his sewing skills — unless you were looking closely, you couldn't even see where he had attached the hair. He stroked the thick, dark hair and cooed quietly, "Not much longer now, beautiful." It was at that moment that he decided to give his Barbie-doll a name. It needed to be fitting of her beauty... 'Camilla' was an Italian name meaning young and virginal...perfect. "I think I'll call you Camilla. Yes, Camilla is a perfect fit for a perfect woman."

He kissed his trophy's cold lips and it sent a shiver down his spine. Just a few more days and she would be complete. The Collector moved his masterpiece back into the refrigerator to await tomorrow's addition. His skin twitched with anticipation.

Thirteen

THREE HOURS OF TALKING to the security staff, managers and waitstaff at the Monte Carlo had produced zero in the way of progress for Holland and Devon. The dead woman was a reliable worker, single, and had a young son who stayed at his grandmother's house when Kenalynn was on shift. She had been at the hotel for three years and wasn't dating anyone, though one of her friends said that she was supposed to be going on a date that evening with someone new. No names, no description, no help.

"How is this guy able to so easily get in and out of these hotels? It's like he's a damn ghost. The Strip has more security than anywhere else in Las Vegas. On top of the countless plain-clothes cops we have out here, the hotels have security everywhere; and then there's the cameras. Yet somehow our guy is slipping by all of them." Devon was shaking his head as he spoke. "This guy has to have balls the size of New York City to try and pull these murders off under that kind of scrutiny."

Holland nodded his head in agreement. "Someone has to have seen something. I guarantee you he's on the surveillance tapes; but which man is he? There's thousands of people who go in and out of the hotel every day. This is worse than a needle in a haystack. But I agree; it's like he knows where the smallest holes are in the security web. Maybe this is an inside job."

"At two different hotels?"

"Let's not forget that Stacy Bailey probably invited him to the hotel, and Kenalynn Markerson, our second vic, was going to meet someone out back of the hotel and outside of the scope of the security cameras. Her car was in the staff parking lot, in the opposite direction. Our guy knew both of these women, *and* knew where to kill them so that he wouldn't be caught on tape. I'm not convinced that anyone outside of a staff member would have that kind of knowledge."

"What about their security company?"

"Do all the hotels use the same security company?"

"Not sure, but it's worth checking out." Holland managed a small smile. It was the first one since the discovery of their first victim. It seemed that the angry outburst from earlier had dissipated once Holland heard about their second victim.

With just two phone calls, the detectives had the answer they were looking for. All of the MGM hotels on The Strip used the same security company, including the Aria and Monte Carlo. Local company Dedicated Defense won the contract three years before, and provided security services for all of the MGM group of hotels on the West side of the Las Vegas Strip. The small boutique company had been in business for the past twenty years, and boasted a 99.999% security guarantee for The Mirage, Bellagio, Aria, Monte Carlo, New York New York, Excalibur, Luxor and Mandalay Bay hotels. The only MGM property that used a different organization was the MGM itself, due to an existing contract with another organization, Protection Plus. They were set to switch over to Dedicated Defense in two years once their contract ran out. The Dedicated Defense contract was set to renew in July. By all accounts, they had done a good job; but with the current flurry of activity, the renewal could be in jeopardy.

Holland was excited. "So, let's say that Protection Plus wants the entire contract for themselves. They set it up so there are major security issues at the other hotels currently being serviced by Dedicated Defense. Protection Plus has no issues, and everyone wants to switch teams. Political pressure and a lot of bad press would make it a no-brainer."

"Do you really think that a security company would set up murders just to get a contract? Sounds like a pretty risky plan to me;

and on top of that, would their management agree to risk everything? Doesn't make sense."

"Okay, I understand your skepticism; but I'm guessing that these contracts are worth millions of dollars each year. It could make or break a business. How 'bout you humor me, and we go and have a chat with the two companies. Who knows? Maybe one of them has a Prince, a Pauper or a Preacher on the payroll."

"Always the optimist," Devon replied with a grin.

For the first time in the investigation, it seemed that there might be a light at the end of the tunnel. At a minimum, it gave them someone with a motive. It was time to go and talk to both firms, to find out who had access to the security grid information.

Fourteen

SURVEILLANCE TAPES IN HAND from Monte Carlo, Devon Cartwright and Holland Grant made a stop at their second victim's apartment. The plan was simple; go to Kenalynn's house, then back to HQ for a debrief with the Lieutenant, then off to visit the two security companies. With over twenty-four hours of straight work, both men hoped there would be time for a snack and another five or six coffees.

Kenalynn's small, upscale space was tastefully decorated in warm, neutral colors, and was spotlessly clean. Even the toys available for her son were tucked neatly away in wicker baskets on the floor. It immediately struck Holland that they still had one more stop to make after this. They had to go and tell the family that Kenalynn would no longer be coming home. By far that was the worst part of the job. The looks on their faces and the heart wrenching sobs were still difficult to take, even for seasoned veterans on the homicide squad. Despite the fact that it was supposed to be 'just work', both men tended to build connections with the families, which was probably one of the reasons that their partnership was still strong.

The two men got to work processing the apartment. It didn't take long to realize that Kenalynn Markerson was first and foremost a mother. The thought of talking to the family just got a whole lot worse.

"She was a straight and narrow kind of girl by the looks of it. How'd she meet our guy? Looks like her whole life was kid-centric.

The books, the toys. There's nothing here that says risk-taker. She doesn't seem like the kind who would chance it and bring a strange guy into her life. She was supposed to go on a date, but she would be careful to make sure he was the right guy...she trusted him. Someone she knew quite well?" Holland was leafing through the contents of the small computer desk as he spoke out loud.

"Take the computer. Maybe there'll be something on there we can use. Seems like the only thing that our two women had in common was that they worked as waitresses in the casinos. Different hotels, but the same job. Feels like maybe a stalker to me. Guy's a high roller maybe. That would fit in with what Stacy wrote. He goes to lots of casinos and knows all of the waitstaff?" Devon was rustling around in the kitchen cupboards.

"I'm kinda liking the preacher angle. Girl like this with a kid might be looking for guidance and help from up above."

"Or how about a security guy? Someone who has access to multiple casinos. I still want to look into that angle. A guard could be friendly with the waitresses. Acts non-threatening. They think he's watching their back. He knows the routines of the loading dock and when to hit."

After finding nothing of value in the house, and canvassing the neighbors with no results, the two detectives got back in the car to go and tell the family the bad news.

Fifteen

THE DRIVE BACK TO headquarters was a quiet one. Kenalynn's mother had not taken the news well; not that they had expected anything different. They had a chance to meet the little boy, who had angelic, rounded features and an outgoing personality. There were lots of tears but nothing that helped the investigation.

Back at the station house, Holland and Devon mulled over the facts in the case, staring at the whiteboard, and adding notes on their second victim. Holland had taken a two-hour nap in the staff room, but Devon had opted for a cold shower and was still going strong.

Maureen Lamont had called; the bullet used on their second victim was a hollow-point Federal Hydra-shok. By design, they were one of the most deadly. While the entry wound was small, the bullet dispersed in the body, the equivalent of running an egg beater on someone from the inside. Not only was their guy a ghost, he was an apparition who understood the benefits of good ammo. Some ballistics fanatics thought of the Hydra-shok as old school; but they were the preferred choice of many former military personnel. Devon was mulling over yet another possible pathway to the investigation when he was interrupted.

"You look like shit, partner," Holland remarked, as he came up to his desk with a fresh cup of coffee for each of them.

"I'll keep working as long as I have energy. I just want a lead — something, anything. There has to be a connection between these women."

"The casino job is the connection, and the fact that they were both single. Other than that, they were polar opposites. Kenalynn had a kid and local family. Stacy had never been married and had no one she even knew well enough to give as an emergency contact at work."

"If he's moving down the picture, our next vic is either arms or torso." Devon swirled his cup of coffee with a plastic stir stick, but didn't drink any.

"What about the eyes? Look closely at the printout. The eyes look funny to me, like maybe they were added later."

"Shit. I really don't want to have to deal with another corpse, let alone one with no eyes."

"We need to identify the outfits on the torso, arms and chest. I think the breasts are another woman, too."

"Okay, so what do we have left here? Arms, torso, breasts, eyes, and legs? Five more vics?"

Holland let out a heavy sigh. "I hate this fucking job some days."

Devon looked at his partner and could tell that something else was bothering him. He debated if he should try to get it out of him now, or wait. He decided that with his own dwindling supply of energy, the conversation could wait; but whoever was next on the killer's hit list probably couldn't. "I think I'm gonna go back to the Aria and see if I can't talk to those waitresses again. Maybe the note we found at Ms. Bailey's will jog something in their memories. Maybe something that Stacy said about the guy she met that'll connect with the note." The frustration in Devon's tone was obvious. They had nothing to go on, and based on the patchwork printout, this was going to be a daily occurrence until they got a lead.

Holland took a deep breath. "I'm going to talk with the Lieutenant. I think we need some more help on this one. I want some more staff to go and canvas the casinos. Maybe someone will recognize one of the body parts on the printout. Then I'll hit up the security companies."

Devon hated to call in for more help. It was failure with a capital F. But with a madman on the loose and lives at risk, he had to put his ego aside. He frowned but nodded his approval. "I'll be back in a couple of hours."

Sixteen

DEVON WAS LUCKY ENOUGH to have arrived just as Stacy Bailey's friend Cindy was coming on shift. He was unlucky in the fact that the same manager was also at the back of the casino floor.

"I thought we agreed that we were going to keep the unfortunate incident with our waitress quiet." The vein in the manager's head was pulsing prominently on his glowing forehead.

"*We* didn't agree to anything. I told you that based on what we understood at the time, we would try to keep things as discreet as possible," Devon replied.

"Yeah, well, since all of this nasty business hit the news today, we've had four of our high rollers cancel their trips. Do you think that's just a coincidence?"

Devon wanted to punch the guy in the head. "I really wouldn't know. I imagine they would feel a lot more comfortable staying in a hotel where their security and management works *with* the police, as opposed to working against them. Look, I just want to talk to Cindy here and ask her a couple more questions. Then I will be out of your hair...so to speak." Devon glanced up at the manager's receding hairline as he spoke the last words. It worked, and the man turned an even brighter shade of red before he walked away, swearing under his breath.

Cindy giggled. "That was fantastic. Can you hang out on all of my shifts?"

"He just irritates me. Sorry." Devon looked at the woman standing next to him and got back to business. "So, do any of these descriptions mean anything to you? We found this in Stacy's apartment, and I'm hoping that one, or all of them, might ring a bell."

The brunette studied the list closely. "She really didn't talk much about the specifics of who she was dating. I can't say that I can put a name to any of these guys specifically. What I *can* tell you is that the preacher might be the guy that hangs around the front of the hotel sometimes. But, I can't imagine why she would want to date him."

Devon's heart skipped a beat — a name to one of the men? A lead? "Who's the guy?"

"Rumor has it that he used to be an actual preacher in a church somewhere, but now he hangs around outside the casinos and tries to get people to donate to the cause — one of those street ministers. I was telling Stacy one time about how he was trying to get me to quit degrading myself and go to work at a grocery store. Can you see me at a grocery store? Minimum wage and no tips? Anyway, the guy starting quoting the bible or something, and I just walked away. Stacy told me that he wasn't that bad of a guy, that he was just doing his job just like anyone else. He might fit the description."

"Any idea what his name is or where we can find him?"

"Reverend Clark. The only way I remember that is because I used to call him Reverend Bark, 'cuz talking to me was like barking up the wrong tree. I like working here. I get to meet lots of great people, and the Aria treats me well — outside of my very obvious manager issues. Anyway, Stacy corrected me and told me that his name was Clark. He's usually wandering this side of the strip around dinnertime. Hey, should I tell the girls to stay away from him? Is he dangerous?" The waitress was looking worried.

"Don't set off any alarm bells yet. We're going to question him and see if he's seen Stacy lately. We're keeping a close eye on all the hotels, including the Aria." Devon thought that she looked a bit more comfortable, but warned her to be ultra-cautious of strangers when she left after her shift. "Any idea on the prince or the pauper she talks about?"

"Well, if there was a handsome prince in here, I would be all over him like a mouse on cheese." Cindy giggled again before she continued, "Honestly; we get lots of rich guys in here, and Stacy did work the high roller room for a few shifts when things were busy. Are they princes? I have no idea. As far as paupers go, take a group of any ten people, and probably at least three of them would fit into that category. I don't think I can be much help with those two. Sorry."

Devon thanked her and reminded her to call if she remembered anything else. He found himself eyeing her up as potential date material as well. He cursed himself mentally and moved on. Once the case was over, he was going to have to find himself a girlfriend. He had never been against the idea of marriage, but he liked his women smart, and wanted someone who could hold her own. Sure he had dated lots of pretty women over the years; but none of them lasted more than a month. He had toyed with the idea of an online dating service, but didn't want to take the inevitable ribbing in the station house. Holland's wife Maggie had mentioned a friend once...with his hormones out of control, he thought he might give love another try.

Seventeen

BY THE TIME DEVON got back to headquarters, Holland had already spoken to management at both the Dedicated Defense and Protection Plus security companies.

"These guys are adamant that no one in their organizations could possibly be involved in the murders. They both insist that their staff are the best in the business, and have been checked five ways to Sunday before they get hired. Neither company is willing to give us a list of their staff members without a court order. They say that by giving out a list of their employees, we would be putting the safety of everyone who works, gambles, or stays in the casinos at risk. I tried to explain that the list would stay with us, but they aren't backing down. And, the fact that we have two murders in their customer's hotels doesn't qualify, according to the DA. We're out of luck for the moment."

"Shit. How does us having a list of employees risk anyone's safety? I don't get it."

"Both CEOs said essentially the same thing, 'If our undercover employees are identified, they won't be able to do their jobs with the anonymity that the role requires'. Can you believe that crap? It's not like we're going to plaster their photographs on the five o'clock news." Holland was pissed off, and it showed.

"Did you push them about the contracts? Any word on what each hotel pays them?"

"The official word from both organizations was that they don't give out the specifics of their financials. But I caught one of the employees in the parking lot, and he told me that each hotel pays in the multi-million dollar range. Times that by the number of hotels, and that's a pretty big motive."

Devon thought for a moment. "Let's keep that one in our back pocket for the time being. We have a bit of a lead." Devon filled Holland in on the conversation that he had with the waitress from the Aria. "It's not much, but based on the fact that we have nothing better, I'm willing to take the drive to go and visit Reverend Clark."

On the drive to the east-side residence, the two detectives went through the limited amount of information they had to date. "Lamont says that the women are being found right after they're killed; so our guy is close by when we get there. I want to set up extra security at the remaining MGM hotels. Maybe we can catch him on video. Or better yet, we catch when he's getting ready to remove a body part — before he hurts anyone." Holland was grasping at the thin hope that they had a line on the killer's next move.

"I disagree. We are all of a sudden making the assumption that our guy is only going to target women from that hotel group. There are another dozen or more big non-MGM hotels on the Strip that could be our next kill site. I don't want to get tunnel vision and think that the security company angle is our only one. This could happen at Harrah's next, for all we know."

"But our first two victims were killed and left in MGM hotels. There has to be a connection."

"You willing to risk some poor girl's life on that? We need to alert all of the hotels and lend them a few of our guys as backup." Devon knew that his partner disagreed with the thought process — his silence said it all. "Look, we both want to get this guy; but I'm not convinced that we have anything concrete. Two kills doesn't really make much of a pattern."

Holland took his eyes from the road just long enough to scowl at his partner. "I don't want to wait for more dead women who are missing body parts to establish one."

Eighteen

REVEREND EARL WESLEY CLARK had made it his personal mission to try to enlighten the masses. Whether it was from the pulpit of the Southern Baptist Church on 50th and 12th where he used to preach, or on the street corner where he spoke now, he was always on the lookout for those who needed his guidance. There were so many lost sheep that needed a shepherd, and he wanted to be their man.

Then thoughts of the Strip would invade his mind. The Godless creatures littered the streets ten-deep. Church Bingos were one thing; but the hedonistic lifestyle being promoted on that four-mile stretch of land was simply unacceptable. He knew that if he could just get one percent of what the tourists spent chasing the big win, he'd be able to spread the Lord's word from Las Vegas to New York and still have money left over for one heck of a church social. And then there were the women — selling their bodies and their souls to the highest bidder. They had no respect for themselves. The Bible clearly states God's teachings in I Corinthians 6:13: "…Yet the body is not for immorality, but for the Lord, and the Lord is for the body." Words to live by, in his humble opinion.

His current mission was to work with the waitresses, the showgirls, and the hookers, to get them back on the straight and narrow. All he wanted was to show them that if they believed, God would give them back their self-respect, and they could be whole again. It wasn't too late to change.

He watched the news and was excited that there was so much

coverage of the two murders on the Strip. Maybe now the women would start to listen to him. Maybe now they would see that they were putting themselves at risk every day. And not just in a physical way, but spiritually as well. His plan was in motion, but he wondered if it was good enough to kick start the moral conscience of the city of Las Vegas. He just wanted to start a spiritual revolution. To get people to realize that it wasn't just their money they were wasting; it was their eternal souls. If all worked well, he would have his parish back, and it would be bigger and better than ever. The scandal would be forgotten, they would respect him again, and he would finally get the accolades that he deserved.

He glanced at the clock. Ten forty five. It was almost time for his guest. It would help clear his head. That and prayer. Maybe he could find the answers that he needed tonight. Maybe God would come to him, take his hand, and lead him down a righteous path. Or maybe it would just be the same as other nights, when he went on instinct, following the scriptures in his heart.

When the knock came on his door, he knew he was mere moments away from a greater connection with God. He opened the door quickly and without looking up said, "Come in. I was starting to think you were going to be late." He was expecting someone very different than the two homicide detectives on his front porch.

"Detectives Cartwright and Grant." Holland flashed his badge as he walked through the doorway and into the small, eight hundred square foot house.

The Reverend, who at six foot two and two hundred thirty pounds took up a large space in the small home, looked up, and his face went ashen. "I...I...sorry detectives. I was expectin' someone else." *Someone who would take me to a place far better than here,* he added in his head. "What can I do for you all?" The Southern drawl that he had tried to minimize for his whole life was coming out, as were the beads of sweat on his brow. He wiped his face with a handkerchief, despite that fact that at this time in March the weather barely got up over seventy-two degrees.

"We'd like to talk to you about your relationship with Stacy Bailey. I understand that you've been speaking with her lately. When was the last time you saw her?" Holland asked, as he shut the door.

Reverend Clark's eyes darted back and forth from his watch to the detectives. Precious time was being wasted. If his connection saw a cop car out front, he would never come up to get his next set of instructions. This was the worst case scenario for today's part of the plan. "I don't know anyone by that name, my son."

Holland walked out of the foyer and into the small living room, where a large cross was the only piece of art, hung over a three-seater beige couch. The house was sparsely decorated, but a bible sat prominently on the coffee table, as did two wine glasses and a bottle of cheap red. He turned back to face the Reverend and pulled out a picture of the waitress. "Does this help your memory?"

Clark's face turned white, and he turned away from the photograph. "She's the woman who was murdered a couple nights ago. I saw her face on the news last night. Tragic loss."

"We were told that you've made it your personal mission to try to get the waitresses on the Strip to change their lives. Maybe get a new vocation. Was she one of them?" Holland asked.

Clark couldn't take his eyes off of Devon, who was wandering around the small space, leafing through his bible and admiring his wine bottle. *Stop touching my things.* If the detective opened the drawer just inches from his hand it would all be over.

"In all honesty, I don't remember her specifically, though I do talk to the waitresses. There are so many who could earn their living in a more respectful fashion. She mighta been one of them." His accent grew along with his anxiety level. This was not the way the night was supposed to unfold.

"Funny you say that Reverend; we have a witness that saw you with her, and we have video surveillance that shows you speaking to her the day before she was murdered," Holland bluffed. "You want to tell us what you were talking to her about?"

Reverend Clark knew that his anxiety was starting to show, and he was dangerously close to passing out. Time for a new tactic…time to get mad. "No, ah don't. Y'all come in my house and ask me about some dead waitress, which ah told you ah don't know. Now y'all tell me that you have video of me with her. What am ah, some kinda suspect or something?" He glanced at his watch again, and calmed slightly. "I have a parishioner comin' over soon, and I need you to leave me be." The accent had subsided with those last words, but his heart was pumping fast.

"It's all about perception, Reverend. You were with her the day before she died. You understand that we're just doing our jobs," Devon said.

"Yeah, well, an elevator smells very different to a midget, don't it son. Obviously you got your heads in the wrong place."

"Do you want to finish this conversation downtown?"

"No sir, I do not."

"What about Kenalynn Markerson. Did you talk to her too?" Devon asked.

The Reverend's face contorted to a bitter-beer squint. "Unless you are chargin' me with somethin', y'all can get out now." Reverend Clark reached behind Holland and opened the front door.

He watched as the detectives gave each other the nod that said it was time to go. "Thanks for your time Reverend; we'll be in touch."

Nineteen

"Arrogant prick. That guy is hiding something for sure," Devon said.

"I know it; but we don't even have proof that he saw either girl before they were killed. We need to get some solid evidence before we can pull him in. Let's get someone to watch his house tonight. Maybe we can rule him out as a suspect."

Holland called in and was told that there would be an unmarked car there as soon as possible. Had they known that the Lieutenant's mood was going to change so dramatically during the twenty-minute drive back to the station house, they might have turned around.

As soon as they walked in the door, the face of the front desk constable said it all. The shit was hitting the fan. "The Lieu wants to see you in his office. Better go quick. He has a visitor," she said.

No eye contact — not good. Devon knew that when co-workers stopped looking at you, things were about to get really bad.

"Lieutenant, you wanted to see us?" Holland was the first one through the door. His relationship with his superior was the better of the two. Devon had rubbed the man the wrong way five years prior on a case where Cartwright had been accused of tampering with evidence. The whole thing was bogus and Internal Affairs had cleared him; but Lieutenant Harvey Miller had a long memory, and was not one to easily forget someone who made his department look bad.

"Mayor Norman, these are Detectives Holland Grant and Devon

Cartwright." One look at the Mayor's face, and no one extended their hands. "Detectives, Mayor Norman is here because he's very concerned about the murders of the two women in our city, and wants to get a personal update on where we are at with the investigation." Harvey Miller was staring at the two with an intensity that could start a brush fire. Having the mayor take a personal interest in the case meant that they would have even more pressure on an already explosive situation.

"Sir, we are doing everything we can to get someone into custody. We've added more people to our team, and we're following every possible lead," Holland said.

"Thanks for the lip service Detective Grant. What I want to know is, how close are you to fixing this issue? This is *not* the week to have a string of murders. I'm sure that you're aware of how many business conferences are here on any given day in our city — in case you need a reminder, currently there are dozens, including one of the biggest fashion exhibits in our history. *And*, we have the added media exposure for NASCAR this weekend, and a heavy weight title match."

Devon was going to interject but the Mayor continued his rant, "Then let's talk about the countless celebrity concerts and appearances. This shit is all over the news and is going viral on the Internet. I can't tell you how many people have phoned me today, expressing their concern about holding their events in our city, when we have a serial murderer on the loose. NASCAR alone brings us close to two hundred million over the weekend. And let's add in that we're trying to get them to give us an additional race each year."

Mayor Norman's face was stone cold. Devon knew that he had won the election handily for the past two terms, and wasn't about to have the police department tarnish his squeaky-clean image.

He turned back to Lieutenant Miller and gave him some advice, "Don't just add a few more people to this Miller; I want every available person on this case. I mean *everyone*. And I hereby officially give you as much budget as you want for overtime pay. Don't you dare use that as an excuse."

With a parting glare of fire for each of the detectives, the Mayor and the Lieutenant exited from Miller's office and walked toward the precinct elevator. Holland and Devon stayed put, knowing that while the conversation with Mayor Norman might be over, the one with their boss was just beginning.

When Miller returned to his office, he looked beaten down. "Shit, who *is* this guy?" He sat behind his desk and ran his fingers through what was left of his thinning hair. "What do we know? Give me everything."

Devon took the lead on the status update of the investigation — whatever he said at this point couldn't really make things between them any worse. "We have a potential suspect and a soft lead, but not much more than that." Devon continued with the entire update, from the minute they were in the Aria, to their suspicions about the security company, to their last visit with the Reverend. Miller didn't look impressed with their progress.

"So you're telling me that we have a nervous preacher who might tie back to a note left in the first vic's apartment. There are two other suspects who we haven't identified — one's a prince, and one's some asshole with no money. We can't tie our two vics together at all, and we probably only have a few more hours until the next murder. Get in the WAR room and gather every breathing person in the office. I want a solid plan in the next hour as to how you are going to use those extra sets of hands. Now get going before all of us find ourselves looking for new jobs."

Twenty

WHEN DEVON AND HOLLAND walked into the WAR room, the walls were bare. The room could hold thirty people comfortably, was equipped with an overhead projector, and almost every vertical surface was covered in whiteboard space. Most often it was used for in-house seminars or staff meetings; but its real purpose was for days like today, when a large team of the force needed to collaborate on one case. The last time the room saw this much action was three months before, when vice set up a multi-week sting on Trick-Rolls, hookers who ripped off their Johns. Once the main pimp had been taken into custody, along with twenty prostitutes and an equal number of their customers, the room had remained relatively empty. Until now.

It took all of ten minutes for the outlying offices to be cleared and the WAR room to fill to capacity. In no time, it was standing room only. Everyone was waiting for their instructions.

The buzz in the room was so loud that Holland had to do a two-fingered whistle to allow Devon to be heard. "Okay, guys. As you all know, we have a killer on the loose, and we are fully expecting him to kill again within a few hours."

Devon updated the roomful of officers with every scrap of information that they had to date. It wasn't much to go on, but as his dad used to say, 'Many hands make light work'. And the more staff that were looking for the killer, the more likely they were to save the next woman.

They split up the team as quickly as possible. Some were sent to the Aria, some to the Monte Carlo. Their mandate was to re-canvass the staff and see if there was any connection to the Reverend. Another team was sent to the outlying hotels to see if anyone could identify the outfits in the printout —there were over twenty to cover. Other officers were dispatched to the public and private airports to find out who had flown in on a private jet recently. Maybe the Prince would be easy to identify.

As people left to complete their jobs, more poured in and were given other duties. Some were kept in the precinct looking at surveillance tapes. Others were tasked with tracking down the connection between the two dead women. Everyone was given only one command — get your job done and report back as quickly as possible.

While the criminals were unaware of it, for the next few hours the streets of Las Vegas were very vulnerable. Every officer from vice to traffic cops was focused on only one thing — find the guy who was killing the Strip's women. The pimps, the gangbangers and the petty criminals would be safe tonight.

Twenty-One

DEVON AND HOLLAND UPDATED their boss and took a few moments to grab a bite to eat. Across the street from the precinct there was a greasy spoon restaurant that stayed open twenty-four hours to accommodate the hungry shift workers. They served egg sandwiches and donuts in the morning, hearty soups and sandwiches in the afternoon and homemade hot meals in the evenings. The detectives grabbed two of the hot chicken pot pie specials to go, and two more barrels of coffee. Holland also picked up a couple of chocolate bars for a quick burst of energy when the inevitable blood sugar crash hit them.

"You need to call home?" Devon asked, as they were eating their late-night dinners.

"I called a while ago. Maggie's not pleased."

"Hey, I can take over for a while; we're just waiting for the intel to get back now. You go home and sleep for a couple of hours. I'm going to call that reporter; see how she knew about the first vic. I can handle that without you."

Holland's face looked hollow and tired. "She wants another kid."

Devon was confused. "Huh? Who does?"

"Maggie does."

"Well, congrats then. When this case is over, you can spend a few hours practicing to make a baby. That's always been the best part — for me, anyway." Devon grinned.

His partner didn't smile back. "I don't know if I can do it. Look at me; I haven't been home in two days. I have a wife at home taking care of a kid already. I can't really expect her to take care of two by herself. I don't want to be like my old man was."

Holland had spoken only once to Devon about his absentee father. He had been a cop as well and, back in the heyday of the Vegas mob, was decorated for his many collars of high-profile gangsters. His father had taught him the value of hard work; but with so many hours on the job, he had divulged little else about growing up to be a man. As a second-generation police officer, Holland had always said that he wanted more for his kids.

"You're doing the best you can. It's not every day that we have to work forty-eight straight."

"But it happens more than it should. I'm thinking about asking for a transfer out of homicide. Maybe they'll find me a desk job or something. It's been seven years of this. Who knows what will happen if I do seven more. Will my kids know me? Will Maggie know me?"

Devon was shocked; he never thought that the successful detective would even contemplate a move down the ladder. Plus, they worked so well together. They could finish each other's sentences and thoughts. It would be a huge loss to him personally, and an even bigger loss to the department. "You're just tired, buddy. Go home for a couple of hours. I'll keep things under control here."

Holland took his last bite of the hot, flaky pie and shook his head. "I'm just gonna lay down in the staff room for a couple hours. I'm seeing double. Thanks."

"No problem. Like I said, I'm going to call that reporter and see what I can find out. I'll wake you up in a few hours." Despite his lack of sleep, Devon was still feeling pretty good. He promised himself a few hours of shuteye as well — after his chat with the reporter. He had the personality of a pit-bull once he got on a hot case...it was his strength and his downfall, all wrapped up in one.

As Holland walked to the back staff room to lie down on a cot, Devon wondered how much he could trust his partner to finish the job. He was worried that the family pressures and decisions might mess with his brain. He had seen it too many times with other detectives in LVPD — once they had some family challenges, be it marriage problems, a sick kid, or even an ailing parent; their work suffered. All the more reason to stay single.

He rustled through his pocket and found his notepad. The reporter had said she was from the Las Vegas Sun, and her name was Mehgan. He insisted that the front desk of the newspaper connect him to her home phone number. She probably wasn't going to be happy about getting a phone call this late, but he didn't really care.

Twenty-Two

IMMEDIATELY AFTER THE DETECTIVES had left, Reverend Earl Wesley Clark blotted his brow with a handkerchief and grabbed his phone. He knew the number by heart. "Don't come here. I'll meet you at our usual place in an hour." He hung up and wondered how badly his last guests were going to screw up his night. He looked up to the ceiling and said a short prayer before he packed a small suitcase — it might be a few days until he could return home.

The interview with the police had not gone well. He came off looking guilty as sin. He had provided spiritual counseling to a cop once, and knew how their suspicious minds worked. The man had given him countless tidbits of interesting information about how the force tracked and apprehended suspects. It was one of these tiny pieces of knowledge during casual conversation that was about to help him out.

He pulled out of his driveway in his Toyota Camry and looked behind him to see if anyone was following. He immediately saw headlights come on three houses down. He drove down his street and made a quick right turn; so did the headlights. The car stayed a few lengths back, but he knew who it was. He made another right and then a left. The headlights followed. His next stop was an easy choice.

The Reverend pulled into the In and Out Burger parking lot one block off of Las Vegas Boulevard and went up to the counter.

"Fries and a Coke, please."

Two minutes later, with his breadbox-sized order of fries, he sat at a table close to the front door — he wanted them to see him. He munched on the salty potatoes and watched to see if the headlights had showed up. It didn't take long to spot the undercover cop in the unmarked car.

He looked at his watch. Time was ticking away. He needed to act…now.

With the majority of his meal remaining, he wandered toward the bathroom in the back corner of the restaurant. He passed by a few late-night revelers and a couple of teenaged Latino lovers smooching in the back corner. He took a right turn before the bathrooms, and wandered through the kitchen to the back service entrance. Two of the cooks in the back yelled at him to get out. He did just that.

Abandoning his car at the front of the building, Reverend Clark walked calmly across the street and into the night. Once he was safely out of the line of sight of the restaurant parking lot, he made a call on his cell phone. Five minutes later, a car showed up to retrieve him from the side of the road.

"Get in, old man," the female driver said to him. "What're you doing wandering around at night by yourself?"

"Car issues. I'll get a towing company to pick it up tomorrow."

"Why didn't you just stay at the burger joint? I would have met you there."

"Too many scary people," he lied. Then he added, "You, on the other hand, have the most beautiful eyes."

Twenty-Three

THE NEWS REPORTER WAS awake and watching late-night TV when Devon called. "I thought you had no comment for me yesterday," she cooed into the phone.

"Yeah, well, I still don't have a comment — only questions," Devon replied.

"Oh, now, you know it doesn't work that way. I'll show you mine if you show me yours." Mehgan had thought that she caught a little spark of electricity from him when they had met the day before, and wasn't above using her femininity to her advantage.

"How did you know that the murder at the Monte Carlo was the second? At the time, that wasn't public knowledge."

"Tell me about the first victim. Where was she found? How was she killed?"

"Look, I don't want to play games with you, Miss Bowman. I need answers and I need them now. Just tell me how you knew."

"I'm not into games either Detective Cartwright. I'm more than willing to give you information, but not without something in return." Her voice was strong and commanding. She wasn't going to give up her source without some sort of payment.

"I'll meet you in person and we can talk about a business transaction. I want to see your face to make sure you're giving me the straight goods," Devon said.

Mehgan gave him her home address. It was twenty-five minutes later that he showed up at her door.

The reporter opened the door wearing her sweat pants and a T-shirt, her blonde hair gathered up in a ponytail. "What took you so long?" she joked.

Devon moved into the house and sat down on the couch without being invited in. "Tell me what you know."

"Let's get this straight right now. I will share my information with you, and you in turn will give me an exclusive on everything that you learn. Deal?" She sat down in a dark-colored wingback chair beside him and waited for an answer.

"You tell me what you know, and I'll give you information when I can. That doesn't mean that you can go around broadcasting whatever you want, whenever you want. I get to control what is printed. You can't use my name, and under no circumstances can you elude to the fact that you are working *with* the police department."

Mehgan considered her options for a moment or two. Insider in the investigation – every reporter's wet dream. As long as she kept the information flowing on her end, she was going to have a long relationship with the LVPD.

"You've got yourself a deal." She held out her hand to seal the agreement.

The detective hesitated, but shook her hand. "Now, how did you know about the first murder?"

"A woman phoned me and told me."

TUESDAY

Twenty-Four

THE CALL CAME IN to HQ at about seven in the morning. The latest victim's name was Barb Goldfinch, and she was lying on the Luxor's casino floor just outside the Starbucks by the west tower elevators.

When Devon and Holland arrived on scene, the ME was already in place, the Crime Scene Unit was on site and the level of sheer panic in the hotel was at a critical mass.

"From what we can tell, at the time of the attack, this area held a string of people twenty deep waiting for their morning cup of coffee. It's the one and only area of the casino floor that has a direct opening to the guest rooms above. The first drops of blood hit a hotel guest on the shoulder as she was walking toward the queue. When she looked up to see what had happened, the body fell from either the third or fourth floor. CSU is up there checking out which one right now. The computer printout was in between her breasts, just like the others. It's been bagged and sent for analysis. She's a Luxor waitress. Still in her blue dress when he mutilated her." Maureen Lamont was, as expected, in full work mode; but Devon could tell that she was shaken.

"Did I hear right — our vic is alive? Why did you get called out?" Devon was ecstatic. Maybe, just maybe, it would result in an arrest.

"The responding officer just assumed…I had about two minutes with her when I realized she was still alive. She's in critical condition. She's taken a bullet to the chest, but we think that as our guy was killing her, something might have spooked him. He missed her heart and didn't have time to take a second shot. But the sick bastard still found time to take her eyes. She's on her way to Valley Medical, but I'm not sure if she's going to make it. She's lost a lot of blood."

Holland looked at Devon, and without speaking, the two knew their next moves. Holland was on his way to the hospital, and Devon was staying behind to process the hotel guests and staff. The difference was that this time, they had a team of people to help.

The entire corner of the Luxor's casino was eerily silent. The slots were still, and the chairs at the machines were full of potential witnesses, none of which were pressing buttons, inserting money or cheering over a big win. Many of them were crying, or holding on to loved-ones for support. A young Starbucks employee in her green apron offered the witnesses free coffee, compliments of the hotel manager. Most took her up on the offer. If it wasn't a crime scene, it would have made a great marketing piece for the popular chain — everyone with a white and green cup in their hands.

Devon and team talked to small groups of the guests and asked all the standard questions. What did you see? What did you hear? Did you notice anything unusual or anyone strange? The answers were all the same. No one saw or heard anything until the screaming started when the body hit the floor, and then it was all-out bedlam. In the world of casinos, where by design the carpets are so bold that you have to look up and the ceilings are so boring you have to look down, it wasn't a complete shock that no one was paying attention to the one small area above where the body had fallen from.

Leaving the remaining team members to get names and contact details from the witnesses, Devon walked under the yellow police tape and was immediately grabbed by the arm. He swung around and almost clocked Mehgan Bowman in the face with his fist.

"I need to talk to you in private."

"It's not a good time," he growled at her. "And by the way, never grab me again unless you want a fist upside the head."

"Look, asshole. I got another phone call. I thought you might be interested in hearing about it." The reporter looked pissed off, but had a slight look of disappointment as well.

Devon grunted and pushed his way through a slew of other reporters. No cameramen had been allowed inside the Luxor's Egyptian-themed walls for security reasons. He imagined that they wanted to keep the other reporters out too; but in the melee, had failed to do so. Mehgan followed him into the Cat House bar a few yards away. The popular night club was being used as a makeshift meeting space for the team.

"When did you get the call? What did she say?"

The reporter explained about the mysterious woman caller who had contacted her less than an hour before. The woman always seemed to be one step ahead of the police. She knew too much, and had her information much too early to be ignored. The two big questions — who was she? And how was she involved?

"She said that the guy's not picking them at random. He knows them somehow. She told me he had hit the Luxor tonight."

"What time did you get the call?"

"Thirty-ish minutes ago. I came right here."

"Bastard has an accomplice? What was the caller ID?" Devon had asked her to track the numbers that showed up on her cell phone. The team back at headquarters would run them down.

"Same number as before. Hey, and I'm not sure that she's in on this. She sounded really scared."

They had already run the number that Mehgan had given him from the first call. It was a prepaid cell with a local 702 area code, and wasn't traceable to a specific person. There was a team of people that were going to track down where the cell was purchased, but they had to wait for the manufacturer to provide the specifics; and so far, they hadn't phoned back with information on the serial number. "Did you bother to ask her how she got her information?" Devon's tone was condescending, and he knew it.

"Of course I asked. She hung up, you arrogant idiot. Quit treating me like I'm a stupid kid, or I won't bother to tell you anything at all."

Despite how much he was coming to dislike the woman, she was right. She was the only source of a credible lead at this point, and he couldn't take the chance of alienating her. He looked her in the eyes, and for a moment thought that he saw a childlike hurt. Maybe he was coming on a little too strong. "I'll call you in an hour. We'll meet for coffee outside of this mess and we can talk more. Okay?" He didn't wait for her to answer. His cell phone buzzed on his hip as he ushered her out of the Cat House and into the slot area of the hotel so that he could take his partner's call.

Twenty-Five

HOLLAND WASN'T CALLING WITH good news. Their victim, Barb Goldfinch, was in surgery to remove a slug from her chest. In addition, she was having surgery on her empty eye sockets. Their guy hadn't been gentle as he removed her eyeballs from her head. The cuts were jagged and deep. It was a miracle that she was alive.

"He used a Federal Hydra-shok bullet, same as our last vic. Lucky for Ms. Goldfinch, they aren't as effective when they go through thick cloth. In Barb's case, she was wearing a padded bra. The hollow-point of the bullet got clogged and didn't disperse properly. The internal damage was a lot less than it was in the previous murder." Holland said.

"When can we talk to her?" Devon asked.

"The doc says, at best, we might be able to speak with her in a day or two. The surgery was a hard one. The bullet pierced a lung and was lodged so close to her heart that every move they made was putting her life in jeopardy."

"Damn it. I'll meet you at HQ when I wrap up here."

Devon finished dispatching the onsite team to all areas of the Luxor. Some were sent to security, some were sent to the front desk to get a list of guests, others were up on the third and fourth floors looking for potential witnesses. The crime scene people were already swamped trying to decipher the evidence from the previous two murders, and now they had a third crime scene to add to their workload. It was a complete and utter chaotic mess.

A half hour later they were back in the packed WAR room, sifting through the first pieces of information gathered by all of the remote teams.

The team that had gone to McCarran, the North Las Vegas Airport and Henderson's Airport had come back with a list of thirty privately held jets that had been in the vicinity during the murders. A total of sixty officers had been sent out to track down the owners of the planes and to try and determine their whereabouts during each of the deaths.

Other teams were coming in with lists of hotel guests from all areas both on and off Strip that were in the city during the last week. There were literally thousands of people to track down and eliminate as suspects. The Aria had four thousand rooms, the Monte Carlo boasted three thousand and the Luxor had another forty-four hundred —almost twelve thousand rooms, with multiple people staying in each — an overwhelming amount of work was on their plates.

Security camera evidence was even more difficult to digest due to the huge volume of people going in and out of the hotels. It was probably the busiest week in the entire year for events, and the NASCAR people were already starting to show up early for the big show on Sunday. The streets and the hotels were packed.

News of the third murder was hitting the airwaves, and there was a low buzz in the city that was starting to gain momentum. It wouldn't be long until the entire city was on high alert. And worst of all, the team that was tailing the Reverend had lost him almost immediately, and hadn't been able to find him again. His abandoned car was still at the In and Out Burger on Tropicana Avenue.

"The CSU team just got finished at Barb's house. She lived in Henderson. The boyfriend works nights and has an alibi. He's pretty shook up from what I understand, and is camped out at the hospital. This is our first vic that was involved with someone." Holland had a few days of growth on his face and was looking like he was the walking dead, despite a few hours of sleep the night before on the staff room cot.

Devon had filled in the team on what the reporter had told him regarding the anonymous woman caller. "What's he doing? Building a perfect woman for God? Divinity's Desire...a reference to religion and what God wants? Or is it that, like the good Reverend said, the women could be doing more "respectable" jobs, so our guy is showing them the consequences of their actions? The *Divine* has a *desire* for them to die if they don't change?"

"Maybe it has nothing to do with the preacher. What if our guy is just a wacko who likes to kill women? Maybe he's like that guy in *Silence of the Lambs* and he's building a woman suit for himself to wear. Maybe he's a woman lover instead of a woman hater," Holland suggested.

"He's been scorned by women, and I seriously doubt that he's like the character from the movie. Plus, the sicko in the *Silence of the Lambs* movie was a compilation of many real life serial killers created by a writer named Thomas Harris," a deep voice said from the back of the room.

Devon and Holland turned their heads as a strange man walked to the front of the WAR room. It only took a couple of seconds for the seasoned men to recognize the signature dark FBI jacket.

"Special Agent Mark Kincade." The man extended his hand.

"Detective Devon Cartwright. This is my partner, Holland Grant." He shook the tall man's hand and was struck by how thin his fingers were. At over six feet tall, the gaunt man must have weighed less than a hundred and eighty pounds. His handshake was firm but skeletal.

"I'm guessing your guy is in his mid- to late-forties. He hasn't had a lot of success with women. He's not shy, but something about him turns them off. He wants to have them, but the rejection is too much, and he's resorting to murder to get what he wants."

Devon's forehead crinkled with anger when he saw the FBI agent. Just another sign that they were failing. However, after almost three days with little sleep and no hard evidence, part of him was relieved to see the lanky agent. "I knew it was just a matter of time before you guys showed up. Take a seat." He motioned to the only empty chair in the entire room. "We were just discussing what we have so far. I'll fill you in on the rest when we're done with the group." Devon wanted to establish the chain of command and power right up front. This was LVPD's case, and Special Agent Kincade was just another worker bee.

It took another hour to document the rest of the information being brought in by the team. Important items were written on the whiteboards, pictures of the victims were taped on the walls, and teams were dispatched to their next assignments.

Kincade sat quietly, asking the odd question, but not being intrusive. When the last few officers left, he got the entire update from Devon and Holland. His only comment at the end was, "Holy shit." The agent filled the detectives in on his background. He was flown in directly from Quantico, and was considered one of the top criminal profilers in the country. For the two men, who typically didn't like sharing cases with the feds, the man was a somewhat welcome addition to the team.

With pods of officers searching the city for information, and now the FBI in tow, Devon finally hit the wall. Holland, who was only in marginally better shape, sent him home for some sleep. The cots in the staff room were already full with other officers who had been on the case for a mere thirty-six hours. Devon was officially beat, and was no good to anyone in his current state.

When he walked into his house on the north end of the city and turned on the lights, it felt like a foreign land. Having been under the florescent lighting at the station house for so many hours, the warm glow from his living room lamps looked unusually dim. He set his keys on the kitchen table and un-holstered his service weapon. In his bedroom, he set his alarm clock for a five-hour nap, and almost as quickly as his head hit the pillow, he was asleep. He didn't even hear his cell phone buzzing on the kitchen table an hour later.

Twenty-Six

THE COLLECTOR WAS FINALLY back at his safe haven. Sweat was pouring down from his temples. Today was much too close a call for his liking. Taking the woman was easy; she was exactly where he was instructed that she would be. The suite on the third floor was easy to access with the room card that had been supplied in his kit. But today had been different than other days. Today he heard voices from down the hallway just as he was about to pull the trigger on the hand gun. Sure the gun had a silencer; but his hand had jerked nervously with the distraction, and he was concerned that it wasn't a clean kill.

For the first time, he was upset with the outcome of the plan. He had done everything to the letter, yet he had risked the whole operation because of his silly paranoia. His host had been right on every item to this point, and he wasn't going to let his nerves get the best of him. So many years of dreaming of the perfection that his doll would be. It was one of the few things that no measure of money or fame could buy, and he wanted it now more than ever. He took the clear plastic baggie from his pocket and held it up to the light.

The eyeballs that stared back at him were the most beautiful that he had ever seen in his life. They were the most crystal clear blue, with a dark line around the irises. Until he had met Barb, he wouldn't have thought that such perfection even existed. But there they were, in the baggie in his hand. Now it was simply a matter of including them in his masterpiece of a woman.

He went through his routine of clearing the counter and covering it with a heavy plastic sheet. Then he removed the head from the refrigerator. It took about ten minutes to remove the existing eyes from the corpse. He had to be careful not to damage the eye sockets, or Camilla's new eyes wouldn't fit properly. He pulled the upper eyelids up and the lower ones down, and cleaned the holes with a surgeon's precision. As he worked, he referred back to the instructions in his kit — everything was happening just as described in the notes. Next step was to clean the perfect eyeballs, and to push them into the open sockets. They felt firm but pliable in his hands as he washed them with warm water. He severed what was left of the optic nerve, and finally felt like he was satisfied with his work.

He was so excited as they slipped snugly into place. He pulled both the upper and lower lids back into a slightly open position. The face that looked back at him was lustful. Camilla was exactly as he had imagined. The stressful events of the day behind him, the woman's head that he was gazing at was more than enough fuel to keep the fires in his loins burning.

He had known for a long time that perfection is a static state. It can only be achieved in a moment of time. It cannot last in a changing environment. That was what he was striving for. The perfect woman who would never change, would never grow old, get wrinkles or get even one gray hair.

Just a few more days. Fortunately, the next murders didn't call for any more risky kill sites. The remaining four pieces of his puzzle would be a breeze to collect. Camilla would be complete.

The stage had been set for the remaining women. He had already done the ground work, and all were expecting his arrival. His host had promised that the next woman would be waiting for him, and ready for the taking. He didn't even have to seduce her. He actually didn't mind making nice with his victims ahead of time; but he found it hard to focus on the body part that he wanted without getting repulsed by the ones that he didn't care for. It seemed to be an unnecessarily lengthy process while he was impatiently waiting for the end result.

Twenty-Seven

THE REVEREND WATCHED THE newscast from a hotel room off-Strip. It was one of the many establishments throughout the city that rented rooms by the month, the week, the day or the hour. He had met his friend here just a few hours ago, as it was a place that didn't require ID for renting some privacy. He took a long pull off of his crack pipe, one of the few guilty pleasures that he still allowed himself in times of stress. The smoke escaped from his mouth and twirled in the air, as he wondered if the murders would be considered a sin, or just a sign from above that it was time for him to make his move.

The murders served a purpose. The Lord was giving him the opportunity to take back his rightful place in the pulpit. After all of the scandal, after all of the heartbreak, God was giving him a chance to make things right. If he allowed the killings to continue, and he positioned himself correctly, the parishioners would surely realize their mistake, and give him back his church. All of his past indiscretions would be erased. God had forgiven him — why wouldn't they?

Three long years had passed since they had turned their backs on him. He was angry; but the Lord taught him that forgiveness was important, even with those who would trespass against him. They had kicked him out without so much as a thank you for all of the inspiring sermons he had given them, for all of the spiritual counseling and love. He had been an addict; but now he had it all under control, only using drugs in the most stressful situations. He hadn't molested the altar boys. He hadn't hurt a woman or a child. He only sin was being needy. And his need had only been there to give him a better conduit to the Almighty.

The friend that had met him in the dirty hotel room earlier had been given his orders. Reverend Clark knew that they would be followed to the letter. His guest was a loyal subject who would never let him down. Just a few more days, and everything was going to be all right.

WEDNESDAY

Twenty-Eight

GRIZ WATCHED AS CHET demolished the speed bag at the gym. Sweat was dripping from every pore after the hour-and-a-half workout, but Chet always seemed to have more to give. "Good, now get in the ring."

He watched as Chet sparred with a partner for ten minutes. His right jab was a little slower than he would have liked. Outside of that, the boy was in pretty good shape. He just had to make it six rounds... had to.

His new boss had phoned again. It was just a couple of days now until he would have to do the best acting job of his life. Hell, every day was turning out to be a test of his acting skills...of which he truly had none. He would never do well as a poker player — he knew his face had lots of tells. Any time he tried to bluff, he failed miserably; and any time he had a good hand, everyone else folded...even sunglasses didn't help conceal the giveaways. Now every meeting with his investors and phone calls with his new boss invoked the kind of fear that could potentially cost him his life. If either of the parties got nervous, he was going to be shit on toast. He knew they could smell a rat a mile away. As a result, he was losing his marbles, afraid that his body would betray him at the worst possible moment.

Chet came and stood beside his trainer. "I'm ready, Griz. I can take this guy." Chet was tired and bored.

The trainer knew that his prize fighter was in Sin City without the benefit of any sin, and it was driving the boy crazy. He nodded at the young man, who was next up to go a couple of rounds with the potential champ. The man walked away, knowing he had been dismissed for the time being. "Okay, take a water break; I need to talk to you anyway."

The two men sat in the gym, which had been evacuated specifically for their workout schedules. Chet didn't need any distractions when he was in training. His temper had always been touch-and-go, and sparring partners were hurried in and out as required. Chet drank from his water bottle, and squirted some on his face for refreshment. "What's up, boss?"

"The fight is in three days, and there's still some crazed killer on the loose. Based on your background, I want you to be a little more visible for the next couple of days."

Chet smiled a wide grin. "You're letting me out of the hotel room? Thanks!" He wiped his face with the towel and was almost jumping up off the bench to go and get ready for a night of women and wine.

"Slow down, buddy. No drinking, no women. Just out in the public eye whenever you aren't working out. We'll do some photo shoots and promo sessions."

"Come on, Griz. You know I can handle this guy with one hand tied behind my back. A few drinks and a pretty girl aren't going to fuck that up. Give me a break!"

The trainer looked at the piece of meat sitting next to him and knew that he wasn't going to win the fight under any circumstances. In reality, a couple of drinks and a hooker or two wouldn't make the least bit of difference. But right now, it was all about appearances. And to the outside world, it had to look like Chet was in the best shape of his life, and was the front-runner to win the heavy weight match. If word got out that he was seen whooping it up, the press and the bookies would have a field day. That couldn't happen under any circumstances, or his ass was grass.

"Look, I've invested a lot of years of my life into your career. You want me to remind you again of how I helped you climb the ladder to get to this point? You want a reminder of how I got you out of that rape charge, and how you wouldn't even have gotten a shot at the title without my help? This isn't just about you kicking some ass; it's about me, too. I call the shots and I make the rules. Got it?" Griz was pleased that he had brought up the rape charge. It was a constant reminder of who ran the show. He didn't think he would have any issues with his meal ticket after that. He would do as he was told, and when it came to fight day, he would lose in the sixth round. Guaranteed.

Chet looked like a puppy dog who just got scolded for peeing on the carpet. But Griz also saw a twinge of determined anger in his face. "Yeah, I *got it.*"

He wondered if the young fighter actually did.

Twenty-Nine

THE ALARM CLOCK WOKE Devon up with a start. He had been deep in dreamland. Nightmare-land was probably a more accurate description. Images of the dead women had been flashing in his brain like a slide show on a computer; Stacy Bailey without her hair, Kenalynn Markerson without a head, Barb Goldfinch without her eyes. Gruesome pictures of a madman's handiwork. But it wasn't just a bad dream; it was what he had to face as soon as he got his butt out of bed and back down to the station house. It was a nightmare, only it was real.

He had a quick shower and ran his electric razor over his face. It didn't get as close as the blade razor that he usually used, but it would at least make him look a little more respectable and a little less like a street urchin. Clean clothes, a swig of mouthwash, and a brush through his wet hair, and he was off to the WAR room for an update.

He drove almost on autopilot, thinking about the case. There wasn't much that got him riled up, but this one was messing with his mind. The kills were coming so close together that they didn't have time to get the update from the ME from the first, when she was already looking at victims two and three. The whole team was off-balance. Never in the history of the Las Vegas Metropolitan Police Department had their systems been this taxed from one perp. It was like the guy was invisible. He certainly knew a lot about when and where to attack without being caught. Was he just the luckiest son of a bitch on the earth; or was someone helping him? Who was the mystery woman calling the reporter? And what did the note in the first vic's apartment have to do with the string of murders?

When Devon pulled up to headquarters, he barely remembered the drive. The scene when he got inside was unfortunately very memorable.

The front lobby of the station house was packed with reporters, cameras and TV video feeds. Lieutenant Harvey Miller was standing at a podium, with all eyes and ears trained on his every word. It looked like the briefing had just started.

"As you know, we have a murderer who has been killing young women in our city. We are looking for a man in his mid- to late-forties, who frequents the Las Vegas Strip. He may live here, or he may be a regular visitor to our city," Harvey Miller repeated the profile that Kincade had supplied. "Anyone with information is urgently asked to call the Homicide Hotline. A reward of a hundred thousand dollars is available for anyone whose information leads to a conviction."

The crowd of people watching went wild with questions.

"So can we assume that you don't have any suspects at this time?"

"What are you doing to ensure the safety of visitors to the Strip?"

"Will NASCAR and the boxing match still move ahead on the weekend?"

Everyone was talking louder and louder to have their questions heard above the others.

Miller spoke again, "We won't be answering any questions at this time. However, I can assure you that we have increased security both on and off-Strip, and do not expect to have any incidents that would require us to reschedule any public events or privately held functions. Thank you." He turned from the podium, and the reporters and their cameras scanned the lobby for any other potential source of newsworthy information.

Devon moved quickly to the secured hallway and was almost out of sight when the door behind him flew open. He looked back, ready to scream about breaching police security, when he saw Mehgan Bowman holding the door open. "Get in here before everyone else sees you." Once again, he was not pleased with her over-eager reporting style.

"I've been trying to call you. Where the hell have you been? You said you would call me hours ago."

Devon reached to his belt clip for his cell phone, and realized that in his haste to get back to work he had left it on his kitchen table. "Damn it."

"She called again. This time she talked a bit longer. She says the guy is going to take another victim tonight. We need to talk."

Devon was shocked at how much had happened in the few hours he had been asleep. He had to get back in the WAR room for an update, but he needed to talk to Mehgan as well. "Follow me. Don't touch anything or talk to anyone. If you so much as take an extra breath without me okaying it, you'll be back outside with the vultures you call colleagues."

He snapped around so quickly that he missed seeing the smile on her face.

Thirty

THE WAR ROOM WAS packed wall to wall with people. In the few hours that Devon had been away, the whiteboards had been filled with information that was coming back from the field teams. Holland was sitting at the front of the room talking to the FBI agent. Both looked tired.

Holland and Special Agent Kincade looked surprised to see a strange woman with Devon. "Who is *she*?" Holland snarled.

"Mehgan Bowman. She's the reporter that's been getting the phone calls from the mystery woman. She was down in the lobby when Miller was talking to the press, and told me that she got another call. It's a circus down there, so I brought her up here to get the scoop. She won't be staying." Devon's lips were thin as he shot her a warning stare.

Mehgan stuck out her hand for a handshake, but was met with indifference.

Holland quickly ushered her from the WAR room and into a smaller interrogation room next door. Kincade and Devon followed them, and watched as the young reporter took a seat in the plastic chair usually reserved for criminals. Devon sat across from her, and the other two men stood against the wall in the crowded space.

"Tell me what she said," Devon demanded.

Mehgan looked around at the three men and understood that she was perhaps in a bit deeper than she had expected to go. While she found Devon Cartwright to be attractive in a hard-nosed-cop kind of a way, the other two men in the room just looked plain old intimidating and serious. There would be no more flirting to get her way. But she reasoned that if she played her cards right, and she was holding the aces right now, she might be able to keep her status as a valued participant in the investigation. She tried to ignore the other men and talked directly to Devon.

"She called me about two hours ago and said that we were on the right track. The killer has some tie to the hotels through work. She said that he's a predator who likes to...." She hesitated for a moment, not wanting to say the next part.

"Who likes to what?" Devon was getting impatient with even the smallest of delays.

"He likes to screw dead bodies," she replied.

"What? The sick bastard likes what?" Holland asked, shaking his head.

"She said that he likes to have sex with dead women."

All three men sat in silence for a few moments. Kincade spoke first, "What else did she say, Miss Bowman?"

"She said that he's building perfection. That's it. She sounds really scared, and said that she couldn't talk anymore; but I think I heard her say that he's already taken the next woman."

"Tell me exactly what you heard, dammit!" Holland roared, as he made a menacing move toward the reporter.

Devon stood up and put his arm in the line of fire to stop him. "Just step back, Holland. Can't you see that she's scared enough already?"

Holland moved back toward the wall, and came up with a question of his own. "How do we even know she's for real? She's giving us nothing worthwhile. Maybe she's just like the hoard of other reporters downstairs and just wants to get in tight with the police."

The look on Devon's face said it all; he was wondering the same thing.

Thirty-One

MEHGAN WAS GIVEN A cup of coffee and was left to sit alone in the white cinderblock room. The small table in front of her was made of cheap laminate, and the light-blue 60s style molded plastic chair was one of the most uncomfortable she had ever sat on. She imagined that the room was purposefully designed to be stark and unpleasant in order to evoke as much information as possible, as quickly as possible, from the suspects.

It suddenly struck her that she was now being treated no better than a common criminal, and that pissed her off to no end. Who did they think they were dealing with? She was helping the investigation, but they were treating her like street trash. The thoughts were getting her blood boiling, and when Devon finally walked back into the room, she was ready for a fight.

"What the hell? I offer to help you, and you stick me in an interrogation room like a criminal. I don't remember part of our deal being that you got to treat me like gutter garbage. I'm out. When she calls again, I'll do whatever I want with the information, and you can find out on the five o'clock news like everyone else." The reporter moved toward the door to leave.

Devon grabbed her arm and pulled her back. "Calm down, Mehgan. Don't act like the child that you seem to be. This was the closest available room, and it's quiet. Don't think that it was meant to degrade you or make you into 'gutter garbage'."

Mehgan felt her face flush as he touched her. She felt the spark of attraction again, but that irritated her as well. Falling for the detective was not in her plan. She hated that he had that effect on her. She had bigger things on her agenda. "Let go of me!" she yelled, as she ripped her arm from his grip.

"Sit down in the chair and let me tell you what we've decided. I think that despite your petty anger issues, you might be interested in what I have to say." Devon watched and waited. She stared him down for a long thirty seconds before she returned to her seat.

"This better be good, or I'm outta here." Mehgan was trying to be tough, but she had softened a little.

"We want you to be a part of the investigation on the inside," Devon said.

Her heart skipped a beat. It was exactly what she wanted. "Under one condition."

"What's that?"

"You never leave me in one of these rooms ever again. I get to go in the big-boy room like the rest of you meatheads."

Devon laughed. "Yes, you can go in the big-boy room."

Thirty-Two

THE PLAN WAS SIMPLE. The FBI was going to put a bug on Mehgan's cell phone and her home phone for the duration of the investigation. If the mystery woman called again, they would be able to tape the call. In the meantime, they were going to use a software program called Trigger Fish to simulate a cell site which could potentially lead them to the cell phone. If the cell was turned on it would give a signal, and the special software could track it to the exact location where they hoped to find the mystery woman. The only problem was, that when the phone was turned off, the software didn't work.

"If you can ask her to keep her phone turned on, we might be able to trace the unique signature with Trigger Fish and find our woman." Kincade was proud that he had access to all of the best technology.

"How long do I need to keep her on the line?" Mehgan asked.

"As long as you can; but more important, we need her to keep the phone powered up."

"Tell her to leave the cell on so that you can call her back," Holland suggested.

"Don't you think that'll look suspicious?" Mehgan was nervous that one wrong move would jeopardize her plan, and wasn't thrilled with the possibilities.

Devon had been treating her very differently over the past couple of hours and he jumped to her defense. "Just do your best. The longer, the better; but we want her to keep calling, so don't make it look obvious."

It was now just a waiting game from her perspective. Mehgan was only useful as long as the mystery woman kept calling; but in the meantime, she wanted to write her story and submit it to the newspaper for tonight's late edition. She had already been told that anything she wrote would have to be approved before she sent it to print; but at least she had full access to the WAR room and was permitted to hear all of the incoming evidence.

She sat quietly in the corner of the room and typed her observations as the team of homicide detectives worked their magic. Every corner of the whiteboards was full, and she documented each and every piece of information into her laptop. She probably wouldn't be able to print most of it; but not knowing what was going to be important down the road, she wanted to have it all.

Thirty-Three

THE PATCHWORK PICTURE WAS itself the biggest clue that the team had in order to figure out who was going to be next in line. Assuming that the next victim was going to be taken for either her torso, breasts, legs, or arms, the team studied those portions of the picture more carefully. The paper had been scanned, and was now displayed prominently on the hundred-inch screen at the front of the room.

"The legs are the hardest to figure out. No real specifics on the picture to tell which hotel the photo was taken in. He wasn't even courteous enough to give us a glimpse of the shoes. Could be legs off of any cocktail waitress on the Strip." Holland was speaking to everyone in the room, and no one in the room.

"You see that?" Devon pointed to the top of one shoulder on the picture, "It looks like a red strap maybe. Just a hint of red there."

Everyone's attention turned to the right shoulder on the screen. The arms were bare, but it certainly did look like a sliver of red material on top of the arm portion of the picture. The torso was also red, as was the material around the breasts; but all three were taken from different photographs and morphed into a single image. From the neck down to the hips, the victims were going to be from hotels with red cocktail uniforms.

"Okay, so, which hotels get their waitresses to wear red outfits?" Mark Kincade asked.

"On the MGM side..." Holland rustled through the field tech's notes, "MGM, Excalibur, and Mandalay Bay. The Mirage, Bellagio and New York, New York are different."

"I'm not sure that we should focus on just the MGM group. I know our first three victims all worked on this side of the Strip, but really; are we going to put waitresses in the other hotels at risk by ignoring the fact that we have no real evidence to support that theory?" Kincade was trying to expand the search to the other side of the Strip as well. Devon wondered if Holland had tried to convince him otherwise.

"We've got people everywhere in all of the major hotels, but I'm liking the MGM angle. The Preacher, Reverend Clark, uses the west side of the Strip as his pulpit. And initial reports from the field teams say that a Saudi prince, Mohamed Singh, is here for a poker tournament at the Luxor. There has to be a connection." Holland was adamant that they were on the right track, regardless of what the FBI had to say. This was his territory, and he had a gut feeling that he was correct in his assumptions.

"I don't agree a hundred percent, but let's assume that you're right, and let's go talk to the waitresses at the MGM and work our way south to Mandalay Bay."

Devon and Mehgan stayed behind to decipher the constant stream of incoming data from the feet on the street. Holland and Kincade were going back to the Strip.

Thirty-Four

WHEN THEY WALKED INTO the MGM, it would have been difficult to tell that there had been one murder on the Strip in the last couple of days, let alone three. The casino floor was full of people. The blackjack tables were packed, and the slot machines were buzzing away, with their occupants fully mesmerized by the spinning reels.

For a split second Holland remembered the days when he used to play the machines. That was a long time ago, and his life had changed dramatically since then. When he played, pre-marriage to Maggie, the machines still spit out real money. The clanging of quarters in the specially-designed trays made a huge amount of noise when you won. Today the one-armed bandits spat out little white tickets instead, and simulated the noise of the rush of money. On the one hand, it was a much more sanitary way to get your cash; no more black hands due to the dirty coins. But on the other hand, it didn't really feel like winning. The tickets could be inserted into the next game, and you never saw real cash unless you were putting more in, or if you were lucky enough to win and smart enough to cash out at the cashier's window.

The old Vegas was long gone. The days of Sammy Davis, Dean Martin and ninety-nine cent shrimp cocktails had been replaced with *Cirque du Soleil* shows, and celebrity chef restaurants. Vegas was evolving and becoming more technologically advanced, just like everywhere else in the world; but for Holland, there was still a part of him that wished that the old Sands Hotel was still standing.

The two men walked toward the front desk and asked to see a manager. It didn't take long for them to be greeted and escorted away from the prying eyes of the public. No one wanted their hotel to be on the killing map, with millions of tourist dollars on the line over the weekend.

"We're hoping that we can talk to your waitstaff. There's a chance that the killer might target one of your girls." Holland said to the manager.

The man looked nervous as he straightened his suit jacket. "Why would you think that the MGM would be a target?"

Holland showed the man the print out. "This isn't common knowledge, but as you can see, there are three images here with red outfits. Your girls wear red every day. We need to talk to them to see if any of them have had their picture taken recently."

"I don't want trouble here. I also don't want to set a wave of panic through my staff. We need all hands on deck this weekend. This one weekend in March can make or break the entire month. If the girls get spooked and don't show up for work…well, you can understand the issue. Did you see all those people out there wearing their NASCAR jackets? Today is only Wednesday. As the weekend gets closer, those jackets are going to dominate the hotel. Can this wait?"

Holland was amazed at the greed that seemed to dominate the landscape, both on the part of the patrons, and the management — everyone was looking for their piece of good old American apple pie. But he reasoned that in tough economic times in a city built on gambling, he shouldn't expect anything else. "I really can't stress enough that another dead waitress will hurt the entire Las Vegas area. We're trying to avoid a situation that might get the MGM in the news."

Reluctantly, the manager agreed to set the two detectives up in the staff lunch room. Kincade and Holland set up camp at a table close to the door so that they could take a look at each and every woman who walked through the doors.

The constant stream of women in red dresses made it feel a bit like a Technicolor Robert Palmer video. By the end of their first hour, they had talked to thirty women. While most were young and beautiful, many of the more seasoned waitresses just didn't fit the bill.

The picture showed what looked like a youthful figure; slim torso, with an hourglass waist. The breasts were high and firm, and arms thin, but toned. It was easy to eliminate thirty percent of the MGM's waitresses.

When a woman in her mid-twenties came bursting into the room and immediately targeted their table, the two men were a little shocked. She was blond and beautiful; but what made her interesting was what she had to say.

"I think the Strip Killer might be after me." The woman sat down without being invited by either of the two men.

"Sorry, your name?" Kincade asked.

"Jackie Temple."

"Why do you think the killer is after you?" Holland was eyeing up her body to see if it fit the bill. She was a tiny girl, perhaps five foot four. Her arms were covered with the fabric of her dress, but her large breasts and small waist could put her in the right physical category.

"The newspaper said that the guy is trying to build a perfect woman, and I heard that you're looking at us because of our red dresses. I'm scared. I mean, look at me." She stood up and spun around as she motioned up and down her body. "I have the best rack in this hotel. I'm worried." Jackie sat back down again and looked at Kincade with a sincere fear in her eyes.

Both men were at a loss for words. Did this woman really have such a big ego that she thought that she was the best-built woman on the strip?

Holland was first to respond, "Has anyone been bothering you? Have you noticed anyone acting funny? A staff member? A customer?"

"No one specifically. I mean, there are lots of men that give me the hairy eyeball all day. It's a bit of a curse, actually. I'm really scared. I live alone. Can you give me police protection or something?" She ran her hand through her hair and gave Kincade a smile that could melt the Arctic ice cap.

"Miss Temple. I would recommend that you be really careful around anyone that you don't know; but we can't offer every waitress in the city personal protection. Take my card, and if you see or hear anything unusual, please give us a call. In the meantime, we've increased security in the hotel so you'll be safe." Kincade watched as her once-beautiful face went sour.

"You aren't going to protect me? Wow. I really thought you would understand my situation and help me out. I guess coming to talk to you was a real waste of time." She gave them a frustrated frown and quickly stormed off.

Kincade looked at Holland and stifled a giggle. "That is one high-maintenance woman. Wouldn't want to be *her* boyfriend."

****

Jackie Temple left the staff room furious. The fucking police weren't going to help her. She looked around at the other waitresses on the casino floor and was flabbergasted that the men couldn't see what was right in front of them. Sandra was pretty, but she already had two kids; her stomach would be cracked with stretch marks. Mandy was at least five pounds too heavy. Brenda had natural breasts that jiggled all over the place when she walked. Nadia's skin was too dark. Reena never worked out. The examples were endless. The stupid detectives were obviously blind. If the killer was going to take someone from the MGM hotel, she was really the only logical choice.

She was going to have to take matters into her own hands. As it was with all areas of her life, the only person that she could count on was herself. If she had to protect herself from a crazed maniac killer, so be it. On her break, she made a couple of phone calls. She was going to buy a gun.

Thirty-Five

THE HOMICIDE HOTLINE WAS buzzing with incoming calls. Ten officers were busy taking calls from hundreds of local citizens who thought that they had information on the killer. Each and every piece of information had to be documented and investigated; but when there was a large reward on the table, there were just as many crazies as there were people who had potential leads.

Officer Glen Bookwell had already taken over a hundred calls, most of which were not worth writing down. There were people who thought that their eighty-year-old neighbor was the killer; others that thought aliens were killing the women. And one caller even insisted that one of Lance Burton's tigers was on the loose. It was tedious work, but when one special call came in, he knew that it had the potential to be something big. "So, you think that your boyfriend has something to do with the murders?"

The female voice on the other end of the line sounded afraid as she whispered into her phone, "I'm not sure; but he works nights, and I know for sure that he knew one of the women."

"Which one?" There was no readout on the call display. Her number was blocked.

"The first one. Stacy Bailey. I found a business card with her face on it. You know, the ones that the Mexicans give out on the Strip. The hookers."

"I want to send a detective out to see you. Can you give me your address?"

The woman seemed to panic at the thought of someone coming to her home. "You can't come here. If he knows that I called you, he'll kill me, too."

"Will you meet one of my officers somewhere then? Maybe a restaurant?" Officer Bookwell was waving his arms around, trying to get the attention of anyone else on the floor. Everyone was engaged with other callers, and no one looked his way. He wanted someone else to listen in on the call to help him get information from the woman. *I'm a traffic cop,* he thought, *I'm in way over my head.*

Ignoring his question, the woman added one more thing, "Reggie is his name. Reggie Matthews. If you want to get him, he's at the liquor store on the corner of Washington and Eastern. He won't be there long."

The line went dead. Bookwell rushed to the WAR room with the information, and wondered if the officers would be able to get there in time.

Thirty-Six

REGGIE CAUGHT A GLIMPSE of his reflection in the liquor store window and had to laugh. It wasn't one of his finest moments. Perched on the back of his ten-speed bicycle, he was wearing a pair of bright pink track pants; only because they were the first thing that he could find on the floor of the double-wide trailer. The pants belonged to his girlfriend, but the sleeveless T-shirt emblazoned with a Motley Crue logo was all his. The beat-up Speed Racer helmet was there to keep his head safe in case he crashed somewhere along the ten-block trip. He was holding a half-lit cigarette in his hand and had a six-pack draped over the handlebars.

Then, two blocks later, the shit-storm started.

All of a sudden four cop cars came at him from three sides — two in the front, one in the back and still one more on his left. To the right he was blocked by a row of apartment-style condos. *Damn it.*

He dumped the bike and the beer and tried to run. That was probably a bad move. He wasn't in any shape for a police chase anyway, having consumed a dozen beers and two big bong hits of pot just before he left the house.

The police weren't gentle when they tackled him. They took him down in the most efficient police way — lights flashing, guns pointed at his head, and a strategically placed knee in his back.

"What's goin' on? I didn't do anything man," he yelled.

"You're wanted for questioning in the murder of three dead women on the Strip," a cop replied.

"No way man. You got the wrong guy."

Then they slapped the cuffs on his wrists. Marla was going to be pissed when he didn't make it back with the beer. The six-pack represented the last few dollars they had before he got paid at the end of the month. She would be a hellfire bitch when he got home.

Little did he know that when the cops came to call, Marla was actually in a good mood. "I've always had my suspicions about Reggie. He's a shitty boyfriend, always eye'n up other women at the bar. He's the Strip Killer, I just know it," she had said with a gap-toothed smile and the stench of booze wafting off her body. She even handed them an incriminating business card with Stacy Bailey's photo. She added "There's lots of times he's late comin' home from work. Damn dog never tells me where he's been."

The officers had taken notes and the business card.

"So when do I get the hundred grand?" she had asked. "The rent's due at the end of the month, and I'm a little short. I won't be turning Reggie in on a handshake and a smile."

Thirty-Seven

BACK AT HEADQUARTERS, DEVON was pacing, waiting for Reggie "Redbull" Matthews to be brought into an interrogation room. His rap sheet showed several charges of possession, and one rather unusual charge from when he was found having sex in a dumpster. In other words, he was one class act.

Devon felt well-armed with what he thought was enough information to start the conversation with the broad-shouldered, dark-skinned man. Reggie had access to all of the hotels with his job as a soft drink delivery driver. He was in his late forties. He was built like a brick shit house from hauling kegs of soft drink syrup all day. His girlfriend says he was missing when all three murders took place, and he knew the first victim. Bingo.

Reggie looked shaken and still a little drunk when Devon met him in the interrogation room. Devon took the lead, while three other officers, including Lieutenant Miller, watched the proceedings over closed-circuit video feed.

"Reggie. I'm Detective Cartwright. Do you know why you're here today?"

"I heard it was something to do with those women that got murdered on the Strip. But I don't know nothin' 'bout that. You got the wrong guy." He looked nervous, and fidgeted with the fraying hem on his shirt.

"We heard that you knew one of those women. Stacy Bailey; does that name ring a bell to you?"

"No, sir. I don't know no Stacy Bailey. I got a jealous woman at home, know-what-I-mean?" The last part came out as one long word instead of the series of words that it should have been.

Devon spoke to the man who was at best five foot seven, and wondered if he was capable of the crimes. "You see, we don't think that's the truth. We found out that you have this card for outcall services with her picture on it. That true?" He put the business card on the table.

Reggie's face changed. Instead of looking afraid, he started to look more confident. It was the opposite reaction to what the detective was expecting. "Lotsa people have that card. I found it on the street. Them Mexicans give 'em out. I tried to call the number to get her services, but they told me that she don't work there no more. They just use her picture because she's hot. Kinda like a bait-and-switch. You ask me, you guys should look into that. Not a good thing to do to paying customers, know-what-I-mean. Anyway, I never met the girl personally. Just have the picture. You can check with my girlfriend; I come home every night right after work. Since she caught me trying to screw around a couple months ago, I'm pretty good about showin' up on time." He grinned, and his body relaxed onto the back of the chair.

"See, that's one of the problems, Reggie. Marla says that you *haven't* been coming home right after work. She isn't going to be your alibi. And then there's the whole matter of you running from us. An innocent man doesn't run."

Reggie looked like the air had been sucked out of his lungs. His face lost its color and he yelled, "No! No man. I ran because you was chasin' me. What else did you expect? Marla's gettin' revenge for that ho' I banged from the bar. I swear man."

Devon knew that he was on to something. "You want to talk to us Reggie? You want to get it off your chest? Three murders is a lot of pressure for a guy to be carrying around with him. Maybe they were just accidents; rough sex gone wrong. But we can't help you if you don't tell us."

Reggie said the one thing that every detective hates to hear, "I want a lawyer." With those four words, the interview was over, and there was a collective groan from everyone who was watching the interview on the video screen in the comfort of the outer offices. They wouldn't be getting a confession tonight; but maybe the Strip would be a little bit safer for a few hours.

Thirty-Eight

DEVON AND LIEUTENANT MILLER regrouped in the WAR room. "Damn it; I was hoping that we would get some answers from him and we could put this to bed," Miller said.

The men dispatched a team to investigate the allegations that Stacy was part of the outcall service. That would certainly shed some light as to why she would be targeted. Hookers were easy marks. If they could prove that all three were supplementing their income, it would narrow down the search.

Many of the police staff were taking turns spending a few hours on the cot in the staff room; but it was becoming more and more evident that none of them was functioning at full capacity.

Mehgan walked over and cleared her throat to get their attention. She was met with icy stares. "Can I add in my two cents?"

Devon scowled at her, but nodded his approval.

"I don't think you have the right guy."

Pissed off for about the tenth time since he allowed her in on the investigation, Devon asked the obvious question, "And why might that be?"

"I've been looking at the boards, and the three victims were really pretty. None of them would go out with the loser that you have in the other room. I mean, the guy was arrested wearing pink track pants and a Motley Crue T-shirt. If that was the best option that I had for a date, I would just slit my throat right now."

"We think that our first victim might have been involved in

prostitution. That would make her more than willing to go on a date with our guy, regardless of what he was wearing at the time," Devon remarked with an air of superiority.

"Look, all I'm saying is that I did a three-week expose on prostitution on the Strip last year, and I can tell you without a doubt that this guy could never afford to pay someone of that caliber. He's living in a double-wide trailer and rides a bicycle. Sure he works doing deliveries on the Strip and has access to the hotels; but he's not your guy. If Stacy Bailey was in the business, she was probably charging two-fifty or more just for the privilege of having her come to your room. That doesn't include any actual sex acts; those cost extra. He would have been looking at maybe five hundred or more an hour depending on what he wanted. The guy in the other room couldn't afford to have her blow him a kiss from a mile away."

"The girlfriend says he was missing when the murders happened. Seems like a few things are working against him right now." Devon was still driving the conversation, but Miller and the three other officers were listening to the exchange.

"Okay; let's say that you are I are dating. I find cards for hookers in your pants. I might be inclined to get revenge. I know you're screwing other women, and you aren't really a keeper anyway. So I hear that there's a hundred thousand dollar reward for any information leading to the killer's arrest. The first victim is one of the hookers that you were using, and I jump at the chance to get the money."

Devon's face turned a slight shade of red as she was speaking. Was it because she had just punched a huge hole in his theory, or because she had suggested that they were dating as part of her example? Either way, she seemed to like the fact that she had made him uncomfortable.

"She might have a point," Miller jumped in. "Those outcall services aren't going to give some guy their best talent for peanuts. She was a seriously built woman. You don't get that for forty bucks."

"Then why lawyer up? He's hiding something," Devon interjected.

"Maybe he knows the girlfriend is setting him up. Maybe he has something to hide. But maybe, just maybe, killing these girls isn't it. He realizes that his girlfriend should give him an alibi, and seeing as she isn't, he knows that she's going to take him for a ride." The Lieutenant was in agreement with Mehgan's theory.

"Exactly what I was thinking." Mehgan looked pleased with herself.

"We can't keep him here overnight, but it'll take a while for the lawyer to show up, and we can see if we get any dead women in the meantime. It's been twenty hours since he tried to kill Barb Goldfinch. It should only be a few hours until the next call comes in, if the sharp-dressed man in the other room *isn't* our killer," Devon said.

Thirty-Nine

THE NEXT SEVERAL HOURS were spent collecting and documenting the information from the field teams. There was so much information to sift through that the team was using Mehgan for an extra set of hands.

"Hey, just a reminder that I have to send in an article today or I am going to lose my job," she said.

"Yeah, I get it. In the meantime you write on the whiteboard," Devon said.

"What because I'm a woman, I have to take the notes?"

"No. Because I have shitty handwriting." He smiled at her. "Of the thirty private jets two of them are owned by Saudi princes. Neither want to talk to us. But they're not in a big rush to leave Vegas either. One's in a weekend high stakes poker tournament at the Luxor, and the other is supposedly in town for the heavyweight boxing match."

Mehgan wrote the information on the whiteboard. "What about the other twenty-eight?"

"Another two jets are owned by fashion moguls in for the conference and another is owned by an oil executive. All were cleared in preliminary interviews."

More notes were added about the active search for the Reverend. With further investigation, it was discovered that the preacher had been involved in a scandal that rocked his church a few years prior. It seemed that the well-respected man had been stealing from the collection plate and buying crack cocaine. When he was caught red-handed in an alley by one of his parishioners, he claimed that it was the best way for him to connect with God. The consensus in the congregation was that, had he admitted to using drugs, he could have gone back to the pulpit; but including God as an excuse wasn't something that they could stomach. He was pushed from the church, and hadn't been invited back. It would explain his reluctance to talk to the detectives, if he was still using.

Mehgan sat down and had a gulp of coffee. "Any word on the woman who lost her eyes?"

"She still in a drug-induced coma at the hospital. The doc said that if he brought her back to consciousness now, she would die."

"Wow, I feel so bad for her," Mehgan said.

"This is the most frustrating case I have ever worked on. The bodies are piling up so fast that we can't even get the DNA evidence from the autopsies processed before the next woman dies. Plus, these are super high traffic areas. The fingerprint evidence from the Aria is in excess of two hundred full or partial prints to run through AFIS. The team got another hundred pieces of hair and fiber from the first hotel. This is beyond ridiculous. The state crime lab can't keep up." Devon was talking to another detective whose name he couldn't remember, while Kincade and Holland called in via a phone bridge.

"DNA evidence will tie all of the women together; but if the guy has never been arrested, you'll be SOL anyway. The ME has already told us that there were no obvious signs of a struggle. We know that he drugged the last two victims before he shot them. But he slit our first girl's throat. Why the change?" Holland asked.

"The guy has to have help; so maybe we're looking for more than one killer," Devon added.

"It's got to be someone local. The guy has to be totally comfortable on the Strip. I know your team is looking at the Saudi prince angle, but I would look a little closer to home. In all the years of tracking serial killers, there's one thing I know for sure; they start out in their comfort zone. Unless the Prince is someone who practically lives here, I seriously doubt that he's flying in to commit murder," Kincade added on the speakerphone.

Assuming that they had the Pauper secured in the interrogation room awaiting his lawyer, and that Kincade was right about the Prince, the Preacher was looking like the next area of focus. Devon decided to take a rest. Mehgan chose to go across the street to get a sandwich and make a couple of phone calls.

Forty

HAVING NEVER SHOT OR even held a gun before, Jackie went to the most famous place in Las Vegas to learn how to protect the body that she called her Temple. Born as Jackie James, a stupid name in her opinion, she had legally become Jackie Temple as soon as she turned twenty-one. The name was much more appropriate for someone with her physical assets, and it was a stage name that she hoped would one day make her a famous Playboy Playmate. Hanging at Hef's mansion was her ultimate goal.

When she walked up to the desk outside of the famous Gun Store, she had a moment of nerves that almost made her turn away. *Thousands of tourists do this every year...I can do it too,* she thought.

After picking the Coalition package (twenty shots with an M9 pistol, twenty-five shots on a M4 semi-automatic rifle, and forty shots on an automatic M249 nicknamed The Saw), she was asked to sign a waiver that absolved the store of any wrongdoing if she got hurt, or hurt someone else. They weren't getting sued if she was mentally unstable in anyway. She signed on the dotted line, gathered up all of her courage and went into the building.

Her senses were immediately assaulted by the dirty smell of gun powder and the constant banging of the fired guns. Equally intimidating were the former military men who staffed both the front desk and the firing ranges. She smiled her best smile, hoping to catch one of their eyes. Having a huge man with a gun for a boyfriend would certainly help her in the days to come. On the flip side, if she could just learn how to shoot with reasonable accuracy, she wouldn't need a man at all. Based on the fact that three women were dead in three days, she realistically didn't have enough time to make nice with one of the specimens behind the counter. She would have to protect herself the old-fashioned way.

The first gun that she fired was the M4. The man from the store towered over her five foot four frame, and showed her how to brace the gun against her shoulder while aiming the sight at the target. She leaned in as instructed, and reluctantly pulled the trigger. Even with eye and ear protection, the blast was deafening. Fortunately, the M4 didn't have a lot of kickback; but it was awkward to handle, and it wasn't really an easy weapon to conceal.

The Glock 9mm was next. This was the one that she wanted to get proficient with. The small gun was similar to what she had requested from an old drinking buddy who ran with a biker gang in the area. He promised to have something for her later that night. The pistol felt more comfortable in her hands, and was easier to line up on the target. The problem with the 9mm was the kickback. Her first shot was her best, but after that she was scared of the movement, and most of the remaining shots missed their intended target. Knowing that she was probably going to be in close range when she shot her assailant, she wasn't overly concerned about her lack of target accuracy. Up close and personal was what she expected. The killer would move in to do his thing, and she would do hers. *Bang, bang, you're dead.*

The M249 was a bonus after the 9mm, and the only reason she shot it was for the fun factor. It sat safely on a two-pronged rest on the counter of the firing range. Jackie was less nervous about accidentally hitting someone else standing around her, and was finally able to relax a little. The massive gun was almost as big as she was, but it felt awesome in her hands. The rat-a-tat-tat-tat of multiple bullets leaving the weapon was intimidating and invigorating. The shell casings flew past her cheek one after the other, gun powder lightly covering her face. Most of the rounds hit the target where she had intended, giving her a sense of accomplishment. It was the most powerful and sinister thing that she had ever held in her hands. She would never be able to use this gun on her stalker, but just pulling the trigger on the massive automatic fireball gave her the confidence that she needed for the next couple of days.

If she could keep the adrenaline pumping as it was right now, and if she could remember all of the details that the range master had just taught her, she would be fine. No, she would be better than fine; she would be alive and well, despite the two detectives' visual impairments.

The range master took away the now-empty guns and gave her a T-shirt to commemorate her Gun Store experience. She smiled a nervous smile, trying to hide her satisfaction, not wanting anyone to know that she planned on using her new-found expertise on the man that was soon to be stalking her — if he wasn't already.

Forty-One

REVEREND CLARK WAS STILL holed up in the disgusting off-Strip hotel. The filth was getting to him, as were the sounds coming through the paper-thin walls. There was far too much grunting and moaning for anyone to be sleeping next door. He knew what was happening in the rooms next to his, and it made him nauseous. There were several times that he just wanted to slam through the door and try to talk some sense into the woman on the other side. He wanted to tell her that all she had to do was ask the Lord to forgive her, and she could move forward to a much better place. He wanted to do a lot of things; but he knew that if he wanted to get his congregation back, he would have to show a little more self-control.

He had given his friend specific orders. He wondered if they were being followed exactly as he had directed. Once the killings started, everything had to be completed as outlined in the plan, or no one would believe that God was speaking through him.

He looked at his watch. The next murder would only be a couple of hours away. He could stop them at any time; but to ensure success, he had to be precise in his actions. If he stopped the murders too quickly, the congregation wouldn't have the appropriate level of fear. If he let them go on too long, it would go against everything that he believed in. After all, murder was a sin of huge proportion. He reasoned that it was all for the greater good. It was God's hand guiding him. No matter how big he dreamed, God could always dream bigger things for his life. God would tell him when to stop the killings. God would put him in to a position where his hard work would pay off.

The Reverend debated on whether it was time for him to head back home. At home he had comfortable surroundings; his furniture, his crosses, his bed, and his bible. He just didn't want to have to deal with the police. If they asked too many questions, they might uncover that he had the power to stop the murders. If they figured that out, his whole plan would go to hell in a hand basket. Even more important, if he went home now, he would lose contact with his friend, and he wouldn't be able to direct the scenes of the play moving forward. Seeing as his livelihood was at risk, it didn't seem reasonable to take that chance.

The prize at the end of the road was huge. He would get his church back, he would get his life back and he would get his respect back. The donation plate would be full every Sunday, and he could finally take his message across the state, maybe even across the country. He wasn't like Jim and Tammy Faye Bakker, not just puffed up egomaniacs who wanted the spotlight; he was a masterful speaker and a leader of the lost souls. That was what God wanted. It was all in the master plan.

His thoughts were interrupted by the banging of the headboard next door against his wall. The grunting was getting louder as the banging got faster. He turned up the small TV to drown the amorous couple out of his mind. It would all be over soon, he was sure of it.

Forty-Two

AFTER A SHORT CAT nap, Devon called his partner to get an update on the road trip that Holland and FBI Agent Kincade were still on. The two men had completed their survey of the waitresses at both the MGM and the Excalibur, and were on their way to Mandalay Bay for more on-site interviews.

So far the men had identified over fifty potential victims from the first two hotels. In Vegas, beautiful women were a dime a dozen, which didn't make their job easier. Devon agreed that the two men should continue to the next hotel while he went on his own road trip. His job was to see if he could find more info on the escort agency where Stacy Bailey had been employed.

Every corner of the strip was littered with business card-sized ads for escort services. The women on the cards were shown in various states of undress, but the key three areas; nipples and between the legs, were covered with stars. You didn't get the full meal deal unless you paid money.

Devon looked at the business card given to them by Reggie's girlfriend and called the number from his cell phone as he was walking to his car.

"I need a girl to come to my room. I want a brunette. And no bait-and-switch; I want a high-end woman."

Devon walked into the Bellagio and rented a room for the night. He could have told the front desk staff who he was and try to get a free room, but he didn't want anyone to tip off the pimps, and therefore the hookers. At this point, he couldn't trust anyone outside of his fellow officers and reluctantly he added Mehgan Bowman to the list. The annoying reporter was a pain in the ass, but she was adding value once in a while.

After checking in, he called the escort agency back and gave them the details on his room number. He was told that he would have a woman to his room in less than a half-hour. He lay back on the bed and turned on the TV news. He watched as the newscasters talked about the headline story — the waitress murders on the Strip. There was so much speculation as to where the killer would hit next. There was even talk that he might branch out to patrons of the hotels instead of just staff. The paranoia was spreading fast.

The days of total focus on the case were taking their toll. Despite his best efforts to dislike the reporter, he thought of Mehgan. He was finding himself liking her more than was safe, under the circumstances.

Devon jumped as the sharp rap on his hotel room door came twenty-five minutes later. He quickly picked himself up off the bed and opened the door. The woman standing on the other side was stunningly beautiful. She looked like a cross between Cindy Crawford and Scarlett Johansson. She smiled at the detective, and he motioned her in.

"Hi, I'm Candi. Nice to meet you." She was quick to survey the room to see if she was in any danger. Devon must have passed the test, because she turned back and smiled again.

"Great to meet you, Candi." Devon was wondering what such a beautiful woman was doing selling herself on the Strip, and for a moment, wanted to have the same conversation that Reverend Clark might have had with her.

The woman sat on the bed and crossed her long legs. "Shall we get the money part over with so we can have some fun? My call-out fee is two-fifty, and everything else is extra. Tips are welcome. What would you like me to do for you today?" She was all business, but she was trying hard to look sexy at the same time, maybe hoping for a tip before she even got started.

Devon reached in his pocket and pulled out his badge. Candi's face went white.

"Fuck. I should have known you were a cop."

"I'm not with vice. I just want to talk to you about Stacy Bailey."

The escort wasn't listening. Devon could see her mind racing, trying to figure out a way to get out of the situation without an arrest.

Devon pulled the photo of Stacy out of his pocket and pushed it in her face. "Just tell me what you can about Stacy, and you'll be out of here in a few minutes."

The woman looked at the photograph and mumbled something under her breath that Devon couldn't understand before saying, "I don't know her."

"Sure you do. You've been in this game for a while. You're one of the high-end girls, just like she was. You've seen her before. Just think about it for a minute." Devon watched her as she pondered her next move.

"I've seen her before, but I don't know her." Candi pulled down on her miniskirt, trying to cover her legs. Devon wondered why, given her profession, she was all of a sudden self-conscious about showing too much skin.

"Where did you see her?"

"There's a few clubs around that cater to men who like more than just your standard hand job, blowjob around-the-world, or Greek." Devon knew that Greek was the code word for anal sex.

"Stacy worked at one of these clubs?"

"Yeah, I worked there for a few nights as well. Most of us have tried to get away from the low end of the business; you know, the street walking shit. We want a safe place to go where you can make good money. That's what these clubs are all about. It's a bit of a tradeoff. You have protection, but to make the really big bucks you have to do things that aren't...normal. That's where I met her. We weren't friends or anything, we just said hi and stuff."

"What's the name of the club?"

"Aphrodite's. It was raided six months ago. There's nothing left now. And I'm happy it's gone. There were some sick sons-of-bitches in that place. Wanted all kinds of perverted crap." With the memories of the sex club in her mind, Candi was no longer the sex kitten that all men wanted. She had turned into a street-hardened woman who had seen far too much sadness.

Devon was thrilled that he had yet another lead to follow. "Do you remember who ran the place? What was his name?"

"It wasn't a man, it was a woman."

Devon was a little surprised, but pushed forward. "Do you know *her* name?"

"If I tell you, will you let me walk out of here without handcuffs on?"

"Guaranteed."

"Stacy, the girl you're asking about, was the one who ran the club."

Forty-Three

DEVON CALLED HOLLAND AND Kincade on his drive back from the Bellagio. He filled them in from his cell phone, and told them his next move. "Stacy Bailey wasn't just a hooker; she was the den mother for a sex club. I'm going to head back, but I need you guys to look into all of the arrests that happened at Aphrodite's. Maybe our guy was a customer there; or maybe one of the girls who worked there can give us some information. Plus, I need you guys to check on any of our other vics to see if they had any ties to the club."

Holland and Kincade were already punching data into the system before the call ended. It was by far the best lead they had. If all things were equal, they would have another victim any minute. Every second counted.

Aphrodite's had been raided about six months prior. Based on the on-line police reports, the club had been a specialty business that catered to men who had unusual desires. When the SWAT team had entered the large two-story home, they found men tied up in chains while they were being whipped by leather-clad women. All of the six private rooms were full, and there were another five or so male patrons waiting in the lobby for their turn on the rack.

There were twenty arrests made, none of which was Stacy Bailey. The proprietor was noted as being a man in his late forties named Bill Baxter. Baxter had a long rap sheet, mostly consisting of pimping and selling drugs. He had branched out a year before the raid and started the fetish club. He was able to charge premium prices, and even had a bar set up to loosen his customers up before their sessions with his girls. The files stated that he was charging twenty dollars a beer to his very captive audience.

Holland was amazed that anyone would pay that much for a drink; and then he caught himself, wondering why with everything else that was going on, that the price of a beer would be the biggest shocker. It was hard to imagine that he had become so immune to the violence. His thoughts drifted off to Maggie again. Her pretty smile and the sight of her holding their daughter for the first time. How could he bring another kid into a world where their father was more worried about the price of beer than a murderer on the loose?

Kincade interrupted his thoughts, "So Stacy Bailey was the den mother to the girls, but Baxter was the guy who officially ran the place? Why wasn't Bailey ever picked up and charged?"

"Her name isn't even on here. But one of the arrests is interesting. Chet Hamilton. He's one of the fighters in the heavyweight match this weekend. He's been here the whole week," Holland said.

"Okay, let's go talk to the fighter. Any idea where Baxter is now?"

"He's out on bail while he waits for trial. No need to say it — I'm on my way. You try to find out more about the boxer."

Devon had just walked back into the WAR room, passing Holland as he was leaving to locate Bill Baxter. The two spoke for less than a minute, trying to update each other as they passed in the hallway. Neither man got where he was going.

Kincade started yelling at them from the WAR room. "Don't leave! We have another victim!"

Forty-Four

DEVON, HOLLAND AND SPECIAL Agent Kincade went together to the Excalibur to get a look at the crime scene. Mehgan took her own car. They didn't want to be seen giving favors to one reporter — they told her it was bad for LVPD's public relations. She didn't fuss over the arrangement, and due to her lack of respect for traffic lights and rules, beat them to the scene.

The victim was twenty-five year old Heather Langdon. She had been a waitress at the Excalibur for the past three years, and had been dating her personal trainer for the last twelve months.

This time the body had been left outside of the hotel, in the manmade moat surrounding the medieval castle. The yellow police tape surrounded the sidewalk for the entire length and depth of the hotel. No one was setting foot around the perimeter of the huge property.

ME Maureen Lamont hadn't shown up yet, but hotel security and the officers who had been stationed at the hotel had fished what was left of the body out of the shallow waters. A street cop that Devon recognized from the WAR room was as white as snow when he spoke to the three men. "She's missing her arms, and her body was cut in half at the waist. The printout was in her cleavage, but it's soaking wet and the ink ran. It's a mess." Devon wondered if the officer was referring to her body, the patchwork picture or both.

Devon thanked the officer and told him to go and secure the northwest corner of the hotel. This was a scene that even he and

Holland didn't want to deal with. It was overwhelming for anyone that wasn't used to homicide. The young officer seemed to be relieved that he was being asked to move away from the dead woman, and scurried off without asking further questions.

Devon was recording his thoughts on his phone recorder while Holland took pictures of the body and the surrounding area. "How did he get her in the water without being noticed?" Holland asked. "I mean, look around here. There's an open sidewalk on all sides of this water. There's no real place to walk up with a body and dump it in without making a splash. Plus, we have a ton of extra staff watching the hotel."

Devon lifted his head for a moment to respond. "Okay, say I'm the killer. I dismember the body somewhere else; there's no way that she was killed here. One, no one has mentioned a big pool of blood anywhere and two, there's too much traffic. The best way for me to dump her in the water isn't from the top of the walkway into the hotel. I would need to get as close to the water as possible."

Devon, Holland and Kincade looked at the surrounding area. The majority of the moat was only accessible from the overhead walkways. One went to New York, New York, and the other went to the tram which ushered passengers from the Excalibur to the Luxor and further on to the Mandalay Bay resort. The sidewalk on the east side of the complex faced Las Vegas Boulevard and was too exposed. The northwest corner had fairly easy access to the water; but the more interesting area was to the south. While it was in full view of the Luxor's pyramid rooms, it was a little more secluded, with large palm trees to provide coverage.

"Are there any security cameras at street level?" Devon asked.

The three men looked around them, but didn't see anything obvious. It was more likely that the hotel didn't bother to monitor the exterior sidewalks except at the entrances and exits. They walked the perimeter of the manmade moat, looking for evidence. Just as they suspected, they found what they were looking for on the south side of the water.

"Check it out." Holland pointed toward the cinderblock wall. "That look like blood to you?" The smear of dark red went across the top of the castle wall.

"Get the CSU team here and get as much as we can for trace evidence. This guy has to have left *something* behind." Kincade was now part of the team, and though Holland and Devon didn't particularly enjoy being told what to do, it took the pressure off the two of them. If the FBI was involved and couldn't get their killer, then they were partially off the hook.

"I'm going to go and talk to the management and see if I can't get hold of the boyfriend." Devon smiled at Holland, knowing that his partner wished that he was the one leaving on a road trip, and that Devon was the one left behind at the scene. First one to call it gets to go, and his partner was slow on the uptake.

Forty-Five

HEATHER LANGDON LIVED IN Henderson, just outside of Vegas. She and her boyfriend had a small but comfortable home with a well-manicured yard. Pride of ownership showed from the moment that Devon walked up to the front door.

The man of the house filled the opening of the doorway. His face was swollen and his cheeks were flushed. He had been crying. "Come in." The man, who introduced himself as Colin Young, motioned the detective over to a living room area with dark leather couches.

"I'm so sorry for your loss. I just need to ask you a few questions."

"Whatever I can do to help. I want you to catch the bastard and bring him here to me. I want a piece of this guy." The veins on his huge forearms were popping out as he clenched his fists into tight balls.

From a brief conversation with the on-site officer, he was told that the boyfriend had come home after work to find a pool of blood on the front hallway carpet. CSU had left an hour before, but the red stain remained untouched.

"When was the last time you saw Heather?"

"Two nights ago when she was leaving for work. I told her to be careful. I told her that she should take a gun or something with her. This fucker is killing MGM waitresses, and guess what — she's one of them. Why didn't she listen to me? Told me that she wasn't worried — no one would go after *her*."

"What time did she leave?"

"Six-ish. Her shift started at 7:30. She works nights and I work days. We only get to see each other when she comes in to do her workouts at the gym and on the weekends. We were just going to get two full days off together. We were supposed to go to Lake Mead for a hike." The boyfriend put his head in his hands.

Devon hated to see a grown man in so much pain. Even after years in homicide, it still made him uncomfortable; so he hurried the interview along. "So you were gone when she got back from work?"

"Yeah. I leave at about three a.m. so I can get my workout in before I start training people at five. We're open twenty-four hours. There's lots of shift workers in the city who need to train at weird hours. We do our best to help them out. Most days, she's home before I leave; but sometimes she stops for a drink with her friends from work. When I saw the blood today when I got home…oh God. What did he do to her? Why didn't you protect her?"

Devon leaned back in his chair, trying not to start a confrontation with the muscular man. He made note of the name of the boyfriend's gym. He would have someone check it out when he left. "Did Heather tell you anything about a strange guy hanging around her at work? Anything unusual in the past few days?"

"Nothing. But yesterday she called me when she got up, about noon. She told me that the hotel was sending someone around to get paperwork signed."

"Paperwork?"

"Yeah, something about a new policy manual that she hadn't signed yet. I can't imagine her opening the door if it wasn't someone that she knew from the Excalibur."

"I'll check that out. Anything else you can think of? Anyone that she was having problems with at work?"

"Not that she ever told me. The only person that she complained about was her boss. He kept changing her shifts at the last minute. She got along with everyone else. Even that damn priest who harasses all the girls, she even got along with him." Colin's eyes had welled with tears, but they hadn't fallen to his cheeks.

Devon looked down at his notepad to give the man some privacy.

Ding, ding, ding…warning bells were going off at the mention of the Reverend. "Reverend Clark?"

"I don't remember his name. She just told me that he bugged the girls, trying to get them to quit degrading themselves. I told her not to talk to him anymore, but she said he was just a harmless old man trying to save souls. She was too damn trusting."

Devon thought back to the Reverend and how he was maybe forty-five years old. Not exactly an old man by his standards; but maybe to a twenty-five year old, he would be considered ancient.

He wasn't sure how to ask the next question without getting beaten to a pulp by the huge man sitting across from him. "Were you guys having any financial issues? Any reason why Heather might have taken a second job?"

The boyfriend looked confused. "Huh? No, we're good. Heather just had the one job. Why are you asking?"

"No reason. Just checking all angles." Colin's look of genuine surprise said that he didn't know anything about a potential link to prostitution. "Thanks for your time. If you think of anything else…" Devon put his card on the coffee table on top of a bodybuilder magazine.

As they walked to the door, the boyfriend's parting words sent a chill up Devon's spine. "You get this bastard, or I will." He looked like the kind of guy who meant it.

Forty-Six

DESPITE WHAT THE PUBLIC saw on TV cop shows, DNA processing takes much longer than you see on Law and Order. After almost four days of investigation, the first samples were just coming back from the lab. Seventy-two hours was pushing it, even with extenuating circumstances. The main problem was that in such a high traffic area like the Strip, there were a lot of samples to check.

Minute traces of hair and skin cells from the crime scenes had been processed and amazingly, they found DNA from the first two hotels that matched each other, but didn't match anything on file. The bad news was, there were still hundreds more to process in the hope that they might get another match down the road.

Holland, Devon and Kincade were back in the WAR room. Every surface of the whiteboard walls was covered in notes gathered from the field teams, and they were starting to tape sheets of paper notes to the walls.

Holland made a recommendation to the team. "I want a more concise picture of all of this. There's too much detail." He moved to the laptop keyboard and opened a new Word file on the screen. "Let's start with what we know for sure about our victims." He started typing, and the rest of the team could see his notes projected on the screen at the front of the room. He wrote the names, locations and the summary of each murder.

"All of the women, except our first, were shot point blank with a .45 caliber hand gun with specialized bullets meant to inflict as much damage as possible; except Stacy Bailey, who was basically beheaded. Barb Goldfinch is still alive because the hollow-point bullet filled with the padding from her bra and didn't fragment like it was supposed to. The first three were drugged with a potent form of tranquilizer before they were killed — same drug in all victims. Lamont hasn't confirmed it, but I think we can assume that our fourth will be the same. No sexual interference with any of the vics." Holland paused for a moment with his fingers hovering over the keyboard as he gathered his thoughts.

Devon piped in, "The only tie that we have with all of these women is that they worked at MGM hotels. There isn't anything else that's similar. Don't forget Stacy Bailey's tie to prostitution; but based on everything that we've learned about the other three, I can't see them having extracurricular activities. Maybe Barb Goldfinch, but the other two — no way. The muscle-head boyfriend that I met today didn't seem like the type who would be into sharing his woman, and Kenalynn Markerson had the kid, who would need a crap-load of attention. Can't see her having the time to do the hooker job on top of waitressing."

Kincade added questions and comments of his own. "Did we hear back from the Hard Rock yet? How did Stacy get the expensive purse?"

"Nothing yet. I'll head over there personally tomorrow morning," Devon answered.

Holland added a few more notes to the screen, and wanted to move on. "Okay, high level. Let's talk about our potential perps. We have the note from Stacy talking about a Prince, a Pauper and a Preacher. It looks like Reverend Clark is the Preacher. He's known to at least two of our women, Stacy and Heather. He works the same side of the strip as all of our vics, and he was kicked out of the church for drug abuse and delusions of talking to God when he's high. Plus, he hasn't been home since we starting staking out his place."

Kincade was next to speak. "We have Reggie in custody right now; though he could have taken her yesterday and dumped her in the water before we cuffed him. Once Lamont gets back to us with how long the body parts were in the moat, we might be able to figure out Reggie's involvement. If we don't charge him with murder in the next hour, his lawyer will have him out on the street. The paperwork is already done."

Holland made more notes on the screen. "The Prince. Now this one is tricky. We have two men in from out of the country who are princes; both are stinkin' rich, and own private planes. But I'm in agreement now that our killer is someone local. Maybe Prince is a nickname. Maybe we should look at the gangs."

"Don't forget Chet Hamilton. The guy was arrested at the fetish club six months ago. He's in the city for the fight, and sources say that he's been here for a few weeks trying to get ready for the title match," Kincade said.

Devon added a couple more items. "We also have the security company angle. How far do you think these guys would go to get a contract? They have the ability to access any hotel, and any floor. They also know the areas where there are holes in the system. They could very easily be involved. Plus, we need to find Baxter, the guy who ran the fetish club — he's a former Marine, and could be a good candidate to use those specialized bullets. I'll get a beat-cop to track him down."

Kincade was shaking his head. "Goddammit; too many angles. Our guy is a ghost, and we've only got a few hours until he kills again."

Forty-Seven

MEHGAN BOWMAN HAD GONE home for a shower, a bite to eat and few hours of uninterrupted sleep. The mystery woman hadn't called to tell her about the last murder, and she knew it most likely because she was camped out at police headquarters. The police and FBI presence could very well have scared her off. She also needed to spend some time writing her article for the paper. She was drastically behind schedule at work, and a repeat of yesterday's short synopsis wouldn't cut it again today.

She sat at her desk and opened her laptop. It had been close to twelve hours since she had connected to email, and her inbox lit up with over sixty new messages. She scanned the screen, looking for anything that was super-important; but other than a note from her boss demanding her copy, there didn't seem to be anything of real value.

Devon Cartwright had given her specific instructions on what she could, and couldn't, print. While she was happy to be in the inner circle, it seemed a bit like having a boa constrictor around her neck. If she made one wrong move, they would strangle the air from her, and she wouldn't have access to the all-important WAR room; but if she didn't print what she had learned, then she wasn't being true to her profession. There was a fine line, and as her fingers flew over the keys, she knew that she was walking on a very sharp edge.

Based on her knowledge of where they were at in the investigation, she thought it might even help them in the long run. She wondered if

Devon would see it that way, or if he would choke the life out of her when he read it. It was a calculated risk. Plus, she thought that maybe she had picked up signals from him. Was he falling for her?

She had noticed him smiling at her more often over the past twenty-four hours. He had the rugged good looks that she was always drawn to. Over the years, she had found men easy to manipulate. A smile here, a toss of the hair there — next thing you knew, putty in her hands. The detective was a bit more of a challenge, but she liked a challenge. There's no way he would kick her off the case. She typed the teaser for the website, which would promote tomorrow's early edition. She read the copy over twice to make sure that it would have the exact impact that she wanted. Pleased with her handiwork, she smiled at the screen...it was perfect.

A half-hour later, her full article was complete, and she hit 'send' on the email to her editor. Let the chips fall where they may. Time for some sleep.

Forty-Eight

THE COLLECTOR WAS BACK at his temporary home, and took all of his prizes from the refrigerator. He couldn't stop staring at Camilla's face. It was too beautiful for words. The lush, dark hair complemented her pale face, which had the most slender nose and full lips. The eyes were the best part of all. The piercing blue irises were the sparkling jewels on his creation.

He took the two arms from the icebox and laid them on either side of his masterpiece. He caressed the slender forearms, and gently touched the length of each individual finger. He was so pleased that the ring finger was empty. Once he had completed Camilla, he would place a gold band on her left hand to make the union complete.

He wanted so much to join the masterpiece together. He had to gather three more puzzle pieces before he would get to consummate their union. It seemed like he had been waiting forever for her. But of course, the thought hadn't become real until he had met Scarlett. If it wasn't for her, he wouldn't have had the knowledge or the guts to do what he was doing now. Scarlett was his savior. Scarlett was the best thing that had ever happened to him...outside of Camilla.

Before meeting her, he had muddled along through life. His successes were measured only in dollars and cents. But he had always wanted more. It was only after he met her at Sirens that she had shown him the way to true happiness and fulfillment. The women before her hadn't understood his particular idea of love. First he had asked girlfriends to perform certain tasks, but they refused. Some just stopped returning his calls; others had called him a "sick, perverted bastard", amongst other hurtful names. Then he moved his sights to women that he could pay to do his bidding. But as time went on, that wasn't sufficient to give him an orgasm either.

He had become so picky, that with most of the escorts, he only allowed them to show one body part, the rest covered with sheets while he masturbated beside them. It was at that point that he heard about Sirens. The private club catered to a more upscale clientele who had unusual tastes. When he first walked through the door, he had wondered if they were going to ridicule his interests, like the rest. But instead of cold, judgmental looks, he was welcomed with open arms. After three sessions at Sirens, he had spoken to the owner of the club and "jokingly" asked for what he really wanted. The look on the man's face had a twinge of surprise and shock; but he had smiled, and the next time the Collector had walked through the doors, the manager of Sirens had come through with flying colors.

Now, many months later, he was sitting in a luxurious home with his dream girl half-built. He could scarcely believe it was true. He spent the next hour removing the pink nail polish from Heather's fingertips, and replacing it with two coats of a candy-apple-red varnish. While the last coat was drying, he leaned in to the head that sat on the table before him and kissed his prize softly on the lips. Her ice cold flesh was so wonderful, so sensual. Not much longer now… he would have her soon.

THURSDAY

Forty-Nine

WITH JUST TWO DAYS before the big fight, Chet "The Hammer" Hamilton felt like he was living in the gym. For the past three months, he had lived and breathed everything healthy and clean— it felt like the life was being sucked out of him. When his trainer had told him that they were going to spend a month in Vegas to get him acclimated to the elevation and the heat, he thought that he was finally going to get a chance to break away from the constant sparring and speed bag routine. That wasn't what Griz had in mind.

The grizzled old fuck was making him work harder than ever. It was grueling, but if he won this match, he would be the Heavyweight Champion of the World. Years of hard work were about to pay off. Maybe. If he could keep his head on straight. The win would mean a couple of million in his pocket, and maybe a big endorsement deal. Griz was supposedly working it all out.

What would one night of wine and women hurt? That was what he had thought each and every night for the past three nights. Griz was off working on PR and schmoozing, and he was alone for a few hours. He wanted to go and meet the cute waitress that had been giving him the eye the last few times that he was "allowed" to play blackjack for an hour. Griz had wanted him to be more visible; but even that small timeout had rules — no booze, no drugs, no women. No distractions. He was so tired of making nice with total strangers. Shaking hands and taking pictures with their boozy breath so close to his nose made him crave all the things that Griz forbade him to do.

Jerking off wasn't going to cut it anymore. He had what he liked to refer to as DSB— Dangerous Sperm Build-up. Griz told him to keep the tension in his body and use it in the ring when the time came. *Bullshit.* He was going to explode. Two hours out of the hotel room — max. Meet the girl, have a drink, get his rocks off and then back to the grind tomorrow. Griz wouldn't even know he had done it.

The girl would be working downstairs in the Mandalay Bay casino just like every other Thursday night he'd been in town; and if he played his cards right, he could get her to meet him in the hotel room for a quickie. He got himself dressed in his best black skin-tight T-shirt to show off his ripped arms, and donned his designer jeans that showed off his rock-hard ass. With one last look at himself in the mirror, he smiled the smile that melted the women's hearts, and headed toward the hotel room door.

The elevators for his room at Mandalay Bay put Chet about thirty feet away from the blackjack table. With a quick glance to the left and the right, seeing that the coast was clear, he moved quickly to the table, and laid out two hundred dollars.

The table was far enough away from the elevators that Griz wouldn't be able to see him first, but close enough that Chet could spot the trainer if he finished his business dealings early and was heading up to the room. If that happened, he had already devised a plan to grab a bottled water from the waitress and use it as an excuse for being outside of his prison cell.

It wasn't more than five minutes before the hottie waitress came around. "Hi beautiful. I'll have a double vodka on the rocks, and a bottled water on the side." He gave her the smile that he had given himself in the mirror before he came down. Based on the huge grin on her face, it seemed to be working.

"You alone tonight? Did you ditch your chaperone?" she asked.

"I wanted to see you. He's pretty protective, but I managed to escape," he flirted.

"Glad you came," she replied with a wink, as she walked to the next card table to complete her round.

The Hammer watched as she walked away. She had the best set of legs that he had ever seen. Lots of girls in Vegas were hot, but this one...well, her legs blew his mind. He wanted to have them wrapped around his...

"Would you like to place a bet, sir?" the dealer asked. He was dressed in a beige, button-down shirt with decorative stitching down the front, which made him look a bit feminine, despite his huge frame and large hands.

Chet was holding up the play at the table. He put a twenty-five dollar chip on the square, and watched as the dealer spread the cards in front of his spot, and the one other player at the table.

After a couple of minutes and a few sideways glances, the guy next to him asked, "Hey, you're The Hammer, right?"

"Yep," Chet replied, not wanting to draw any further attention his way.

"Can't wait to see the big fight this weekend. You'll kick some major ass."

Chet looked at the man and wished that he would have met him some other time, not when he was breaking Griz' no booze or gambling rule. He didn't want to be rude — bad for PR — but today, he wanted to stay low-key.

"Yeah, thanks for the support. Just help me out a little buddy, and don't let on who I am. I'm taking a little R and R break that my trainer doesn't know about." At that moment, the waitress showed up with his vodka and the bottled water. It wasn't his favorite beverage, he preferred a good whisky; but vodka didn't stink like whisky, so it was the least likely to cause suspicion if he ran into Griz later on. He gave the girl two five-dollar chips as a tip for the free drink. She smiled again.

It was three vodka on the rocks and an hour-and-a-half later that he finally made his move. He was up about two hundred dollars, and if he wanted some sugar from the girl, he would have to move fast. The next time she came around, he whispered in her ear. She smiled and nodded, accepting his offer. His groin started to throb.

Ten minutes later, with his bottled water in hand, he went back upstairs to his hotel room to wait for his nightcap to arrive.

Fifty

DEVON AND KINCADE DECIDED to pair up to question Chet Hamilton. His reputation in the ring was one of unbridled rage and determination. Neither man wanted to be on the receiving end of the huge man's anger alone. Devon found himself secretly wishing that Kincade wasn't so skinny. Sure he was tall, but a tall twig is still a twig, no matter how you look at it.

When the door in Mandalay Bay's "the Hotel" opened up, they were surprised to see a withered old man standing in the doorway.

"We're looking for Chet Hamilton," Kincade said.

"Who the hell are you?" the old man barked.

Devon and Kincade seemed to pull their badges out in unison. It looked like a choreographed move, though it was just dumb luck that the timing worked out. "Is Mr. Hamilton here?"

"Crap. Sorry officers; there's a lot of people who want to talk to the champ, you know, reporters and stuff. Why do you want to see Chet?" The old man looked nervous, maybe afraid that his star boxer would get arrested just a few days before the big fight.

"Is Mr. Hamilton in the room or not?"

"He's next door. I'll take you over there. I'm his trainer and agent, Sammy Hanson." The man stuck out his hand, but neither man accepted it.

"Chet, open the door!" the old man yelled. He looked to Devon like his head was going to pop off. Anger? Nerves? Who knew?

Moments later, the boxer filled the entire doorway. He was wearing just a towel. Devon relaxed a little, knowing that naked is a great equalizer.

"Can we come in, Mr. Hamilton?" Devon demanded more than he asked, as he pushed forward into the well-appointed hotel suite.

"Doesn't look like I have a choice," Chet replied.

"We need to ask you a few questions about Stacy Bailey."

"I don't know anyone named Stacy Bailey. Is this about that waitress downstairs? She came on to me. I just agreed to let her come up and see my room."

Griz shot Chet an angry glare before he spoke, "Gentlemen, we don't know anyone named Stacy Bailey. What's this about?"

"I'm sure you've heard about all of the women who have been murdered on the Strip this week. Ms. Bailey was one of them, and it also turns out that she was involved with a club called Aphrodite's, where Chet was arrested a while back. Is any of this starting to ring a bell?" Devon saw both men's faces and attitudes change in a heartbeat.

Griz looked at Chet and shook his head. The message was clear to everyone in the room – don't say another word. "While Mr. Hamilton was arrested at the scene, he was cleared of any wrongdoing at that club. I'm sure if you look in your files, you'll see that he was just out having a drink with friends. He didn't know the type of club he was walking in to. If that is what this is about, I'll ask you to leave. As you know, we have a heavyweight boxing match in just two days, and Mr. Hamilton needs his rest."

Kincade jumped at the chance to play the bad guy. "Did you pay someone to get the charges dropped, just like you did five years ago with Chet's rape case, Mr. Hanson? I would protect my meal ticket as well if I were you; but now we're talking murder. You want to add to your title of manger and agent, and include accessory to murder? You're pretty old to be going to the pen, don't you think? Those young bucks in there will have your ass on a platter."

"Look guys; I understand that you're just doing your jobs. But I can guarantee you that Chet has nothing to do with the murders of those women. I can give you an itinerary of his every move for the past week, if that would help."

"That *would* be helpful. But we'll need a little more than that. Would you be able to give us a DNA sample for comparison purposes?" Devon asked.

"Do you have enough to charge Mr. Hamilton with the murders of those women? I'm guessing the answer is no, or he would already have cuffs on him. We'll come down to your offices tomorrow morning; but for the moment, I need you to leave so that Chet can be rested for the morning. We have a very tight training schedule that we have to follow. And as you know, we aren't going anywhere, with the heavyweight title on the line."

Hanson was trying to be cocky, but Devon thought he heard a hint of doubt in his words. The mention of DNA had made both men cringe. What were they trying to hide? Did the trainer really know where Chet had been for every moment of his Vegas trip? He wanted to bring both men in for questioning, but if they were wrong, doing so could potentially ruin the boxer's shot at the title. It was a risk that he wasn't willing to take. There was already enough pressure on the department. They would post a man outside of Chet's door for the rest of the night. It was the best they could do without causing a bigger scandal. No one wanted to have the headlines read "Police Cause Heavyweight Title Loss".

"We'll see you tomorrow then," Devon said.

Though Devon hated to admit it, celebrities did get special treatment in some cases; at least they did in Vegas, when the stakes were so high.

Fifty-One

EVERY TIME MONICA SAW him, she melted. She had seen the man many times; he was a regular at the hotel. While he wasn't the most handsome guy she had ever met, there was something about him that got her juices flowing.

Things had gotten more heated last week after the blowout fight with her boyfriend. The bastard had accused her of cheating — honestly? She was as loyal as a Saint Bernard; but someone, an anonymous caller supposedly, had told him that she was screwing someone at work. Nick was a jealous hot-head at the best of times, and the call had set him off. He ranted and pointed an accusing finger her way, and in return she had stopped taking his bullshit, and his calls, for a few days.

So when she saw the regular at the blackjack table and he had smiled, it made her want to rip his clothes off in the middle of the casino floor. It was one of those smiles that was mischievous and sly; but with a little boy's innocence that turned her on. That same day, he had touched her shoulder as he was talking to her, and her body felt like a bolt of electricity had traveled all the way down to her toes.

Ever since that moment, every single time that she saw him in the casino, she immediately had a triple-X-porn reel going on in her brain, with the two of them in starring roles. It was absolutely crazy. If you had asked her a few months ago, hell a few *weeks* ago, she would have said that he wasn't her type. He was too old, too nice, too polished. He had glasses; she never liked guys with glasses. He had touches of red in his dark hair; she liked blondes. He looked like a businessman, and she liked the bad boys. Then *whammo*, everything had changed. It was like a switch got flicked in her brain, and now she found herself thinking about him during the day, hoping that she might catch a glimpse of him when she was on shift. If Nick didn't trust her, then maybe she'd give him a reason to go ape-shit.

He always showed up on Wednesdays and Thursdays to play blackjack. She had never been much of a gambler herself, never having learned the proper way to play, and not wanting to lose her measly income as a result. But when he played, it seemed to be so easy that she thought she might have to learn the nuances of the game. She only understood the basics; hit on sixteen or lower, stay on seventeen or higher. There were lots of other things to know as well, like when to take a card based on what the dealer had showing, where you were sitting at the table, and how many decks were being played at once. It all seemed so confusing when you really didn't care about the game. And up until the fight with Nick, she couldn't have cared less.

She looked at her watch; it was closing in on eleven. She was off shift at midnight, and she still hadn't seen him. She so much wanted to get another one of those smiles. She wondered if he had in fact intended to give her that kind of signal, or if it was all just in her head. But why, if he wasn't interested in her, had he touched her shoulder? He must be at least a little interested, right? She wondered if he was married — she hadn't seen a ring, but that didn't mean that he wasn't taken. Monica wondered if that really mattered in the end. She was so hot for this guy, that maybe she could turn her moral compass down for a few hours while she ravished his body. Maybe sex with a married man would be worth it, if he was as good in bed as the porn-reel in her mind.

She wandered through the casino floor, taking drink orders and checking her watch every few minutes. He was usually here by now. Maybe he was out on a date with someone else. Maybe he had found another waitress in another hotel to smile at. Dammit, she hated that he was dominating her thoughts.

She turned the corner from the back waitress station with a full tray of drinks on her arm, pissed off at herself for acting like a silly school girl. She walked back to her section and served the first drink off of the tray to a couple who had won a three thousand dollar jackpot earlier in the day, and seemed determined to put it all back in the casino's purse before the night was done. She looked up and walked toward her next customer, when she saw him out of the corner of her eye. She was so excited that she almost dropped her tray. The triple-X film started, and she couldn't wait to get close to him to see what would happen next.

Fifty-Two

THE COLLECTOR SAT AT the gaming table, determined to make eye
contact with the pretty waitress wandering around the New York,
New York casino floor. The hotel was one of his favorites, as it
always reminded him of better times. Having spent five years of
his childhood in the Big Apple with his father and step-mother, the
bustling casino took him back to his teenage years.

The designer of the casino had done a great job of recreating
the real streets of New York. They had the neon signs, the delis, the
rowdy bars and best of all, the pretty women. The waitstaff here
wore black and burgundy bustiers on top of short, black skirts. Their
bodies were perfectly framed by the satiny fabric.

He was later than normal today. *Normally,* he would have come
into the casino to double check that his prey was working; but the
plan specifically stated what he was to do — show up at eleven, no
earlier.

Now he just had to make eye contact with the waitress and make
her feel comfortable. He had parked his car in the guest parking lot,
and had already scoped where the leggy waitress had parked hers.
Day five was looking to work out perfectly, as he caught a glimpse
of her delivering drinks to a packed house.

The NASCAR patrons were well-lubricated, and easy to pick out
in the crowded casino. The obvious ones were the men, and a few
women, wearing brightly colored racing jackets covered in corporate
logos. The others, those who looked a bit more rough and tumble,

were most likely a mix of racing fans and boxing fans. The smallest part of the casino patrons were those who were dressed up for dinner and a show, again very obvious. A tiny percentage were just regular folks looking to score a big win.

The Collector wondered which category most people would put him in at first glance. Today he was dressed in a business suit, minus the tie. His dark wig, cut into a spiky, modern cut, was only worn when he came to this particular establishment. The staff, and the cameras, had seen him with this look many times. Nothing too fancy, but something that said he was well-off. The city was on high alert looking for their killer, and he had been told that from this point forward, he would have to play it smart.

An older woman, he guessed to be sixty, was sitting two seats down, and took a quick look at his ring finger as she introduced herself. She was a talker, name of Loretta Lovely, from Texas...in Vegas with a girlfriend who had already gone to bed, not winning but hoping to get on a streak, dealer was doing okay for her, but she was hoping for more. She gave him a wink, which seemed to suggest that he was the 'more' she was looking for. She continued to talk, blah, blah, blah, and the Collector smiled but kept his eyes on the prize as Monica emptied her tray. She would be at the table in a couple of minutes.

Her legs seemed to go on forever. He guessed her at five foot ten, with the majority of her height coming from her legs. They were muscular but lean, strong but feminine, hard but soft. He was thrilled with his choice for the bottom part of his masterpiece. Monica was perfection.

She was just a few feet away now. She was a statuesque blond with a beautifully displayed cleavage; but while her chest was interesting and distracting, he only wanted one thing. He leaned back in his chair to get her attention. "Can I bother you for a drink?"

She smiled and nodded. "Same old, same old?"

"Please," he replied, and gave her his best, most sexy smile.

She smiled back, and her eyes lit up like a Christmas tree.

The Collector turned his attention back to his cards and the unfortunate woman sitting next to him. Loretta was yammering on about something or other to do with Houston and her favorite seafood restaurant, True-something or other...Trulucks, she remembered. Had he ever been? No. Did he like seafood? Yes. Had he ever eaten the crab-stuffed lobster tail at the Brand in Monte Carlo? Yes.

The mention of the Monte Carlo brought back images of Kenalynn Markerson, his perfect head girl. His mind drifted briefly to Camilla, and her beautiful beginnings in the refrigerator at the house. After today, he was going to be so close to the finish line. There were only three more pieces to collect; the legs, which would be in the refrigerator tonight; the torso, which he would have tomorrow; and finally, the breasts, which he would have on Saturday. He was starting to feel invincible. His host had given him perfect instructions, and he had never felt more confident. By Sunday, Camilla would be complete, and after the embalming process, he would have the perfect woman at his disposal whenever he wanted.

The woman sitting next to him kept talking and it continued to bore him; but he had to keep up appearances for just a little bit longer. His first two cards were a ten of hearts and a nine of clubs — it was a no-brainer win. He waived his hand in front of his cards to signal that he didn't want any others. Both Loretta and the dealer went bust; the woman with a twenty-two, and the dealer with a whopping twenty-six. The night was turning out to be very profitable on every front.

Monica returned a few minutes later, and he gave her a ten dollar chip and a huge smile as a tip for the complimentary drink.

See you in an hour, he thought.

Fifty-Three

WITH AN OFFICER POSTED outside of Chet's door, Devon and Kincade were summoned back to the station by their boss, Harvey Miller. Holland had called, and said that he would be on site by the time they arrived. They rode in relative silence, both trying to decipher the clues that were in front of them. So many things were in play, so many tidbits of information, and so many people. It was getting difficult to keep it all straight.

The Lieutenant met them at the front door, where he had been pacing for the past thirty minutes. His face was as red as a ripe apple, which most certainly meant that his blood pressure was skyrocketing. "Get into my office." He turned and stomped away at an alarming pace.

Holland was already sitting in one of the seats across from Miller's desk, looking sheepish, when the two other men arrived.

"What the fuck is going on with this investigation?" Miller turned his computer monitor around so that the three men could easily view the screen. "Do you have any idea how many phone calls I've taken in the past couple of hours? Mayor Norman is getting pressure to have all of us fired, and to make sure that our 'idiot offspring' don't work in the city when they grow up. You should be in control of what's happening, not letting some reporter jeopardize a high-profile investigation. Do you understand the implications of what she wrote? You've got every single officer who can take a breath on this case. What the hell is wrong with you people?"

The screen showed the Las Vegas Sun website. The newspaper was posting a teaser to get excitement for the following day's printed material, in hopes of boosting sales. Devon's face turned the same color as his boss' as he read the headline on the monitor. The little bitch hadn't cleared any of this with him.

Miller continued his rant, "Did you tell her she could write this bullshit? *Strip not Safe?* Dammit...you better get this guy tonight, before he kills again. And get a muzzle on that reporter. NOW!"

Holland just nodded, and the three men left without another word.

"Where is she?" Devon yelled, as he burst into the WAR room. The twenty or so people who were working on updating the whiteboards all turned to face the angry detective. "Where is Mehgan, the reporter?" he asked again.

Someone in the back answered, "I think she went home. Said she'd be back in a few hours."

Holland had already pulled up the newspaper's website on his laptop so that he could get a look at the fine print underneath the headline. He scanned the wording. "Shit on a stick. She really fucked this up."

Devon was pacing behind his partner as Kincade sat opposite the two men. "Read it to me. I'm too pissed off to focus on the screen," Devon demanded.

"Strip not Safe? The LVPD are chasing a killer who has taken four women from our city in the past four days. In the only press conference held this week, Lieutenant Harvey Miller stated that we should be on the lookout for a man in his mid- to late-forties, and assured our citizens that he had increased security both on and off Las Vegas Boulevard. Yet despite his words of comfort and a hundred thousand dollar reward, the body count is still rising. On one of the most profit-inducing weeks of the year for our city, is the Strip safe? The LVPD will tell you not to worry; but for waitresses and guests of the targeted MGM group of hotels, words don't stop bullets. Local reporter Mehgan Bowman is deep inside the investigation. Read her insider's view in tomorrow's Las Vegas Sun." Holland looked up. "That's it."

"Shit." Kincade spoke first. "That's going to cause some problems."

Devon was still pacing back and forth behind his partner. "I'll be back. I'm going to talk to her and get the article stopped before she causes any more damage."

Fifty-Four

AT 11:45 P.M., THE Collector gathered his last few dollars from the blackjack table and walked toward the cashier's cage. There was a lineup of about three people in each of the four open windows. He would have plenty of time. He had to be in the parking lot at 12:15, no later. After a few minutes in line, he made it to the front of the line and handed over thirty-five dollars in chips. The woman behind the counter smiled as she passed him paper money; he smiled back.

He walked to the east escalators and climbed to the second level, where he purchased a New York pretzel at the kiosk at the top of the stairs. He was starving, and the night was just beginning.

Five minutes later he was back on the casino floor, and walking toward the self-park entrance. Guests of the hotel and staff parked in the same lot; but the staff were instructed to position their vehicles as far from the doors as possible, in order to save the best spots for the paying guests. He had followed the staff parking rules, and was just two cars down from Monica's blue Jeep Liberty.

Halfway to the parking lot entrance, a woman's high-pitched scream pierced through the clanging of the machines, a mere two feet away from his path. The Collector jumped and had immediate thoughts of being recognized. He was sure that he hadn't left any witnesses. Wasn't he? His eyes shifted left to right to see which direction the ambush was coming from. He turned his head toward the woman on his right. She turned toward him and screamed again — higher pitched and louder, and she was waving her arms in the air.

"Ahhhh, Ahhhh! Holy shit! Ahhh! Ahhh!" Her voice was carrying, and she was getting a lot of attention from the busy gaming area — security was sure to be on their way.

The Collector wanted to run at top speed out of the casino. Fighting the overwhelming urge to bolt, he started to walk faster, his hands and armpits wet with perspiration. He looked back several times and saw security guards surrounding the screaming woman. What was she going to tell them? How the hell did she recognize him?

He turned back a few more times. No one was following. Did the woman see where he had gone? Did she know that he was heading toward the self-park?

He reached his car at 12:10 a.m., and seriously thought about calling tonight's adventure off. With shaking hands, he fumbled with his key fob and finally had a chance to catch his breath. That was close. Or was it? The Collector took a few deep breaths to clear his head and slow his heart rate. He looked in his rear-view mirror to see if anyone else was in hot pursuit of him in the parking lot. Nothing. Either the woman hadn't seen where he went, or the security staff didn't believe her story.

It was less than fifteen minutes later that he had to make his decision. His head resting on the seat back, his heart slowly returning to its normal tempo, he spotted Monica walking toward her car. He had to decide — follow through with the plan as stated by his host, or take the safer route and abort today's mission. *Think, think, think.*

Not wanting to betray the trust of those who had given him the opportunity of a lifetime, he did the only thing that felt right; he put his car in reverse.

Monica was just a few feet from her car when he pulled up beside her. She jumped a little, and the Collector watched as she fumbled in her pocket and pulled out a small canister.

"Hey, stranger; are you just getting off shift?" he asked.

"Wow, you scared the living crap out of me. You almost got a faceful of pepper spray." She flashed the canister his way.

The Collector recoiled at the sight. He didn't remember getting sprayed in the face with dry fire being a part of the well-documented plan. "Don't shoot, it's just me." He put his hands up in the air as a sign of submission. He watched as she smiled, knowing that it was probably the last time she would do it in her life.

"Lucky it's you. Anyone else would be writhing in agony by now. There's a killer on the Strip, as I'm sure you've heard."

"Sorry, I didn't mean to scare you. I just saw you and thought you might want to go for a drink. I'm tired of the NASCAR crowd. Maybe somewhere off-Strip?" *Smile, smile, smile.* Was that lust in her eyes?

"Sure."

"How about the Freaking Frog on Maryland?"

She paused for a second and nodded. "Sounds like fun."

"Okay, just a second. Let me pull back in and I'll write down my cell number. That way you can call me when you get there and I will be your escort to the door." *More smiles.*

He pretended to write down a number. Folding the paper in half, he took his gun from the passenger seat.

"Here you go."

Monica leaned forward to grab the paper. He grabbed her arm and pulled her toward him.

"Hey, what are you…"

The gun was already at her temple and the trigger pulled before she could finish her thought. It was messier than he expected. Little chunks of hair and scalp flew in to the driver's side window and coated the car next to him.

Less than thirty seconds later, the leggy blond was in the trunk of his car. No time to dawdle; he would dismember the key parts when he got home.

Fifty-Five

DEVON DIDN'T USUALLY LIKE to use the standard-issue cars with the lights and sirens, preferring to use an unmarked car to investigate crime scenes; but today he wanted to drive fast and hard, without worrying about traffic signals and other vehicles. *Get the fuck out of my way,* was all he was thinking as he whizzed through each intersection. He was as mad as hell, and with each heartbeat his fury was increasing.

He was normally pretty even-keeled; but the stupid reporter had gotten under his skin. He cursed out loud in the car, pissed off at himself for letting her get involved in the inner workings of the case. Why had he trusted her? He was normally more guarded. Why had he allowed her to come into the WAR room? He didn't really want to know the answers, afraid of what he might find if he did too much analysis of his mind.

He barely got the car in park before he rushed to her door and started pounding his fist on the wooden exterior.

"Mehgan!" He smashed his fist into the door another half-dozen times. "Mehgan! Get your ass out here!"

The outside light came on and the door opened quickly. "What the hell is your problem? Get in here before you wake up the whole neighborhood." The reporter was dressed in jeans and a T-shirt. "I was just heading back to the station house, so there was really no need for you to come here. What's going on?"

Devon pushed past her and stormed into her living room. "Good question. You tell me what's going on. Nice fucking post on your website tonight. I thought we had a deal. Get on the phone right this second and get the article stopped before I jam your laptop into the toilet, along with your career. Do you honestly think that anyone, and I mean *anyone*, on the force is going to talk to you *ever* again once I tell them what kind of woman you are?" Devon grabbed her by the wrist and pulled her toward the phone on the coffee table. "Do it now, before I lose the last shred of control in my body."

She pulled her arm from his grip. "What the hell are you talking about?"

"Don't play dumb with me. 'Strip not Safe'. Does that ring a bell?"

Mehgan rushed over to her laptop which she was in the process of packing up. With a few keystrokes she had the Las Vegas Sun website on the screen. "Damn it!" She turned to face Devon with a shocked look on her face. "I didn't tell them to post that, I swear. I'll show you the article that *I* wrote." The reporter hit a few more keys and brought up the full article on her screen. "Look."

Devon pushed her aside from the screen and read the Word document. His breaths were short and hard as he tried to focus on the monitor...Police working hard...Increased security with additional FBI assistance...Strip safer than ever...

"See, I told you. I didn't break our agreement. My editor must have embellished a bit to try to increase sales of tomorrow's morning edition."

Devon got up from the desk chair and turned toward the door. "Consider yourself banished from the station house."

Mehgan cut him off and stood in his path. "That's not even close to being fair. I didn't do anything wrong. I'll talk to my boss so this doesn't happen again. But you read the article. You can trust me."

"Even if I can trust you, I can't trust your stinking newspaper, so the deal is off. Plus, the one and only reason that you were allowed in to start with was the phone calls, and low and behold, you haven't had one lately. Coincidence? Did you make all of that shit up? Anything for a better story, right?"

Mehgan positioned her face closer to his. "You self-obsessed asshole. You think that I lied? Maybe you lie to get information out of suspects, but I hold myself to a higher standard. You've seen me get the phone calls. I've given you the number so that you could trace it. Just because she hasn't phoned today doesn't mean she won't." She took another step closer to the detective. "I'm so tired I can barely think and you, Mr. Bigshot Detective, are pissing me off. Maybe you're right and I shouldn't be a part of your investigation; then I can print whatever I want, whenever I want."

Devon's blood was boiling, but his body and mind seemed to have a disconnect for a moment or two. His mind said, *push her out of the way and drive like hell back to the station;* but somehow his body forced his hands to her face and pushed his lips onto hers. It was a hard, animalistic kiss that took both of them by surprise. The anger turned to unbridled lust in a heartbeat. Her body was responding to him as well and, despite his better judgment, groping hands and warm, probing tongues got the better of him.

Fortunately, or unfortunately for the brain below his belt, before any clothes were shed, Devon's cell phone buzzed and he was able to take control of his body for a moment.

He answered the call with his left hand while his right hand re-buttoned his pants. "Shit. On the way."

"What happened?" Mehgan asked as she pulled her T-shirt back down over her chest.

"Guess," he replied, returning to his previously angry tone.

"I'm coming with you." Mehgan grabbed her purse from beside the front door.

"No, you're not." Devon was firm, but a look into her eyes and he was cursing himself for allowing her to complicate things yet again. "Go to New York, New York. The security guard found someone's brain splattered all over the parking lot."

Fifty-Six

BACK IN THE SAFETY of his house, the Collector took the lifeless corpse out of his trunk and placed it onto a thick plastic sheet in the garage. He was under strict instructions as to his next move, and he had less than an hour to complete the next step in the plan. After placing Monica on the concrete floor, he took a moment to admire her legs again. He carefully removed her black shoes and her dark nylons. Her skin was even more perfect than he imagined it would be. He ran his hands up and down the woman's legs. He wanted to spend more time lost in the fantasy; but while the legs were perfect, the rest of her body wasn't anywhere near good enough for Camilla. For most men it would have been enough; but he wasn't most men; he deserved perfection.

He grabbed the rechargeable miter saw from the garage shelf and turned the power on. He wanted the cuts to be perfect. He would need to cut above the femur and through the hip bone so that he would have enough skin to reconnect the legs to the torso once he retrieved it tomorrow. The saw ate through the first layer of skin and fat without issue. Once it reached the hard hip bone though, it began to struggle under the immense load. It was more challenging than he had anticipated. The removal of Kenalynn's head and Heather's arms had been much easier, but then the bones and tendons were smaller in scale.

After a half-hour of careful dissection, the two perfectly proportioned legs were free of their less-perfect host. The Collector was covered in blood. After a quick shower, he realized that he had only fifteen minutes to get to the hotel. He was at least thirty-five minutes away. He reasoned that a twenty-minute difference was not the end of the world.

He double checked the instructions one more time. He was supposed to add the printout to the woman's cleavage and put her body into a 36" black suitcase lined with a green garbage bag that had been provided as part of his kit. Then it was off to the Mirage hotel. He changed his wig to a longer, redder version, and added a full beard. He looked nothing like the man that he was earlier in the night. He had transformed from a smartly dressed businessman to a NASCAR hippie, complete with the colored jacket and denim jeans. He looked like thousands of other people who were checking in for the weekend's festivities.

Thirty-five minutes later, he walked through the casino's lush tropical entrance, suitcase in tow. He was nervous and felt the buzz of excitement in the hotel. Were they looking for him? Did the screaming woman point him out?

He crossed over the wooden bridge flanked with colorful vegetation to the left of the front check-in desk. Straight to the back was the entrance to the men's washroom. He walked past the many urinals and into a stall. He caught the eye of another man who looked at the suitcase. "Can't wait to go through the check-in line?"

"Not a chance." The Collector grimaced and shuffled himself and the suitcase into the handicapped stall. Despite the oversized space, he felt claustrophobic. He couldn't wait to get this part of the mission completed so that he could go back home. This hotel didn't feel busy enough and for this mission; there was safety in the crush of a large crowd. He sat on the toilet fully clothed, with the dead woman next to him and wondered who would find her. Would it be someone in a wheelchair? Somehow he hoped not; it didn't seem fair to give them the burden when they couldn't even run screaming to the front desk.

After a few minutes of sitting and waiting for an appropriate amount of time to pass, the Collector walked out of the stall and calmly exited the washroom. He didn't feel the need to wash his hands.

Fifty-Seven

AFTER THE RUN-IN WITH the two detectives, Griz had turned into a basket case of major proportion. What seemed like a really good idea a few months ago was now looking like a huge cluster-fuck. Not only did he have the businessmen breathing down his neck, he had his new "boss" to deal with, and the added pressure of cops nosing around his business. He hadn't anticipated that they would ever figure out the connection between the first murdered woman, Aphrodite's, and Chet — he had been assured that the tiny strings that held everything together would remain in place. Chet, on the other hand, had nothing to worry about. He had never met Stacy Bailey, and under pressure in an interrogation room, would hold up well. The only concern was if Chet talked about Griz' involvement with the club.

The tabloids had jumped all over the fact that Chet was arrested in the fetish club so long ago; but Griz had fixed the problem with a few bundles of hundred dollar bills and a fabricated story about a friend who took the boxer to the club without knowing that it was a brothel. It had worked brilliantly. The criminal charges were dropped, and eventually bigger stories took over the headlines. In reality, Griz had taken Chet to Aphrodite's as a congratulations gift after a hard-fought battle with Graham "The Grenade" Jacobs. The trip to Vegas included some drink, some blackjack and some dirty dancing with the girls at the club.

While Chet was enjoying the fruits of his labor in a private room, Griz was fed thirty year-old port and Cuban cigars in the lounge. It was there that a pretty woman named Stacy had introduced him to a potential business partner who could make him very wealthy. After a couple of hours with the rich port coursing through his veins, the two men had struck up a friendship. With Griz lubed up with booze, the man had proposed a business deal that Griz had immediately dismissed as a joke. It was so far out of his comfort zone and he was so offended, that he had left Chet at the club alone. He politely excused himself, using the booze as an excuse, and poured himself into a cab. He left the limo behind for the champ, to ensure his safe return to the hotel.

That night he got two calls. One from a frantic Chet in jail, and another on his cell phone from the man he had met at the club. The second call was promising to make the news from the first call go away. Griz knew what that meant, even with a hangover pounding in his brain — he was going to owe the man in a big way. Somehow, that was okay in the moment.

Then a month ago, he had received the call — the man was calling in his favor. It was a horrible deal, but the man was offering big money — he thought it was a deal that he could live with, based on what he was told. What he didn't realize was the extent to which his boss would go to get what he wanted. Dead women weren't originally part of the deal...at least not the deal that he thought he was agreeing to. He was told there would be a distraction. He never asked what that meant. In hindsight, he thought that perhaps he should have.

Thoughts and considerations for what he should do next were interrupted by the buzz of his cell phone. He looked at the displayed number, and knew that regardless of what he decided in his mind, there was only one option — do what the caller wanted him to do, or die. Despite how shitty he was feeling about himself and his choices, he still wanted to live.

"Yes?" Griz answered.

"It's time to have the conversation with the promoters. Call them now, and get a breakfast meeting set up for the morning," Scarlett said.

"Sure. Yep."

"Don't act smug with me. Just get the fight venue changed tomorrow. You know what to do."

Griz hung up on her this time. He was tired of being ordered around. He would do what she asked, but by ending the call, he finally felt a bit of power, however minimal and temporary it was. He felt the tears welling up in his eyes, and then chuffed out a nervous laugh. He was a grown man who had set himself up for this...in fact, he had invited this stress. Time to suck it up and act like a man.

Ten minutes later, he had the meeting arranged for Friday morning. The fight promoters and Laz Butte's team were all in agreement that they should discuss their options for Saturday's big event. If Griz did his job right, there would be a lot of people scrambling in the next twenty-four hours.

Fifty-Eight

THE ENTIRE PARKING LOT of the New York, New York hotel was locked down. No one, staff or customers, was getting in or out, no matter what their excuse... a sick kid, a dying parent, husband waiting at home for dinner, a flight leaving in an hour...none of it mattered. Every single car and every single person was stuck. Holland, who was first on the scene, suggested to the hotel manager, who was continually in his face, that he should give his staff and guests taxi vouchers, or he would lock down the entire hotel complex, casino and all. The threat was taken seriously enough that the man hadn't shown his face in the last twenty minutes.

Holland was standing in the middle of the concrete parking lot, directing the team which was thirty-strong and growing by the minute. When Devon showed up, he was relieved to have some help.

"No body?"

"No body. This goes against what he's done in the past. He's always left the woman behind once he takes what he wants. Where is she, and who is she?" Holland replied.

"What do we know so far?" Devon asked.

"Not a lot. The hotel has a security guard who patrols the parking lot. His last round in this area was about eleven o'clock. The murder had to have happened after eleven, but before the blood was found by another staff member at 12:30 a.m. The car that's covered with bits of brain belongs to a sixty-year-old woman who works in the cashier's window. She's still on shift. There are another hundred cars on this level, most belong to staff. We're running the plates and trying to find out who's missing."

"Anyone see anything?"

"Nothing so far. He obviously came in and out of the parking lot, but there isn't any surveillance video on this level. We've got people checking the parking lot's hotel entrance footage. That's the only area where they have cameras. If our guy went into the hotel tonight from a vehicle that had been parked here, we'll have a picture of him."

"He's changing his pattern. He knows that we have hundreds of cops on the Strip, so he's taking the women somewhere else so that he can cut them up in peace." Kincade, who had been sleeping in a hotel room off-Strip, walked up to the two men. "The guy is smart, but he's being more cautious than before. Our first three women were killed on-site in the hotel; but Heather Langdon, and whoever *this* is, were moved. He'll leave us the body...have the team check every inch of this hotel. She's here somewhere."

Preliminary reports were coming back in from the detectives who were interviewing the staff and running the license plates. It looked like there were three people who weren't accounted for, and only one was female. Monica Cantrel, a twenty-six year-old cocktail waitress, had gotten off shift at midnight, and wasn't answering her cell or home phone.

With the investigation into the missing woman in full swing, Devon, Holland and Kincade headed inside the hotel, where the manager had provided one of the hotel's suites to serve as a makeshift meeting room.

"This guy has to be changing his look every time he enters the hotels. He's going to look like anyone else in for the race or the fight. He has to blend in for any of this to work." Kincade was looking as puzzled as everyone else. "What about using face recognition software in conjunction with the hotel security tapes? We could try to match faces that have shown up in each of the hotels the day of each murder."

"If he's changing his look, would the software be able to pick it up?" Devon asked.

"There's new software that we've been working with at the Bureau. Pretty high-end stuff. The big casinos use something similar to track cheaters on the gaming floor; but our software algorithms are smokin'-accurate compared to anything here. If we can find images from men entering the hotel from the parking lot, and then compare it against the other hotels...well, you get where I'm going with this. It's a long shot based on how many people are on the Strip right now, but it might work."

"It's our best bet, considering that our only eyewitness is in a coma with no eyes," Holland replied, then thought better of his comment.

The other two men nodded their approval, and set out to take the next step in their plan. Then the phone call came in...the body of their missing woman was found in a bathroom stall at the Mirage.

Fifty-Nine

BACK AT HOME AFTER making his deposit at the Mirage, the Collector was watching the news, wondering if he was going to see his face on the screen. Instead, he was pleased to see that the screaming woman in New York, New York was not a witness to an unspeakable crime, but was instead a jackpot winner. The newscaster was bubbling with excitement, talking about the Canadian woman who had won the Mega Millions jackpot of ten million big ones.

The Collector felt all of the tension leave his body in one gigantic *whoosh*. He hadn't even realized how many of his muscles had knotted up until the moment he saw the picture of the woman on the screen. It was his 'eyewitness'. There was no mistaking her dark hair and pale, white skin. He wondered if Canadians even got to see sunlight — he had never met one who was tanned. The newscaster interviewed the woman, who seemed like she might have had a few drinks since she won; her cheeks glowing red.

Now able to relax, he took the two legs from the refrigerator, and carefully cleaned them with warm, soapy water. He squeezed one of the calves and was pleased to feel strong muscle tone beneath the flesh. Her thighs were feminine, but muscular as well. He was surprised to see that despite the fact that his victim had perfectly smooth, supple and hair-free legs, she didn't have any nail polish on her toes. He wondered why, with such beautiful legs, that she hadn't taken care of such a small but significant detail. It was like baking a perfect cake, and forgetting to add the icing.

The Collector truly didn't mind fixing the problem, as it gave him more time to caress his newly acquired prizes. He soaked the feet in a bath of warm Epsom salts for fifteen minutes, then carefully cut away the cuticles. He took the biggest, fluffiest towel that he could find and dried each foot with the tenderness of a mother caring for an injured child— nothing was too good for Camilla. He hummed Alice Cooper's "I Love the Dead" as he applied the same color polish that he had put on her perfect hands. Two coats in long, smooth strokes. If he did it right, the varnish wouldn't have to be reapplied for at least two weeks.

While the last coat was drying, he couldn't resist the urge to put all of Camilla's parts on the table at the same time. He was so incredibly close now. He positioned the two legs at the bottom of the table, and then added the arms and the beautifully assembled head. He stepped back to get a better look at his work. If you had told him a year ago that he would be standing in a kitchen in Las Vegas looking at a collection of stunning body parts, he would have laughed— mind you, a year ago he hadn't been offered the chance at such a big payoff. He mused at how quickly life could take you in different directions. This was one road that he was super-excited to be on no, matter where it led next.

Sixty

THE SUITCASE HAD BEEN discovered about ten minutes after the Collector had left it in the bathroom stall. The cleaning staff had taken it to the front desk assuming it should go into lost and found. A few minutes later, a staff member from the bell desk, trying to find identification that would point to its rightful owner, had opened the case and discovered the gruesome contents inside. The panicked screams were heard as far away as the taxi line outside.

Holland checked his watch; it was after 3 a.m. when he and Devon arrived at the Mirage. Adrenaline was coursing through his veins like a freight train; but he knew that the entire team, himself included, were at the breaking point. This just couldn't keep happening. It was ludicrous. He wanted to call Maggie, but she was asleep hours ago.

Surveillance tapes showed a man entering the Mirage washroom with the suitcase at 1:50 a.m. Their guy was finally caught on tape, but that did little to help the investigation. Long hair and a scraggly beard left only a small portion of the killer's real face to compare to the tapes in other hotels.

"Can you zoom in on the face?" Devon asked the hotel's security manager.

"Sure thing; but honestly, our best camera work is done at the tables and the slots. We don't have video in the washrooms, for obvious reasons, so it might be a bit grainy."

The face of the man came into view and filled the computer screen. Devon and Holland scrutinized every part of the picture, looking to see who it might be. The face looked like a furball with eyes. The long wig and facial hair obscured the majority of the killer's true identity.

"This truly tells us nothing. Anyone could be under all that hair," Holland said.

Kincade jumped in. "Zoom in on the eyes for me."

The security guard did as instructed, and just the two eyes were visible on the monitor. The black and white image was unfocused — they could belong to anyone.

"Can your software work with something that grainy and that small?" Devon asked.

"I'll send this to the lab and see if we can clean it up. There's a chance, a small chance, that we can use the facial recognition software to match this image with the tape from the other hotels. It's a long shot, but worth trying at this point," Kincade replied.

FRIDAY

Sixty-One

THE LVPD GATHERED THE entire team in the WAR room. The room that was designed to hold thirty was now standing room only, shoulder to shoulder, with people spilling out into the adjoining hallway. The added body heat had the room at about eighty-five degrees, and everyone was wiping sweat from their brows.

Holland stood at the front of the room, and summarized their status and the day's assignments. He divided the team into twenty-eight groups.

The room was as quiet as church at the beginning of a Sunday sermon.

"Okay. Based on the silence, I assume that everyone understands their assignments. I want a radio update from each of the groups to either Detective Cartwright or myself every hour. Now get out there and get this guy before he kills another woman."

The room emptied out quickly. Only Devon, Holland and Kincade remained at the boardroom table. "The answers are here, but they're just not coming together," Devon commented.

"I know. It just seems crazy that with all of this manpower, we can't get a break here. The best leads that we have are from our first murder. I can't even see a connection with the other women. The only person that makes sense is the Reverend. We can't find him, and he seems to have had access to all of the victims. He would have their trust. He's a man of God. Who would suspect him? The girls would let their guard down, which would give him a chance to strike," Holland added.

"I just can't see how a preacher would have access to security cards to let him into the hotel rooms. How would he get them from someone? What would be his excuse? I still think we are dealing with multiple people; but that doesn't sit right in my brain either." Kincade's eyes were getting dull from overwork.

"If there are multiple people involved, what's their motivation?" Devon asked. His mind flashed quickly to the last moments that he had spent with Mehgan the night before. What was her motivation? She made a mistake; but she seemed to genuinely want to help with the investigation. Had he misread her? Was she really one of the good ones? He wanted to see her again and apologize for his outburst.

"That's an interesting question. Who's benefitting from the killings other than the whack-job who's collecting the body parts? Especially on such a busy weekend? The only hotels that haven't been targeted are owned by people other than the MGM. Would someone from the other hotel chains try to sabotage the MGM group to increase business? God knows there's a mitt full of cash floating around the city right now." Holland was thinking that he might be on to something. "But then again, how would they get access to a competitor's security grid?"

Devon leapt up from his seat. "I just can't put it together. We normally try to solve one murder at a time. Now we have five in five days. The bastard is just trying to keep us off balance, and he's doing a good job."

Sixty-Two

JACKIE TEMPLE WAS AT the ready every time she went anywhere. Her drinking buddy had come through for her the very same day that she had called, and for the past two days she had been carrying her new protection — it was a well-spent three hundred dollars. The small handgun was fully loaded, thanks to her friend, and had been within arm's reach any time she left the house. Even at night when she felt most safe, she kept it on the nightstand beside her bed.

She was watching the news every moment that she wasn't working, and wasn't surprised to see that the killer was closing in on the MGM hotel. So far he had hit the Aria, Monte Carlo, Luxor, Excalibur and New York, New York, and he had left one of the bodies at the Mirage. If what the newspapers, TV and radio were saying was true, the only MGM-owned properties left on the strip were the Bellagio, Mandalay Bay and the MGM itself. If the killer took another woman tonight, it would either be her or a waitress at one of the other two resorts. The thought was terrifying. She was scheduled to work from noon to nine, and wondered when he would strike. It seemed to make sense that she would be most at risk after her shift, rather than early in the morning; but he was an unpredictable foe — she couldn't let her guard down.

Jackie went over the plans in her mind a million times. She had devised separate scenarios if he tried to take her at home, on the casino floor, in the back hallway, in the parking lot or even in public places like the grocery store. She practiced getting the gun in and out of her purse, in and out of her jeans, and in and out of her red waitress outfit. She was starting to feel like Clint Eastwood in an old spaghetti western. Some moves proved more problematic than others, especially concealing a gun in her MGM uniform; but she was starting to feel more confident than afraid.

Jackie took the gun, went to the full-length mirror in her bedroom, and held the weapon in front of her. She practiced the stance that Scott from the Gun Store had taught her — hands overlapping, back and arms straight, knees slightly bent. She held the position for a few minutes, and turned to admire herself from the front, the left and the right. "Pretty impressive, girl," she said out loud. Even if the dumbass cops couldn't see that she was the only logical target from the hotel, she knew in her heart that there wasn't anyone else who could hold a candle to her body. He was coming, she was sure of it.

As a pre-emptive strike, she had even given an interview to the Channel 3 news crew earlier that morning. They wanted to know if she felt safe working on the Strip, and what she thought about the current police protection that was being provided. At first she was reluctant to talk on camera, afraid that it might make her a bigger target. But knowing that she was the only one pretty enough to be a target anyway, she agreed, hoping that the extra camera time might speed up her journey to the Playboy mansion. Did Hugh Hefner watch Vegas news? Probably not. But she reasoned that seeing as everything was available almost immediately on the Internet, and because the killings were now famous all over the world, there was still a slight chance he might see her. All she needed was for Hef or one of his people to take notice and invite her for a visit. Once he got a glimpse, she was sure that he wouldn't be able to resist. She had seen the likes of his current girlfriends, and knew that she had a good shot, based on her attributes.

Maybe this killer thing wouldn't be so bad after all. As long as she survived, she would be all over the news, then Playboy was sure to take notice. A thought flashed in her mind, and it made her grin from ear to ear...what if she was the one who killed the killer? The press coverage would be absolutely massive. Her face and body would be plastered all over the Internet. Everyone would want an interview.

This string of murders might be just the break that she needed to catapult her career.

All of a sudden, she couldn't wait for the killer to approach. The others had no idea that he was coming for them; but in contrast, she *knew* it.

Yes, the killer was coming; but now she was ready.

Sixty-Three

COLIN YOUNG, HEATHER LANGDON's boyfriend, was equally as obsessed about the killings as waitress Jackie Temple. It was all he had been able to think about since he heard about Heather's murder. The guilt that he was feeling was overwhelming. He hadn't slept more than a few minutes at a time since the moment that the police had contacted him with the bad news. To make things worse, they had grilled his coworkers and his neighbors, looking for any dirt that might implicate him in the murders. Top that off with the fact that everyone he knew was phoning, texting and sending emails with their heartfelt sympathies, and he was feeling like he was going over the edge.

He looked around the room and could still see hints of blood visible on the carpet. The police weren't responsible for the cleanup... no one was. He did his best, but the stain just wouldn't go away.

Why hadn't she listened to him? He told her to watch out, to be on her guard at all times. Why didn't he take her to and from work, just to be on the safe side? Why hadn't he told her to take some time off until they found the killer? There were so many 'What Ifs' going through his brain, that he felt like he was going to explode. He wanted to go back to work and throw himself into the weight room for hours on end, but everyone at the gym insisted that he take a few days off to grieve. So now here he was, sitting on his couch, an angry mess of a man who wanted revenge on everyone involved with the situation. He wanted to kill the man who took his girlfriend, the cops that failed to protect her, and most of all, everyone who reminded him that the love of his life was never coming home again.

The national news channel was broadcasting the murders almost 24/7, so there was ample information to keep the fires of his obsession alive. There were no new leads, too much evidence to process and not enough manpower to deal with it all. He thought that he might be better off if he took the easy way out. He had a gun...always had a gun. Surely no one would judge him for taking his own life under the circumstances. If they put themselves in his situation...for the rest of his life, he would be known as the boyfriend of the poor dead woman killed on the Strip. There would be constant reminders every day from this point forward. One of the hotels would certainly put up a memorial...that's what Americans do to keep the memories alive. He would be expected to visit it...that's what grieving boyfriends do. His entire body was in pain, but his heart felt like it was going to rip in two. He *couldn't* and *wouldn't* do this for the rest of his life.

The experts say that people have defining moments in their lives, and just as he was thinking about going and getting his gun from the bedroom that he used to share with Heather, he saw something on the screen that changed his path. The petite blond was talking to reporters about her life as a waitress at the MGM, and how she was afraid for her safety. The interview only lasted a few minutes, but the message was clear — the blond waitress felt that she was a target for the killer, and she was concerned that the police couldn't protect her. Colin hit pause on the screen. The woman's name was on the bottom of the screen — Jackie Temple.

Colin wiped the tears from his cheeks, and a look of determination came across his face. Even though he failed Heather, he wouldn't let another woman feel fear; and most of all, he wouldn't let another husband or boyfriend feel the pain. It was time to take action.

Sixty-Four

FRIDAY MORNING HAD COME so quickly, and Griz had almost no sleep. Once he had set up the breakfast meeting, he thought that he might be able to rest his brain for a few hours; but the importance of the next day was weighing heavily on his mind. Now sitting in a private room on the Mandalay Bay's tenth floor, directing the placement of the breakfast buffet he had ordered, he was so jumpy that the clattering of two metal dishes had almost made him crap his pants. This week couldn't be over quick enough. Tomorrow's fight was scheduled for 8 p.m. in the Mandalay South Convention Center. If all went well this morning, that was going to change.

Four men from the Boxing Commission and three men from Laz Butte's management team were seated around the large boardroom table. Once everyone got a coffee and a plate of food, Griz stood up at the front of the room and started to talk.

"Gentlemen, thank you for coming here on such short notice. As you are all aware, our fight is tomorrow; and while it is unconventional for all of us meet the day before a title bout, the situation that we're in is really unusual." Griz paused for a sip of water. He was wearing a suit and tie for the meeting, and felt like he was being strangled by the fabric. "As of this morning, there have been five victims on the Las Vegas Strip, and to my understanding, there are no immediate suspects in the crimes. I've had countless conversations with Chet, and he's worried not just for his own safety, but also for the safety of the fans who paid hard-earned money to watch the fight."

One of Butte's men interrupted with a smile on his face, "So you're conceding the match?"

The Boxing Commission suits gave Griz an annoyed look and were about to interject, when he spoke again, "Not a chance. Hear me out. We want the fight to go forward, just like you do. I'm just proposing a change of venue. Mandalay Bay is one of the MGM group of hotels which seems to be the focus of the killer's rage. We don't want to be associated with another killing, nor do we want our fans to be subjected to any more police scrutiny than necessary. I spoke to the owner of the Hard Rock Hotel, and they are willing to let us use their location for tomorrow's fight." There, he had said it... let the chips fall where they may.

Laz Butte's manager took a few moments to digest the suggestion. "What about Caesar's Palace? They've done lots of fights in the past. They're set up for it."

Acting time. "That was my initial thought too; but they're still on the Strip. You wanna take the chance?" Griz replied.

"What do we do with all of the ticket holders who have already bought tickets?" one of the commission's men asked.

"We issue new ones that they can either pick up today at Mandalay Bay, or at the Hard Rock's box office tomorrow."

More questions came in at a quick-fire pace from all around the table.

"Can the Hard Rock handle the number of people?" Yes.

"Would they be able to set up a regulation ring in time?" Yes.

"Were they willing to have extra staff in their sports book for betting up to the first bell?" Yes.

"Was Chet comfortable with the situation?" Yes.

"Could they get out of the contract with Mandalay Bay?" Yes.

"Could the Hard Rock accommodate the high rollers?" Yes.

Griz fielded another dozen questions, and then sat in silence while both parties decided on their feelings toward the proposed venue switch. Good sales people might be comfortable with silence, but to the trainer, it was deafening. *Just keep quiet — don't oversell the idea.*

Laz Butte's management team were first to speak up. "I think that it's a good idea, as long as we don't lose any seating, and we can still broadcast on Pay-per-view. I agree with Mr. Hanson; staying at Mandalay could pose a risk, and Caesar's could be an issue."

One down and one to go, Griz thought. He crossed his gnarly fingers behind his back.

The Boxing Commission people nodded in agreement. "As long as Mandalay Bay agrees to let us out of the contract, we would support the move. If there's even a possibility of a lawsuit, then we go ahead as planned."

Griz was pleased that he wore a dark suit jacket — his shirt was soaking wet. "Once we remind them of the potential for bad publicity, I'm sure they will agree to whatever we suggest. We'll promise them that the next match is theirs, once all of this has blown over."

The men remained at the table and chatted about the logistics for another half-hour. The suits from the Boxing Commission agreed to have the paperwork drawn up for signature by two that afternoon. Then, all of the men shook hands and left Griz alone in the room.

He walked back to the hallway and watched as the men got on the elevator to the lower floors. It was only then that he went back into the suite, closed the door and made a phone call.

"They agreed. Let the boss know that we need to get ready for the next phase of the plan."

Remarkably, Scarlett's tone of voice was softer than usual. "Good job," she said, before hanging up the phone.

Sixty-Five

HOLLAND WAS STARING AT the whiteboards, trying to find inspiration from the scribbles on the walls. Devon and Kincade were in the station house kitchen getting more coffee. For the first time in a week, it was quiet in the WAR room. Everyone was out on assignment, which left the three lead detectives behind to strategize on their next move.

Just as the other two men came back into the board room, one of the officers who was manning a call center phone burst through the door. "You might want to turn on a TV. Reverend Clark is about to make an on-air announcement."

The local news station was interrupting its regularly scheduled program to broadcast the Reverend's message. News reporter Kimberly Vince was on the screen. Standing on the corner of Tropicana Avenue and Las Vegas Boulevard, her backdrop was the green and gold of the MGM hotel.

"Today Reverend Earl Wesley Clark is with me in front of one of the most famous landmarks on the Las Vegas Strip. It's a destination hotel for travelers from all over the globe; but more recently, the MGM group, which includes nine local hotels and three resorts outside of the city, has become the target of a serial killer. The man who has taken five victims in the last five days has eluded police and put fear into the hearts of our citizens and visitors alike." The TV reporter turned her attention away from the camera and faced the Reverend. "Reverend Clark, I understand that you have been on a sabbatical of sorts, trying to connect with God to help solve the murders. Is that correct?"

The tall man towered over the young reporter, and adjusted his round glasses before he spoke. "Thank you for having me on, Ms. Vince. As soon as the first murder was announced, I knew that there would be more. God told me there was a powerful evil at work. After days of praying, the Lord has revealed to me who the killer is, and we can now breathe easy."

"Have you already spoken to the police? Do they have a man under arrest?"

"I am on my way there now. I wanted to let the good citizens of the city know that there will be no more murders on the Las Vegas Strip this week." He looked directly at the camera. "You can rest now, my children."

"How can you be sure that the man you suspect to be the killer is really the one the police are looking for?"

"God told me, Ms. Vince. I know that many of your viewers are spiritual people. I just happen to be lucky enough to have a special connection with God. He talks directly to me, and I will do his bidding as he instructs. I am merely a messenger that delivers his word. I assure you Ms. Vince; with God's guiding hand, we will have a man under arrest before dinnertime tonight."

"I hope you're right, Reverend Clark." She turned back to face the camera. "We'll keep you updated as the day goes on. This is Kimberly Vince, reporting from the MGM hotel on Las Vegas Boulevard."

Holland was already on the phone getting in touch with the team that had been dispatched to the MGM hotel earlier in the day. "Get out front; get the Reverend in a car and bring him to me now." He disconnected from the team leader and looked at his partners in the room. "He's going to come and tell us who's behind the murders? Does that mean he's going to confess?"

"Wouldn't that be a nice twist," Devon said.

"Hmmm...I don't know guys. I get the feeling that he might be a tough nut to crack. Even if he is our guy, I'll bet he blames it on someone else first. His little speech there didn't sound like a guy who was going to turn himself in," Kincade said.

The three men moved quickly to prepare an interrogation room specifically for their soon-to-arrive guest.

Sixty-Six

IT WAS A LONG thirty minutes later before the Reverend walked through the door to the precinct. Kincade and Holland had agreed to take the lead for the interview, and Devon watched from an adjacent room on the TV. Devon was a bit put out that he wasn't able to join in; but two's company and three is definitely a crowd when it comes to interviews.

"Can I get you a coffee, Reverend?" Kincade asked, after he introduced himself.

"No, thank you, I'm just fine with the water that Detective Grant gave me earlier." The Reverend looked excited about the possibility of talking to the two men, which was a total turnaround from his earlier encounter with Holland and Devon at his house. "Are you all taping this session? Ah would really like to have a copy when we're done, if possible."

Kincade gave a sideways glance to Holland. Neither man expected the question. "Actually Reverend Clark, it's standard procedure that we videotape all interviews. So, yes, we are being recorded."

The man had very little hair on the top of his head, but the sides were longer than most people would find acceptable. Holland's eyes must have stayed on the sides of the man's skull a little too long, because his hands smoothed the hair back. "Sorry gentlemen; in my rush to get here after my sabbatical, ah didn't have time for a haircut." His Southern accent grew a little stronger.

Holland wanted to laugh — he was in such a rush to get to the station that he didn't have time for a haircut, but still had time to set up an on-air interview with the local TV station. Maybe the guy was just a loony — at this point, he wasn't ruling anything out.

"So you were talking to Kim Vince today from the TV station, and we heard you say that you knew who our killer was. Can you fill us in?" Kincade was anxious to move forward.

"Yes, of course. Ms. Vince, nice girl with a good job. I guess it's time to get started. That is, after all, why I'm here. Where are the cameras positioned? Is there an area where I should specifically talk to so that the cameras can see me?"

Devon watched on the closed-circuit video feed along with three other officers, including the Lieutenant, and shook his head. "What the hell is going on?"

Kincade spoke gently to the man, "The cameras can see all areas of the room, Reverend. Let's just move forward. Who do you think our killer is?"

"Well, I think you need to hear some more of the background first, so that it all makes sense. You probably know that up until a short time ago, I used to have a church, where I spoke every Sunday. My parishioners were loyal, and we worked together to spread the Lord's word and do the Lord's work. We did good things for the city, and the people who live here. We fed and clothed the homeless, we built parks, helped battered women find shelter, and along the way, we saved souls...well, y'all know what we did — you were there." As he spoke, he was looking around the room, searching for a visible camera that he could address directly. When he found none, he focused back on the two men in the room. "Then I fell out of grace. I did some terrible things that I am still ashamed of. I tried to deceive my flock, and I deeply regret that decision. But God has chosen me to teach Las Vegas an important lesson."

"Is that why you killed those women? You wanted to teach all of us a lesson about the evils of gambling?" Holland asked.

"No officer, y'all have it wrong. Murder is a crime not only on earth, but in heaven as well. I didn't kill those women; I was trying to save them. My hands are clean, but God has spoken to me and told me who did. His name is Paul...Paul Gregory."

Sixty-Seven

SIRENS WAS BUSY. THE common area, which included a bar and several big screen TVs, was full to capacity, and the private rooms were just as packed. Paul Gregory walked in for the third time that week, and went directly to the bartender. The buxom, raven-haired girl was dressed in a low-cut, short sequined dress, which accentuated the curves of her body. She knew what he wanted to drink, and quickly poured him a vodka and coke.

"Nice to see you again." The woman smiled at him with a lustful look. It was what the patrons paid for — unbridled sex appeal and fantasy.

"And you too." Her name was Rosie, but she would never know his. No one here used their names. It was part of the extensive security. He signed for the drink using only an account number, and added on a fifty percent tip. It was customary to pay the staff well; after all, they were keeping so many secrets.

Paul had been coming to the club for about a year, faithfully, a couple of times a week when he flew in for business. He had started out in life as an IT geek like Bill Gates, and then in the last five years had built up a thriving Internet security company. He had done so well over the years, that he now had access to a private jet, and could travel easily from his home in San Diego to Las Vegas. No fuss with airport security. He simply drove directly to the hanger and boarded the plane. That one purchase had totally changed his life. Up to that point, he was just a rich businessman with certain eccentric tastes;

but the plane had catapulted him into playboy status, and all of a sudden he was invited to parties that were previously out of his league. Access to Sirens was one of those privileges that was worth every penny of the ten million he paid for the used jet.

Standing at the bar, drink in hand, Paul glanced up at the bank of large, plasma TVs. One was showing the closing stock prices for the day, another one was broadcasting a college basketball game and on the third was hardcore porn. Everything a man could want. He focused his eyes on the basketball. Neither team was of interest, but March Madness was just starting, so it was worth five minutes of his attention.

Ten minutes later, one of the club's hosts came over and gave him a red key. "Sir, your room is ready for you whenever you would like." The bowling ball-shaped man smiled with the grace and charm of any butler you would encounter in the most wealthy neighborhoods. Another of the perks of being a member at Sirens.

"Thank you," Paul replied, as he took the key and held it firmly in his hand. This was when his engine started to rev. He wanted to savor the moment. His body was already anticipating what was waiting for him just down the hall. He turned the key over and over in his left hand, while he brought the glass of vodka to his lips for a final sip. The bartender smiled playfully at him as he handed her back the empty glass.

This time he was in room five. He had pre-ordered something special tonight. The woman on the other side of the door wasn't someone that he had played with on his last twenty-plus trips to the club. His old playmate was no longer available.

When he walked into the room it was dark just as he had requested. He flicked on the light and saw his playmate, dressed in the most trashy lingerie. The cheap, gaudy fabric turned him on, but not nearly as much as the fact that she lay dead in the middle of the king sized bed. Her dark hair was splayed out on the pillow, and her head lolled to one side. One of her arms covered her waist just below the bright-colored bra, and the other hung off of the side of the bed. Her legs were slightly bent, and twisted in the same direction as her outlying arm. He walked over and placed his hand on her skin — it was cold to the touch. He couldn't believe his eyes. Once again, the staff had come through with flying colors.

Sixty-Eight

MEHGAN WONDERED IF SHE should call the handsome Detective
Cartwright and try to weasel her way back into the investigation. The
only way that she could possibly get back in at this point in time was
to get another phone call, and even that was questionable. Otherwise,
she was out on the street like any other newspaper reporter. She
couldn't stop thinking about that damn kiss. Before that moment,
she had been attracted to the man; but certainly hadn't felt any urge
to rip his clothes off with her teeth. *Funny how things can change so
quickly,* she thought. One minute you think you have your life's path
set up the way you like it, and then you get a whack upside the head
that makes you consider driving on a cobbled road instead of the
highway. But, she was already on the highway, and her destination
was a sweet one.

She wondered what she would say if she did get him on the
line. "Hey, just wanted to chat about the fact that we made out like
monkeys the other night?" or "Just wondering if you have time to
bump uglies." *No, it was never going to happen.*

If things worked out like she had planned, once the murders were
solved, she would be off on a plane to Mexico for a long rest from
the newspaper business. There would be plenty of eligible men down
there that were more suitable than an arrogant, self-centered cop.

As if on cue, her cell phone rang. She smiled when she saw who
was on the other end of the line. "Hi lover."

The man's voice was strong and breathy, "I can't wait until tomorrow night. Are we still on?"

"Of course we are. Did you make the dinner reservations?"

"Prime Steakhouse at the Bellagio, six sharp," he confirmed.

"Great. I can't wait either... romantic dinner, I rub my foot up and down your leg under the table, then back to your place...well, you know what you have in store for you after that," she teased.

He groaned into the phone. "Awww...don't do that to me. I'm getting excited just talking to you, and I have customers out on the floor. I can't have a bump in my pants trying to sell diamonds — it sends the wrong message."

Mehgan giggled, "Just don't be late. You know how grumpy I get when people aren't on time for important dates. I think you would agree that what I have planned for you is pretty important, right?"

The man was like a salivating dog on the other end of the line. "Honey, tomorrow is *the* most important item on my calendar. I guarantee you that I won't be even one minute late."

Mehgan smiled from ear to ear as she heard those words. She had the man in the palm of her hand, exactly as planned. He was putty, and she was about to mold him into a sculpture of a perfect financial provider.

Sixty-Nine

IT TOOK ABOUT A half-hour to get a SWAT team organized for the raid. Reverend Clark had given the team the details that they needed. For the first time in almost a week, things seemed to be moving in the right direction. Despite the fact that the Reverend was of questionable morals, the story that he told them made sense. The puzzle pieces fit perfectly based on what they knew to date.

Paul Gregory was an ex-IT-geek who owned an Internet security company. He was worth an estimated one and a half billion dollars, and had his own Lear jet. While he had been interviewed by one of the teams earlier in the week, Devon knew that using the inexperienced officers had been risky from the start. They weren't trained in working with murder suspects, and had most likely missed the nuances that people show when they are lying.

Gregory was in his early fifties, but based on his passport picture, could have easily passed for someone five to ten years younger. He was fit and handsome, which would have positioned him as non-threatening with the women. He was a constant fixture on the Las Vegas Strip, flying in from his San Diego home several times a week to play cards. He was considered to be a bit of a playboy, and exactly as described in Stacy Bailey's note, he had an accent, having grown up in the heart of New York. Best of all, he had confessed to the good Reverend Clark when the preacher had approached him one night looking for money to further his cause.

According to Reverend Clark, Mr. Gregory, while in a drunken stupor, had wanted to confess his sins. So in a makeshift car-confessional on the corner of Sahara Boulevard and Las Vegas Boulevard, he had admitted to the fact that he was obsessed with necrophilia. Despite his slurred speech, the Reverend was able to understand that the man was going to a club called Sirens, to fulfill his needs with women who were willing to play dead for a rather large fee. But the drunken man confessed that he wanted more. Gregory admitted that he was worried that he might one day want to experience the real thing.

Reverend Clark had doled out a suitable penance. As a thank you for the impromptu session, the Internet mogul had given the Reverend his card, and told him to call his assistant the next day to arrange for a sizable donation so that he could continue his good work.

When asked why he had waited so long to come forward with the information, the Reverend had simply said, "I couldn't betray the privacy of the confession. I was waiting for the Lord to give me His blessing. He speaks to you now. I am merely his messenger." He added at the end of the interview, "Y'all are gonna remind the news people about that, right? I want my flock to know that I'm as good as new, and ready to lead them again. Don't forget to send me a copy of this interview. I want to show them what a man of God can do for them."

Holland and Kincade had left the Reverend Clark detained in the comfort of the interrogation room while they investigated his allegations. Despite the fact that it seemed he wasn't particularly worried about the women, and instead was more interested in improving his own reputation, the team was happy that he had showed up.

"According to the intel that the Reverend gave us, Sirens is about ten blocks east from the Boulevard, just off Freemont." Devon was excited. If they were lucky, they would catch Paul Gregory inside the club. If not, they would at a minimum be able to get information about where he was staying.

Thirty armored trucks, police cars and vans converged on the building less than an hour after the conversation with Reverend Clark. The large building, which had no visible identification, could have passed as an industrial warehouse. The front door, just off the large, empty parking lot, was made of steel, and wasn't guarded by security. The building looked empty.

"Doesn't look like much of a swinging illegal club from *this* standpoint. We still doing this?" one of the SWAT officers asked in his radio.

Holland, Devon and Kincade were standing out of harm's way behind their car at the other end of the paved parking lot. Kincade looked at the two other men and nodded his head. "Let's check it out."

"Roger. Move in," Holland replied to the SWAT leader.

When the first wave of officers, dressed in combat gear and ready for a fight, entered the front entrance, they were surprised that they were faced with another cinderblock barricade.

The dimly lit wall, which was perhaps three feet in front of them, ended abruptly to the left; but was open to the right and formed a long hallway the length of the building. The team cautiously followed the narrow passage to the end of the warehouse where it took a turn, realizing that they were being tracked from several ceiling-mounted cameras.

Seventy

"RED ALERT." THE VOICE came out over the speakers in every area of the club. It was the first time that the warning alarm had been sounded since the owner had opened the doors to the private establishment three years before. Everyone, staff and patrons, knew what to do — it was one of the many items that was discussed in their orientation on their first visit to Sirens.

In each of the private rooms, people scrambled to put on clothing, smooth down their hair, tidy the beds and rush to the safety of the common bar area. Rosie the bartender was rushing to change the porn channel to something more PG, while with her other hand pour enough drinks to sooth the nerves of what would be a very anxious clientele.

They had been told in orientation what to do in case of emergency — they had been told to keep calm. The club's owner would take care of everything. In fact, he was so sure of himself, that he offered to pay the legal fees of anyone who was arrested as a result of being in the club during a raid. It was a guarantee that, to this point, had never been tested.

****

At the end of the dark hallway, the SWAT team found themselves in front of a large, lacquered red door which was guarded by a beast of a man. "Police, move aside!" the lead officer yelled.

"Look man, I don't want any trouble. Do you have a search warrant or something? I'll be happy to move once you show me that." The man had his arms in the air. He had been schooled on what to do and say — block the door and stall, to give the patrons a minimum of five minutes. He estimated that he needed to delay for two more. All of the SWAT team were dressed in black and wore face shields. The small lighting fixture above the red door did little to illuminate the group. The doorman wished he could get a look at their faces to gauge how long he would be able to push his luck. He was paid well to basically do nothing; but it wasn't worth risking his life.

"Move NOW!"

Even with the low light and the confined space, he saw that there were a dozen or more weapons trained on his head and chest. He moved as slowly as possible to the right of the doorway. Two seconds later, twenty full-suited men rushed by with a clatter of boots, guns and shields. He hoped that he had given everyone time to get organized. Whether he got arrested tonight or not would depend on it.

The doorman was pushed up against the exterior wall, frisked and handcuffed. He was then taken inside the brightly lit inner sanctum of Sirens. He looked around and tried to count the people that he knew were in the club. He was meticulous about keeping count. So far tonight he had let forty in, and twenty out. Staff included, there should be forty-five men and women in the bar area. He tried to look around, but from his position he could only account for fifteen... *dammit.*

Police were yelling, and more military-style commandos were piling into the space. It was cramped, but the perspiration on everyone's brows was from something entirely different.

"We're secure," the SWAT leader said into his radio.

Seventy-One

DEVON, HOLLAND AND SPECIAL Agent Kincade entered the building. It was a brilliantly designed space. From the outside, it looked like an empty warehouse; but once you walked through the red doors, it was an opulently decorated club. The main bar area was on par with anything that you would find in the high-end hotels on the Strip. Devon had to admit that whoever had thought of the idea was pretty smart, as far as the criminal element was concerned. The hallway provided lots of advance notice if there was trouble brewing, and because of an underground parking lot, no one would suspect a thriving club in the industrial area. From Beemers to Ferraris, the parking lot was a testament to the level of wealth that sat upstairs.

The guests were standing around, cocktails in hand, looking nervous, but not overly concerned about the SWAT team's presence.

The manager was summoned, and chatted freely with the detectives. "Gentlemen, I think there's some kind of mistake. This is a licensed, private club. We aren't doing anything wrong here."

Devon had dispatched the team to check the rest of the space, and had gotten word about the private rooms. Unfortunately, Paul Gregory was nowhere to be found. "Let's not kid ourselves. You're running a brothel, and that's illegal in Las Vegas."

"Not so, officer. The rooms in the back are merely here for any of our customers who have one too many to drink, and don't want to drive. We have a zero-tolerance policy when it comes to DUIs. In fact, if one of our members is arrested driving under the influence after leaving our club, their membership is immediately revoked. In essence, they are barred for life from coming back. I hope that puts your mind at ease."

Devon watched as the man spoke with ease about Sirens. He was too polished with his suit, French cuffs and gold cufflinks, and it irritated the already-exhausted detective. "Listen, you little piss-ant. I have a zero-tolerance policy for bullshit. But I'm going to give you a bit of a break. Tell me where we can find Paul Gregory, and we'll be out of your hair tonight. Then you'll have an opportunity to clean up your club before we come back for another inspection next week." Devon knew that they would be able to keep tabs on the club from this point forward, and that shutting down the brothel was trumped by a string of very public murders.

The manager spoke quietly. "Come into my office."

"Where is he?"

He almost whispered his response. "Honestly, I have no idea. He was here earlier today. He left about three hours ago."

"Where is he staying? Which hotel?" Devon demanded.

"Look, I don't know for sure, because we don't ask for a lot of information from our members. Their privacy is as important to us as it is to them."

Kincade, in a surprise move to the other two men, grabbed the manager by the neck with lightning-fast precision and threw him up against the wall. "Tell us where he's staying."

The manager waved his hands in submission. When Kincade lowered him to the floor, he answered the question. "All I know is, that once, I saw him pull out a room card for the Bellagio. That's it, I swear."

Devon had a hunch that he hoped would pay off, and wanted to run with it. "Which of the women that got killed this week worked for you?"

The manager looked like he was about to deny the allegations; but after glancing at the face of the FBI agent, who was still within arm's reach, he changed his mind. "The only one who has ever worked here was Stacy. Once she was murdered, half the girls quit. Some of them decided to find a different line of work. Stacy was a nice girl. It was sad to hear about what happened. I swear I don't know the others."

Seventy-Two

WITH ONLY TWO DAYS left to complete his masterpiece, the Collector was starting to get nervous. The next kill was the most problematic, just because of the sheer space that a woman's torso would take up in his car, and ultimately, the refrigerator. That, and the fact that his next victim was going to be more on guard. He had a couple of hours to prepare, both mentally and physically.

He watched the Internet news to see where the police were at with their investigation. The net was closing in at a rapid pace. The talk on the street was that he would take his next victim tonight, and that there would be increased security at all of the hotels on the Strip. The public was warned to expect to be searched entering the boxing match, which had been moved to the Hard Rock Hotel at the last minute. Anyone entering and leaving all hotels were also told that they may be subject to random searches. Many vacationers and NASCAR fans had moved their hotel rooms to other off-Strip establishments. The owner of the Orleans Hotel was interviewed, saying that they were over capacity, and couldn't take any additional reservations — he didn't look particularly upset with the situation. There was even word that dumps like the Travelers Hotel on Freemont were filling up.

The Strip was clearing out. It wasn't optimal, but he could live with the situation.

He enjoyed a good workout almost as much as he enjoyed the physical pleasure that a corpse brought him... almost, but not quite.

He went into the workout room and positioned himself on the treadmill. He ran for two miles on a medium speed to get his blood pumping before doing a hundred squats and three hundred crunches. He admired his body in the mirror, and was pleased with what he saw. He might not be a young man anymore, but he was holding up quite well. Money can't buy health, but it had given him a personal trainer and the best quality food — everything helped.

He looked at his watch...almost time to go.

After a quick shower, he put on the second-last of his disguises. This was the most elaborate of all of the costumes that he had worn during the week, and it was really heavy. Thank God he was in such good shape, or the bulk of the outfit would have been murder on his back.

He looked at himself in a full-length mirror just before leaving and laughed out loud. This was the worst that he had looked in his entire life. *Oh well, dead eyes can't see.*

Seventy-Three

AFTER MAKING A PHONE call to HQ, Devon, Holland and Kincade jumped into an unmarked car and sped off to the Bellagio. They needed to find out if Paul Gregory was one of their guests. Devon was starting to get used to the idea that his two-some had become a three-some, but still found himself getting a little jealous that his longtime partner was so friendly with the FBI agent.

While the two ran over the details of their next steps, he found his mind drifting to Mehgan Bowman. He hadn't even had a chance to read what she had been writing lately, but knew that if there had been anything earth-shattering, he would have gotten an earful from the Lieutenant.

The men pulled up to the front entrance of the massive hotel and were greeted by the valet, who opened their car doors, probably looking for a tip. Devon flashed his badge and threw the man his keys. "Sorry, we don't have time to talk. Just get it out of your way, but leave it close by." Sure it was rude; but every minute was critical. The valet nodded — everyone was on their best behavior with law enforcement. No one wanted a dead body in their hotel.

Devon pushed past a line of people and went directly to the front of the check-in line. In his mind, the Bellagio still had the most beautiful reception area. In a word, it was grand. The huge flower arrangements, Dale Chihuly sculptures, and massive ceilings all worked together to create the pinnacle of opulence. When he was still gambling, he would come here just to admire the scenery. But that was a distant memory, and he had more important things to deal with now.

He flashed his badge at the front desk clerk. "We need to find out if you have a Paul Gregory staying in the hotel."

The clerk looked flustered as she punched a few keys on the computer keyboard. "Yes, sir. Mr. Gregory has a standing room with us, and has been here for the past week."

"A standing room?" Kincade asked.

"Yes, sir. He usually stays with us several times a month, and is guaranteed a room even when the hotel is booked to capacity."

"We need his room number and a master pass card to get into his room."

The clerk looked around nervously for confirmation that she was allowed to do what she was being asked. "I'll need to confirm with my manager."

It took a long five minutes for the manager to come over, look at the three men's badges, and confirm that he approved their request. Every moment felt like a lifetime. Would this finally be the end of the week from hell? Devon knew that once they arrested the man, it was really only the beginning. The interview and paperwork would keep them busy for at least a few more days.

They were told that Gregory was staying on the fourteenth floor, and according to the staff, he *always* stayed on the fourteenth floor.

In the elevator, Kincade was first to notice a correlation to their case. "Think about this — the fourteenth floor of the hotel is really the thirteenth floor. They just don't put it on the elevator panel because of superstition. The number thirteen is considered bad luck because there were thirteen people at the last supper with Christ. Paul Gregory insisted on staying on the fourteenth...really the thirteenth... floor of the hotel. Another religious reference? Divinity's Desire and the Last Supper? Plus, the guy confesses to a Reverend about his perverted sex needs. I'm liking this more and more."

"Let's hope you're right," Devon replied.

Seventy-Four

LEE FISHER HAD BEEN working as a waitress at the MGM for three years. Her real passion was photography; but even though she was talented, she was still waiting to get her big break.

Her frustration level was starting to reach the breaking point. She wondered why her career wasn't taking off. She had done everything right...the portfolio of photographs, the website, hours searching for the perfect locations with the perfect light, and the long nights pouring through photography magazines, fine-tuning her knowledge. She had the talent, everyone told her so; but exposure was the bigger issue. It was a catch-twenty-two; she had no work because she couldn't pay for advertising, and she couldn't pay for advertising because she had no work. It was mentally exhausting trying to figure out how to improve her situation. And now, there was a killer who was targeting the MGM hotels. It all felt overwhelming.

She looked at her watch; she was running late. She was scheduled to meet a woman for a photo-shoot right after work. It was her first paying job in a month, and she couldn't afford to lose it. The woman, who had seen Lee's website, had called asking for a session at Lake Mead. Lee had asked to see a picture of the woman so she would know who to meet, and to check out what she would be dealing with. She looked like a regular run-of-the-mill housewife; mousy brown hair, thin lips and small, piggy eyes. She said that she wanted to give her husband a glamour shot for their wedding anniversary, and was willing to pay the five hundred dollar session fee. Things seemed to be perfect. The light would be beautiful, and Lee knew that she could bring out the woman's inner beauty. Regardless, it was a paying job, and it gave her one more item to add to her portfolio...not everyone was a model. It would show the depth of her talent.

She pulled up to the parking lot and started to unload her equipment. A middle-aged couple was off in the distance walking hand in hand, the light hitting them from the West. For a moment she wanted to snap a photo of them. It was a curse of her passion; she always needed to have a camera handy for those times when she saw a perfect shot. They walked on, and the moment was lost. Her customer was nowhere to be seen. *Well, at least I'm not going to piss off the customer by being late.*

As she removed her tripod from the back of her trunk, she heard a car approaching. Turning to look, she saw a woman, a rather large woman, in a polka dot muumuu...not her customer. Damn it, the good light wouldn't last forever.

The woman parked beside Lee's car even though there were very few cars in the parking lot. She glanced at the woman, who looked to be eight months pregnant, and smiled. Her head was back in the trunk fishing around for her light reflector when the woman from the other vehicle spoke.

"Honey, can you help me? I seem to have dropped my keys."

Lee looked down to see the keys on the ground. The last thought that went through her mind was that the woman really needed to shave her legs.

Seventy-Five

JACKIE TEMPLE WAS WALKING from her car with an armload of groceries, and humming happily to herself. In the last two days the sky seemed to be opening up and pouring good news on her. The interview with the TV station had garnered lots of attention. Not only were there more requests for on-screen spots, but she had also been contacted by local radio and print media. She imagined that at least one or more would be interviewing her again as the week progressed. According to everything that she had learned over the years, there was no such thing as bad press – just exposure. She had the opportunity to promote her body, and if all things were equal, she was going to be famous really soon.

She put the two bags of vegetables, bread and chicken breast down at her feet and fumbled around in her pocket for her keys. She felt the hand gun in her pocket, and felt a sense of comfort in the cold metal shaft. After work she was going to make her famous stir-fry and sit patiently, gun in hand, waiting for the killer to make his move.

Just as she heard the tumblers click into place, she felt a presence behind her. She turned to face an unfamiliar face.

"Jackie Temple?" he asked.

Oh my God, it's him. The killer had finally made his move. He even fit the profile that was on TV – mid-forties, fairly attractive, and the final factor that convinced Jackie she was right — he had his hands in his pockets. That had to be a guaranteed sign that he was holding a weapon of some sort.

Pull the gun out! Pull the gun out!

It look longer than expected but she got the weapon out of her pocket and flipped the safety. She pointed it toward him and pulled twice on the trigger.

Bang, bang.

Double shot, just like Scott at the range had taught her.

It went perfectly smooth... just as she had practiced in the mirror. The man fell to the ground and was lying face down on her front steps, blood spurting from his shoulder.

"Holy shit, I did it," she said out loud.

She pushed her front door open, jumped inside and slammed it behind her. She peeked out through the front window and looked at the guy who was bleeding all over her nice clean cement stairs. She could barely believe what she had just done.

Realizing that she couldn't just let the guy die on her front stoop, she picked up the phone and dialed 911.

"What's the nature of your emergency?" A voice on the end of the line asked.

"I've just shot the Strip Killer. He's lying on my front steps. Please hurry."

Jackie looked at herself in the mirror and thought that she had better put on a touch more makeup before the camera crews arrived.

Seventy-Six

DEVON, FLANKED ON EITHER side by Holland and their FBI tag-along, knocked on room 14320 on the Bellagio's thirteenth floor. They didn't hear anyone or anything moving inside.

"Police. Open up." Devon knocked again with a little more force. All three men had their guns drawn.

Still nothing.

Kincade swiped the master key-card into the slot on the door and watched as the light turned green. He turned the door handle and pushed the door open with his foot, gun pointed chest height, ready for whatever was on the other side. He quickly moved into the space and trained his gun to the left, and then to the right. Devon and Holland followed directly behind.

The manager had given them a floor plan of the Tower Suite before they went upstairs. The suite had over fifteen-hundred square feet of space, but the men could only see a few hundred from their position in the front foyer.

Kincade signaled with a toss of his head that Holland should go to the left and Devon was to take the position to the right. The three men moved quickly into the main area of the suite, guns at the ready. The living room was empty, as was the dining room. The bedroom door to the right was pulled shut, but didn't look to be latched. All three men moved slowly toward the bedroom. Devon's heart was pumping at an alarming pace. They heard movement in the other room.

Kincade gave another nod and kicked the door in. "Police! Get your hands in the air!"

In an instant they had surrounded the man who was lying face down on his bed. "Paul Gregory! Get up from the bed slowly, hands in the air!" Devon yelled. The man didn't move.

"Put your hands in the air and sit up slowly!" Devon yelled again. Still nothing.

Kincade went over and pulled the covers off the bed. Finally their naked suspect stirred. He grumbled something, and with his right hand tried to fumble for the covers. The stench of liquor was thick in the air. "Crap, the guy's almost comatose."

"Let's get him cuffed and down to the station. Hopefully we can get him sober enough to talk," Holland said.

With the threat of Paul Gregory out of the way, Devon's heart rate was starting to slow to a regular beat. But now instead of excitement, other emotions were taking over — happiness and disappointment. He was happy that their man was in custody, but disappointed that they weren't going to get a confession for at least a few hours, maybe more. Were they really sure that Gregory was the Strip Killer? He seemed like the logical choice, but without a confession, they wouldn't know for sure. Physical evidence and DNA would take a few days.

More than anything, he wanted to get this case wrapped up. Holland was still acting moody; he wanted the feds to go back home, and he was getting tired of Mehgan Bowman's face turning up uninvited into his brain.

Kincade and Holland dragged Gregory through the hotel hallway to the elevator after covering him with a hotel robe. He could barely stand upright. Devon stayed behind to meet the Crime Scene Unit and to process any hard evidence that he could find.

Ten minutes in, as he was searching through drawers and suitcases, his cell phone buzzed. "Cartwright," he answered. He listened for a few moments, and cursed out loud, "No! This can't be happening."

Devon phoned Holland as he left the hotel room, "Looks like we aren't done yet. Have Kincade drop Gregory off at HQ and tell him to meet us." He rattled off the address. "A woman says that she just shot the Strip Killer."

Seventy-Seven

"THIS SUCKS," JACKIE SAID.

She was surrounded by a sea of reporters, but she was told that she couldn't talk to any of them. Her entire front yard was secured with yellow police tape, and little red traffic cones were everywhere in sight on her front lawn. Each one marked a piece of evidence that the police wanted to gather. It was taking forever. Then there were the hundreds of questions that the officers insisted that she answer. It was one long, boring conversation where she was forced to repeat the same thing over and over and over again.

"The man tried to jump me from behind at my front door, and I shot him in self-defense." It seemed like the tenth time she was asked to tell the story. What she really wanted was to go to the other side of the police barrier and talk to the people who really mattered. All those cameras and reporters were sure to ask more interesting questions than the swarm of unsympathetic officers.

Five minutes later, Jackie was thrilled to see a familiar face. Time to remind them how stupid they were for not listening to me, she thought.

"Glad to see you, Detective. Don't you wish that you'd believed me? I told you this would happen. You should have given me protection. It breaks my heart that I had to kill a man." Honestly, she couldn't care less; but in the moment, it was what any good actress on TV would say.

"Why don't you tell me what happened, Ms. Temple," Holland said.

Jackie let out a long sigh, "Again? Don't you people talk to each other?"

"Just humor me, okay?"

Jackie told the same story one more time. She sped through it in one very long breath. When she was done, she leaned back. Impatience was oozing from every pore as she spoke to Devon and Holland. "Is that good enough? Can I go now?" What she really wanted was to get past the confines of her front walk so that she could tell an even more detailed version of the story — one that would be seen from coast to coast...maybe even by Hugh Hefner himself.

"Did you clean up and get changed after you shot the man?" Devon asked, looking her up and down. No blood spatter on anything.

"Of course. I wasn't going to sit there with some murderer's blood all over me. I'm working tonight."

"Right...Ms. Temple, I think you need to call your boss and tell him that you won't be in. We'll be going to the station for a few more questions."

"What the hell? I've told you everything. The fucker had a gun on me. I didn't do anything wrong. In fact, you guys should give me the hundred thousand as a reward and a medal for bravery as well."

Holland grabbed her by the arm and was putting her into the back of a police car when she noticed the FBI agent from earlier in the week.

"What you got?" he asked.

"Remember the blond from the MGM? She shot Colin Young, Heather Langdon's boyfriend. He's at the hospital. The guy's lucky that she missed all of his internal organs. The piece of crap gun that she hit him with broke a couple of ribs and punctured his shoulder, but he'll be okay."

Jackie, listening in, was disappointed that the shots weren't fatal.

The cameramen were coming close to the squad car. Jackie tried to look relaxed and pretty...all was right with the world.

Seventy-Eight

THE INVESTIGATIVE TEAM GATHERED in the WAR room.

"Time to regroup." Holland had cleaned a whiteboard off and was starting to write notes with a thick blue marker. "Paul Gregory fits our profile on so many levels. He's the right age, give or take a few years. He owns a jet. Vegas is almost his second home. Once he's sober we can ask some questions. Colin Young had an alibi for Heather's murder, but we never even looked at him for the others because he seemed to check out. He's in intensive care courtesy of Jackie Temple. The boxer's been under surveillance, and hasn't caused any issues, so we can probably scrub him off the list. The Reverend is locked up for the time being. No murder yet today, so we could have the right guy somewhere in this mix. Reggie Matthews is on the street but based on what we know about his situation at home, he was probably being set up by a pissed off girlfriend." He paused. "What am I missing here?"

"We still have the possibility of a conspiracy with the security company. How else is this guy getting access to the women?" Devon said.

"Do we still have someone watching Reggie? I don't want to rule that out. It just doesn't play right in my mind that a guy who owns a jet is going to be doing this. And I didn't get the feeling that the owners of either security company are involved. I think it's someone lower down."

"But then what's the payoff? They aren't going to get money if they lose or sign another contract. The only one who gets cash is the owners."

"Maybe they're just trying to save their jobs. The economy sucks."

"I just don't see it. You're going to risk going to jail for killing a half-dozen women to save your job? That seems a bit extreme to me."

"But what if the guy has weird sexual tendencies already? Maybe he's just given up hope and is getting revenge."

"Gregory's our guy; I can just feel it. All we have to do is get him to sober up and we'll be able to prove it. Colin was just in the wrong place at the wrong time."

"I really hope you're right. Either way, we've got every hotel on the Strip locked down. No one is getting in or out without showing a room card and a picture ID. If our guy is still out there, he won't be going far."

A young officer burst through the door and rushed to the front of the room. "Detective Grant. Remember you told me to check on that Baxter guy. We just got a call. He's dead."

"What? Give me the details."

"Bill Baxter, the guy who ran that brothel…we tracked him down to a house just south of the city. He was shot and killed. ME is on her way now."

Holland tried to make sense of what he was hearing. "Coincidence? Or Connected? Are we getting too close to our killer with the Aphrodite's angle and he had to silence Baxter?"

Devon shook his head. "Not sure but I guarantee that Stacy Bailey has more to do with this than just meeting the wrong guy at the wrong time. I just can't put the pieces together."

Seventy-Nine

MARCUS BILLINGS FELT SICK to his stomach. The gurgling and churning was getting worse by the minute. This was his do or die moment, and the latter seemed like a real possibility. Sweat was trickling down his back, and the band of his Fruit of the Looms was soaking wet. Could he do this? Did he want to do this? Those were the big questions, and the only thing on his mind was to get a breath of fresh air before he passed out. He wanted a smoke bad…real bad. The fact that he had quit two years before didn't matter one iota.

Lanny, his best man, came over and put a hand on his shoulder. "You look like shit man; are you okay?"

"Just nerves I guess."

"Jessie's an awesome woman. Don't be nervous. I wish I was marrying someone that looked like her."

Marcus nodded his head in agreement. It was true; Jessie was one hot woman. She could cook, and she was super nice to top it off. It was just that he was scared of settling down. Twenty-five somehow felt overly young all of a sudden. He knew that she was going to want kids in the near future. Was he ready? He could barely take care of himself, let alone a third person. His head swooned again. "Can you just give me ten minutes, buddy? I just need to sit down."

"Sure. No problem. I'll keep the wolves at bay. Go sit in the reception hall. Until you guys finish up the 'I Do's', no one'll be in there." Lanny was proving once again why he had been chosen best man.

Marcus gave his friend a man-hug — close together, but with a hearty slap on the back. "Thanks, man."

The ceremony was set to take place in the MGM's chapel, and just a few doors down was the reception hall. He walked through the big doors and saw the room that would soon be filled with his relatives and friends. The MGM staff had done an awesome job decorating the space. It looked like a crystalline cave, littered with bouquets of red roses and perfectly pressed white tablecloths. He smiled — Jessie was going to be really happy. It was her dream come true. He walked around to the head table and imagined what it would be like with Jessie at his side when he was looking out at their guests. He pulled out the chair that would soon be his and slipped into place. He tried to push himself back into position, when the chair caught on something.

Marcus lifted up the long tablecloth and peeked underneath. The long cry that came from his mouth sounded foreign to his ears; but then what he saw laying on the carpet by his feet was definitely foreign to his eyes.

Eighty

"ANY IDEA ON HOW long she's been dead?" Devon asked. When the call came he had decided to take the lead at the MGM, while Kincade and Holland stayed behind babysitting their suspects.

Maureen Lamont looked like the death that she investigated when he arrived on scene. Dark circles were prominent under her eyes, and the small, thin laugh lines that were always present on her face looked more like deep cut lines in a mountain. Devon had heard through the grapevine that she and her team were working sixteen-hour days to try to catch up. Normally the coroner's office could process more than one body a day; but under the current circumstances, even one body a day just didn't seem realistic. Every single woman had to be combed looking for stray hair, fingernails, fabric fibers, anything that would help catch the killer. It was tedious and time-consuming work and it was obviously taking its toll on the ME.

"You're asking me for the impossible, detective. I don't even have a whole body here. Usually we have the core temperature to check, but I have no core. All I have is a head, two legs and two arms. I need to get her back to the morgue so that I can get a better look. My best guess is that she was killed in the past twenty-four hours. I know that doesn't help much, but it's all I've got."

Devon walked over to the witness who had found the body. The man was as white as the tablecloths that were on the reception tables. His fiancée was holding him close, tears streaming down her face and onto her flowing, white gown.

"Can you tell me what you saw?" he asked the young groom.

"I didn't see anything. I just wanted to have a minute to myself before the ceremony. I came in to check on the reception hall and found..." he broke down in tears.

What a way to start your married life, Devon thought, and had an overwhelming urge to put a bullet, or ten, into their killer's face.

"Did you see anyone before you came into the room? Anyone who was hanging around?"

The man looked around the hall, trying to control his emotions. "There was just the one guy leaving with a push cart. I thought he was there putting out plates or something. He went that way." He pointed toward the back service entrance.

Devon told Marcus and Jessie to stay seated, and he walked through the staff entrance. The space was teeming with people, both MGM staff and his own CSU team. "Check all of the service carts," he yelled. "And don't touch anything without gloves on."

It only took the team of seasoned investigators five minutes to find what they were looking for. The silver room-service cart was draped in pristine white fabric, but both of the lower shelves were covered in blood.

Eighty-One

DEVON WAS BACK IN the WAR room with both good and bad news. He started by filling in the team with the good news. "The guy finally got sloppy. CSU lifted three full prints off the cart, and five partials. There were a shitload of people in the back getting ready for the wedding reception, but one of the staff remembered that our perp was there to drop off flowers for the head table. Guy said he was called in at the last minute to replace the red roses with pink ones."

"No one questioned him? Is everyone brain dead in this city?" Kincade yelled. "We have a murderer on the loose, and they just let him waltz in?"

"From what I understand, the guy had a business card from a local florist and he had an armload of flowers. Plus, they say that they get shit like that all the time. Maybe they're just covering their asses, but they said that there are last-minute changes by brides in almost every wedding party. To them it seemed like par for the course, and the guy seemed legit."

Holland was pacing back and forth. "Anyone who can tell us what he looks like?"

"We've got the groom and a few of the MGM catering staff in with a sketch artist. It'll take a few hours to get something we can work with," Devon replied.

"What about the fingerprints from the cart?"

"CSU is on it. They have it as the highest priority; but you know it's a process, just like anything else."

"Video surveillance?"

"Okay, here's where the bad news comes in...remember how there weren't any cameras out back of the Monte Carlo? Well, the MGM is no different. They added more security guards on the back gate, but we still don't have a picture of our guy."

"So you're telling me that Paul Gregory, Reverend Clark, and Colin Young are definitely not our guy? Especially Gregory? He fits the profile like a glove," Kincade chimed in.

Devon looked disappointed. "I hate to say it, but, no. They were all accounted for when the body parts were dropped off. They could still be part of it, but none of them is working alone."

SATURDAY

Eight-Two

THE SKETCH ARTIST HAD worked through the night with the eyewitnesses and had finally produced a hand-drawn facsimile of the killer. He wasn't confident in what he was putting forward. "They couldn't agree on anything," he told the detectives. "We poured through the standard photo arrays to try and pick out significant facial features; but when I got three to agree on a nose, the fourth one would talk and they all started to second-guess their choices."

Holland was fresh from a trip home to see his wife and daughter, but was still looking like a man twenty years his senior. "Did they agree on anything?"

"Just that the guy was white and blonde. From there, he may or may not have had a moustache, may or may not have had a goatee... hell, he may or may not have had ears."

"Eyewitnesses are unreliable at the best of times. I guess we shouldn't have expected anything else."

Just when Holland thought that things couldn't get any more chaotic, Devon crashed into the room.

"Good news. Our eyewitness is awake."

Holland and Devon were at Valley Medical in under ten minutes. It was another full siren blaring, gas-pedal-on-the-floor kind of trip.

The two were ushered into the ICU by a doctor who warned them not to get Barb Goldfinch too excited, and to limit their visit to a few minutes. Most of all, he warned them not to get into specific details of her injuries. She was still in shock, and was just coming to grips with what had happened.

They entered the room, not sure of what they were about to see. The woman had lost both of her eyes, and had a bullet removed from her chest. Both took a deep breath before they set foot over the threshold to the hospital bed. Their victim was hooked up to several machines and intravenous bags, and had both eyes bandaged. They couldn't tell if she was awake or asleep.

"Ms. Goldfinch? Are you able to talk to us for a minute?" Holland probed.

The voice was almost a whisper when she replied, "I'm awake."

"I'm Detective Grant, and I have my partner Detective Cartwright with me. Do you remember the night that you got hurt? Can you tell us who did this to you?"

The two men waited for what seemed like an hour before the frail woman spoke again. "I don't remember much," she said.

"Did you know the man?"

"Not really. I just wanted to buy some shoes. I was promised shoes."

With the last statement, the machine to Holland's right startled him with a blaring siren.

"Who was going to give you the shoes?" Devon asked.

The doctor that had showed them in earlier was now rushing them out.

Devon was adamant that he get the answer. "Who was going to give you the shoes?" he asked again.

The doctor grabbed him by the arm and was forcibly removing him.

"The Prince," was the last thing the woman said, before the two detectives were out in the hallway.

Holland could almost watch the light bulb turn on in Devon's brain. "Shit, I should have figured it out! We aren't looking for *a* Prince; we're looking for *the* Prince!" Devon yelled.

Holland was surprised by the outburst. "Like the guy who changed his name to a symbol and plays funk music?"

"Not even close." Devon was running through the hospital hallway on his way to the car.

Eighty-Three

BACK AT HQ, THE team was called back in for another debrief. Pictures of the killer were handed to each and every person as they walked in. Once everyone was in place, Holland started the briefing.

"Our killer is Warren Frank. The picture that you have in your hands was taken about three years ago, and we think that he is constantly changing his appearance. He's forty-five years old, and an ex-lawyer. He's more famous for his on-line shoe store, which has made him a billionaire in the last ten years. His nickname is The Prince of Pumps, referring to his Internet success. Consider him armed and dangerous. You see him, call for immediate back up."

The team dispersed to hotels and the racetrack. Devon finally spoke to Holland and Kincade. "I can't believe I missed that angle. The Prince of Pumps should have been obvious to the officers that interviewed the private jet owners. Women died because I was too focused on that damn preacher?"

"Don't beat yourself up. We all missed it. But at least we know who we're looking for tonight. He's going down," Kincade replied. He stared at the photograph of the wealthy well-kept man.

Before anyone could comment further, another officer came in to the WAR room. "Detective Cartwright, there's a woman downstairs who says she needs to talk to you urgently. Says she has information on where the killer is going to strike next."

Devon jumped up and went to the front desk of the station house,

Holland and Kincade following close behind. When the three men saw who their informant was, all of them groaned.

"Didn't I tell you to stay out of my face?" Devon snarled at the reporter.

Mehgan looked sheepish, but also had an air of determination in her tone. "I know what you told me, and you don't have to believe a word I say. But I thought that you might want to know that she called again. This time I told her to keep the phone on so that I could call her back. She just hung up a few minutes ago. You need to hurry."

Despite the angry feelings that he was still harboring, Devon couldn't take the risk that the reporter was lying. If what she was saying was true, maybe they could get to the bottom of the mystery surrounding the woman, and potentially find out where Warren Frank was before he tried to kill again.

The three men were quick to get suited up in bullet-proof vests, and grabbed a laptop to run the cell phone tracking software. Mehgan was allowed to ride along in the cruiser just in case she was needed to place a call to the mystery woman.

"Tell me again what she said," Devon asked as they drove through the streets, looking for the unique signal from the phone.

"Just that he was going to take his last woman tonight. She said he's staying in Henderson. She said she was scared that if he didn't get what he wanted, that he would kill her, too," Mehgan said.

"No word on where he's going to hit tonight?"

"She said he was going to make a big splash. Whatever that means."

The Trigger Fish software, which simulated a cell tower, was only able to give them a signal once they were in a five mile radius from the phone. They would have to drive around all the streets in Henderson until they got a hit.

Kincade was punching information into his laptop. "Warren Frank doesn't own a house in Henderson. Is he staying at the woman's house?"

"I'm telling you everything I know. Sorry."

For a half hour the occupants of the car remained quiet, listening to the steady beeping of the tracking software.

Beep. Beep. Beep. Beep. Beep.

"Slow down, we got a hit!" Holland screamed. "She's close by!"

The unmarked car creeped along for another three blocks until they found the strongest signal. The cell phone was in the house directly in front of them.

"Get SWAT here. We aren't doing this alone."

Devon was already getting backup ready on the police radio.

Eighty-Four

TWENTY MINUTES LATER, DISTRICT Attorney Nathan Liam had arranged for Judge Jones to sign the search warrant for the Henderson residence, and the team had the verbal to move ahead with the SWAT team. Holland, Devon, Kincade and Mehgan moved to a parking lot three blocks away to meet the rest of the team to discuss the plan.

The SWAT team made an intimidating show of power in their full body armor and automatic weapons. Several passing motorists did a double take.

Mehgan was secured in the back of a cruiser. She wasn't going to be allowed to participate in the raid.

Devon had the team's full attention as he discussed the plan with the SWAT leader. "The house is a bungalow, built about ten years ago. This is where we think Warren Frank has been hiding out while he was committing the Strip murders. We aren't sure what, or who, is in there so be careful. The goal is to secure the property as quickly as possible, without injuring anyone."

The huge man nodded and spoke to the group, "Team A, you'll be taking the north side of the house. Team B, split up to the west and east sides. Team C will take the front, or the south side of the home. Any questions?"

The large group of men just nodded their approval. No questions were raised.

"Let's get going." The SWAT leader circled his arm in the air, and the group dispersed into six separate vehicles: two windowless black vans, two black Hummers that had been modified into armed tanks, and two squad cars. They drove single file to the house, just a few blocks away. Everyone's hearts were racing.

As the massive convoy of black reinforced steel made its way down the residential street in Henderson, Devon started to wonder what or who they were going to find. Were Warren Frank and the mystery woman home? Were there other people involved in the murder plot?

The team was pulling up to the home and Devon heard the SWAT leader speak into the radio. "Get into position, and wait for my signal."

The house was surrounded by firepower. Guns and shields were in place, everyone was ready for battle. Devon confirmed that everyone was in place and yelled toward the front door with a bullhorn, "This is the Las Vegas Police Department. Come out with your hands in the air."

No response.

He repeated the demand, and was still met with silence. He nodded at the SWAT leader.

The large armor-clad man gave the signal, "NOW!"

The doors, both front and back, were smashed in with battering rams, and a massive wave of men followed behind. He wanted to stay calm, but Devon found that his heart was pounding fast. Every moment felt like a lifetime as he waited for the all-clear signal.

An agonizing three minutes later, and the detectives were told that they could come inside. The house was empty. Sort of.

Eighty-Five

THE FIRST THING THAT Devon noticed when he entered the home was how normal it looked. The house was decorated with neutral furniture, but the walls had bold, modern art that gave the sense of a well-appointed owner. No one was home but the SWAT team had made an interesting discovery in the kitchen. They pointed to where they wanted Devon to look.

"Ah, fuck," Devon said. He had sworn more in the last week than he had over the course of the past month.

All of the shelves in the oversized industrial refrigerator had been removed to make room for the naked patchwork woman. He immediately recognized Stacy Bailey's brown hair, Kenalynn Markerson's face, Barb Goldfinch's eyes, Heather Langdon's arms, Monica Cantrell's legs and their latest victim's torso. Each part was sewn together with clear fishing line, and the effect was nothing short of horrifying. Lying next to the body was a jug of milk, a carton of eggs and two takeout containers full of pasta and Caesar salad.

Devon looked out of the kitchen window and saw several of the SWAT team outside on the lawn throwing up whatever they had for breakfast.

"Let's get to work. We still have a chance to save the last one," Devon said. It wasn't much but it was the best he could think of to say.

Holland and Kincade started taking pictures and making notes. Repulsed as they were, they had to keep focused to save the next woman. They couldn't waste any time, regardless of how ill the body in the cooler made them feel.

"It's just like the picture. He's going to take the breasts tonight to complete the body." Kincade pushed on.

"I want to take this bastard out myself," Holland replied.

The Henderson house was filled with dozens of people. The Crime Scene Unit was out in full force, collecting fingerprints and trace evidence. Dozens more were canvassing the neighbors to try to get information about Warren Frank. The woman next door confirmed that Frank had been staying in the home for the past two weeks. He was a nice, quiet man, she told the officers. He had even given her a pair of Jimmy Choo's as a gift.

With some digging, Devon found out that the property was owned by a numbered company, whose ownership was still in question. Several officers back at the station house were tracking down the specifics. Devon was searching drawers and cupboards, looking for information, while another group of men was looking through the bloody garage.

"Crap, look at this!" Devon yelled to his partners, who were working in other areas of the house.

When the other two men arrived, he showed them a large, brown envelope, which he had dumped out onto the kitchen island. Several papers lay on the large counter, along with room keys to three of the major hotels.

"It's a manual on how to do every murder. It says where to go and when to do the kills. There's even diagrams on how to cut the bodies apart."

Kincade picked up one of the papers with a gloved hand. "Check this out — there's a bloody fingerprint on this one. We've got him cold."

The three men were ecstatic. Not only had they found their killer, but they had solid evidence to prove it. The week just got a whole lot better. For the first time in days, Devon smiled.

Holland spread each of the pages out on the island in order of the murders. There were pages for each location: the Aria, Monte Carlo, Luxor, Excalibur, New York, New York, Mirage, and the MGM.

"There's nothing that tells us where he's going to hit tonight.

Dammit," Devon said. He looked at the envelope again and turned it over in his hands a couple of times. "Think about this for a second. All of these papers explain what to do. Like a teacher. The envelope is from the Hard Rock. The owner of the Hard Rock bought the Louis Vuitton for Stacy Bailey. The Hard Rock is where the fight got moved to. And the damn guy still hasn't returned our phone calls."

"Crap; we've been so busy that I totally forgot about him. No way; you think Peter Tamis is behind all of this?" Holland asked.

"I'm gonna get him picked up, and then we can ask him personally," Devon replied. "But first, I want to talk to Mehgan Bowman. I think we can use her."

Devon walked through what seemed like a hundred reporters and cameras before he retrieved Mehgan from the cruiser. "Come with me," he said.

When the two were out of ear shot of the mass of media, he told her what he wanted. "Get Warren Frank's picture out on the Internet. If anyone sees him, tell them to call 9-1-1. Got it?"

"Got it." Mehgan was thrilled. Everything was falling into place.

Eighty-Six

PETER TAMIS WAS BUSY getting ready for the big event. He surveyed the massive conference space that was set up for the heavyweight match. In just a few hours, the hotel would be full of gamblers, and he was going to get millions of dollars as a result.

When Scarlett had suggested that she could create a distraction to ensure that the fight came to his location, it didn't seem like a big-money proposition. At best he thought that he would get some of the ticket proceeds and a full hotel of fight fans. He needed quick cash to keep the mob at bay.

But then she told him about the rest of the plan, and it all made sense. Not only would she get him the fight in his hotel; she would also guarantee that Chet would go down in the sixth round. But the candy coating was the Chinese businessman who loved Scarlett's special services. At her request, he had checked in to the Hard Rock two days ago. He had already lost over five million playing roulette. All of a sudden, the sun was looking a lot brighter in the desert sky.

He had called Griz' cell phone earlier to confirm that his partner was ready for the big night ahead of them. By all accounts, things were about to go off without any hiccups.

"Mr. Tamis, I need you to come with me."

Peter was shocked when he turned to face three uniformed police officers.

"What's up?" He suddenly remembered his assistant telling him that the cops had called, and wanted to talk to him about a purse that he had bought for Stacy Bailey. With all of the excitement, he had forgotten to call back. It wasn't a big deal. She was a friend, and he had bought her a birthday gift. Nothing to worry about.

"We need to bring you down to the station house to answer a few questions," the cop said.

"Yeah, I just realized that I forgot to call you guys back about that purse. Let's go to my office, and I can give you all the details."

"Sir, we need you to go downtown."

What the hell? He didn't have time to dick around with cops on fight night. "Can this wait? I'm sure you know I'm hosting the big fight tonight."

"Look Mr. Tamis, we can do this one of two ways. I think you would prefer if we didn't drag you out of your hotel in cuffs."

Not seeing a quick solution to the problem, Peter agreed to go to the station house for a brief conversation. He called his lawyer from the squad car.

Eighty-Seven

THE LVPD INTERROGATION ROOMS were filled to capacity. It was starting to get hard to remember who was in which room, so the detectives reverted to putting sticky notes on each door. When Peter Tamis arrived, they had to relocate a team that was working in the Lieutenant's office to get more space for their latest suspect.

"Mr. Tamis, I'm sure that you know why you're here today. We just want to ask you a few questions about what's been happening…" Devon said.

"I'm a busy man, detective. Let's cut to the chase," Peter cut him off.

"Fair enough. It seems that you bought an expensive purse for our first victim, Stacy Bailey. In addition, tonight's boxing match was moved to your hotel at the last minute as a result of the Strip murders. Then let's add in the fact that we found a Hard Rock envelope filled with a how-to manual for the murders. That all seems to add up to a good reason to have a chat."

Peter's lawyer didn't allow his client to respond. "That is all bullshit gentlemen. Mr. Tamis was personal friends with Ms. Bailey, and he bought her a birthday gift some time ago. As far as the fight goes, he was approached by members of the Boxing Commission and asked if he could do them a favor by hosting the event at the Hard Rock. Finally, anyone who has stayed at the hotel has access to their stationery. Your killer has no tie to my client, and we resent the allegations."

Devon had expected the answers, and was ready to drop the bomb. The news had come in just five minutes before, and he was bursting trying to keep it in. "All true. But let's see how your client explains the fact that our killer was using *his* house in Henderson to store his victims' body parts."

The lawyer gave Peter Tamis an angry look before he spoke to the detectives. "I'd like a few minutes alone with my client."

Holland and Devon left the room. The two men were met by Kincade, who was almost jumping out of his skin with excitement.

"I've got some good news. When we ran the facial recognition software from the Mirage against the other hotels, we discovered something very interesting. In every hotel that our killer has hit, we are seeing the same guy at the blackjack table. He shows up within an hour before each murder. Same guy, same 49ers baseball cap. He leaves before the kills happen. We showed his photo to a few people, and he's an employee of Dedicated Defense. Guy's name is Lyle Hants. We have a team on the way over to his house right now."

"Does he have any ties to the Hard Rock?" Holland asked.

"Not that I can tell so far; but once we get him back here, we'll have to ask that question."

Holland and Devon hadn't noticed, but Peter Tamis' lawyer was standing in the hallway, signaling for the two men to come back to the office.

"My client would like to clarify his involvement with Stacy Bailey."

After hearing Peter Tamis' account of his relationship with Stacy Bailey, you would have thought that the man was a saint of major proportion. According to his lawyer, Tamis had fallen in love with the pretty escort a year before. He wanted her to get away from prostitution but she refused — said it gave her power.

Then a few months ago, she called him crying, in need of a place to stay for a few days. She was so distraught that he offered up his house in Henderson as a safe haven. They had become lovers again, and she promised that she would change her ways.

"I was still in love with her. I thought that if she took some time off, she might be able to get her head clear and see that I was the best thing for her."

"Great story, Peter. It still doesn't explain how the killer got access to your house," Devon said.

"Can't you see? When he killed Stacy, he must have taken the key. After she died, I couldn't bear to go back in and see her things. I haven't even set foot in there all week."

Devon thought that he looked sincere, but something still didn't add up. He wished that they had access to the Dedicated Defense employee to confirm that Tamis was tied to the murders. Most murders happened for one of two reasons; love or money. In Peter's case, there seemed to be a case for both.

"See detectives, there's a logical explanation for everything. So, unless you are going to be charging my client with a crime, we'll be leaving. As you know, his hotel is hosting one of the most important boxing matches this year." The lawyer looked confident that he had proven his point.

"Sorry, but as of this moment your client is under arrest for accessory to murder. And don't worry about the fight; we'll take care of that for him," Holland said, as he pulled the man up out of his chair. The cuffs were on in seconds, and Peter Tamis looked more confused than ever.

Eighty-Eight

"Sorry sir, but I really need to close up." Grady looked at his watch, he was supposed to be closed twenty minutes ago. But, the guy with the 49ers cap was flashing a wad of cash and looking hard at one of his largest engagement rings. "I have an appointment but if you want to come back in the morning, I would love to spend some more time with you." If he hurried he could still make it on time.

"Hot date?" the man asked.

"You understand. Ladies don't like to be kept waiting," he said as he ushered the man out the door.

Any jewelry store owner worth their weight did the same thing every night; they put their most valuable assets into a safe in the back of the store. Grady Tellam was no different. The owner of The 3 C's, named after carat, color and clarity, the three aspects of a good diamond, was meticulous in his closing routine.

Except for today.

Today, Grady was in such a rush to get out of the store, that he had changed his routine, promising himself that he would go back to the store to secure his diamonds after dinner. Tonight there was promise of a rather raucous romp between the sheets. Mehgan loved punctuality and he would be punished if he wasn't on time. At fifty-two years old, he didn't get the chance to screw beautiful women like Mehgan very often. Instead of screwing a ten, like the pretty reporter, he usually settled for screwing five women who were two's.

She was something else, and he wasn't about to give up the

opportunity to get his hands on such a high-quality piece of meat. Most women wanted him because of his access to the sparkling stones that they all desired; but Mehgan wasn't interested in jewels in the least. She seemed to be more interested in him, despite the almost twenty-year age gap between the two. She had originally come in to do a story about the allure of diamonds. The 3 C's was the most famous of the independent diamond brokers in all of Nevada, having designed rings, necklaces, bracelets and the like for most of the performers that graced the Las Vegas Strip. Custom bling and high-end stones were their specialty. They even had access to some of the rarest colored diamonds that even the high-end stores in Bellagio and the Wynn couldn't get their hands on. Grady was the rock star of the diamond world.

Grady's problem — he knew that he wasn't even remotely attractive to most women. He had gray hair, but some seemed to like the sense of experience that it suggested. He had dark brown eyes that seemed to be in proportion, his nose was slim and his ears were small. The problem, in his mind, was the slight harelip. It didn't affect his speech, but the indent in his lip was hideous in his eyes. Three surgeries later, it was much improved; but to Grady, it was the only thing holding him back from finding his dream woman. He noticed that every woman he met, hell every person for that matter, immediately moved their eyes to his mouth, allowed their eyes to rest on his deformity, then moved their gaze back to the top of his face. They all saw it, they all looked at it, and he knew that they all hated it. It happened every goddamn time. Until he met Mehgan Bowman.

She had sat across the table from him at The Brand in the Monte Carlo, leaned in when he spoke, and listened intently to every word that left his lips, never once looking at his mouth during the entire hour-long interview. Then she picked up the bill, and had touched his hand in a gesture of thanks at the end of the lunch. She was a hundred and fifteen pounds of pure pleasure.

She had come back several times since that day to get more information from him, to get a quote or two, to show him drafts of the articles...he hoped that it was to get to know him better. The three articles were posted in the newspaper and business increased, as did his fondness for the young reporter. He invited her to a private celebrity party where his jewelry was going to be showcased, and she accepted. He was thrilled; but at the end of the night when he tried to kiss her, she pulled back. He was devastated. But instead of turning away, she held his face in her hands and kissed him softly on the cheek and whispered in his ear, "I want you too, but I've been hurt before — I need to take it slow." He had walked back to his car with a smile on his face and a bump in his pants.

They had gone on four dates since then, and things had worked up to a full-mouth kiss last week. She was busy working on the serial killer case with the police, and had very little time to spend with him. But she had promised that tonight would be the night...*the* night.

Despite the fact that he had a rather large shipment of uncut diamonds in the store, despite the fact that he had an unsecured inventory of almost twenty million dollars, and despite the fact that he was one of the most cautious men on the earth, he had left the store in a panic, practically throwing his final customer of the day onto the street. He didn't want to keep his lovely sex kitten waiting — she was really particular about punctuality. How many times had he dreamt about what she would do to him when the night finally came? Tonight it was finally going to come true.

Eighty-Nine

GRIZ WAS STANDING RINGSIDE, surveying the crowd. The buzz in the room was electric. To the left he saw his investors. The man with the gold teeth was grinning from the first row. Griz knew that if Chet didn't win tonight, the black monster of a man might have him killed. The businessmen had doled out hundreds of thousands of dollars to make sure that he was in top shape for tonight's match. They had also bet a substantial wad of money on the outcome of the match. For them, anything less than a win would cause a ton of hurt for both Chet and himself.

He smiled and scanned further around the room. Peter Tamis was nowhere to be seen. The fight was starting in a few minutes, but the boss wasn't around. Griz wiped sweat from his forehead. The moment of truth was about to happen.

The ring announcer beckoned both fighters to the ring. Chet looked good with his gold and black trunks sparkling under the bright lights. Lax Butte was in red and white, and was chiseled to perfection. It was going to be a hard-fought battle, but Chet knew what he had to do.

At the first bell, both fighters came out a bit sluggish. By the second round, Chet had taken about five body shots that he should have deflected.

Griz talked to him after the second round. "Get out there and defend yourself. You look like a wet rag up there."

"What's the point?"

"The point is, I told you to do it."

The third round was much improved, and the black monster was showing off his gold, toothy grin in a ringside seat. Chet had connected a great right uppercut that had dropped his opponent to the mat.

By the end of the fourth round, both men had an equal number of cuts and bruises. Things were moving along according to plan. Griz was still looking around the crowd, nervous that he hadn't seen the boss. He was supposed to be ringside...*promised* he would be ringside.

The fifth round was even — both men had delivered and received some nice blows. The crowd was going crazy. Griz spoke to Chet again as he poured water over the boxer's face, "Give it a few minutes. You know what to do."

The animal instinct in Chet was raging through his blood. "Yeah," was all he said; but Griz wondered if he was actually going to take the fall. Just before the start of the sixth, Griz got a tap on his shoulder. Black Dracula was talking in his ear, "Butte looks tired. Tell the Hammer to take him out this round." And there it was — he had two men who wanted the fight to end in the sixth, and both wanted a different outcome. Black Dracula wanted Chet to win, and Peter Tamis was expecting Chet to take a fall. It was time to do or die...or maybe both. Griz looked up to the ceiling and prayed that he would know what to do. He promised God that if he got out of this alive, he would never do anything this stupid again. Having never prayed in his life, he didn't expect a miracle. There was no way out.

The bell chimed for the start of the sixth round. Chet and Laz touched gloves, and moved back and forth in the ring. Chet was the first to connect with a punch. A strong left. Laz was able to hit his opponent with a few hard body blows. Chet threw a right, and another sharp punch to the stomach. The crowd was going wild.

Griz knew that any minute his fighter would be on the mat. Left, right, uppercut. The punches were coming fast and furious.

To Griz, the entire stadium seemed to go quiet — the noise of the crowd disappeared, and an unearthly calm settled into his body.

There was commotion in the ring but Griz didn't bother to look up. He knew what he would see. The ref called the fight. Snapped back to reality, Griz looked up into the ring, expecting to see Chet on the mat. Instead, he saw both fighters standing upright in the ring.

What the fuck had just happened?

Ninety

"WHERE IS HE?" DEVON was standing in the security booth at Mandalay Bay. "He should have been here by now."

Mehgan had received the phone twenty minutes prior. It was the mystery woman again but this time she was calling from a different number. More importantly, she told them exactly where their killer was going to be and at what time.

The walls were lined with computer screens monitoring every nuance of the casino floor, and now included other camera views of all entrances and exits, as well as several make-shift cameras in the parking lot, the hallways of the guest floors, and the pool area.

"You guys sure that he's coming here? Didn't you say that he was supposed to hit at eight? It's almost ten." The head of security was jumpy. "I can't wait until all I have to deal with are drunks and cheaters."

Devon nodded. He understood – that was something that they could relate to, and had countless hours of experience doing. This killer thing was taking the security staff far out of their wheelhouse.

Devon called Holland on the cell. "Anything on your end?"

"Nothing so far. Maybe the woman was wrong. She's been toying with us for days."

Devon paused and thought about the comment. Mehgan's source had been right so many times, that it was hard to believe that she was going to steer them in the wrong direction now. However, the possibility still existed that they were dealing with someone who was working in conjunction with the killer, and was leading them down the garden path. "Let's hold tight for a bit longer. If he keeps up his MO, he'll kill again. He hasn't been back to Henderson. He's here somewhere."

"Maybe he's tired. I know I am." Holland's voice was strained.

Mehgan had left hours ago to broadcast Warren Frank's picture over the Internet, and Devon started to miss her. She had become somewhat of a fixture in his life in just a few days, and he thought that maybe once the case was closed, that he would ask her out on a date. His mind only had a few moments to wander before one of the security guards sitting three chairs down yelled, "I think I got something!"

Devon, who was standing up against the back wall of the room, darted forward and leaned in to get a better look at one of the screens.

"See him? The guy's wearing a long coat. Why the hell would you wear a long coat in Vegas in March? Looks like our guy with a ponytail. He just came from the walkway to the Luxor. He's walking past the Sports Book. See him?" The guard almost jumped out of his chair with excitement.

"Zoom in on his face!" Devon screamed.

The camera got a close-up, and Devon's pulse quickened as he spoke into the handheld radio. "Everyone close in to the west wall of the casino; could be our guy. Long dark coat, long dark ponytail, glasses. He's walking toward the cashier's windows. He's moving fast."

Devon watched the man's pace pick up as he moved past the cashier, past the Mandalay Bay security desk, took a right, and moved toward the elevators.

"Do you want one of our guys to grab him?" the Mandalay security guy asked, with more than a hint of apprehension in his voice.

"No. Let us take care of this," Devon said. He watched as the man pushed the down button on the elevator. Into the radio Devon spoke again, "He's going down in the elevator. Get your asses over there NOW!"

Ninety-One

DEVON WATCHED AS THE elevator doors opened and the man got in. Devon started to second-guess himself — was the man that he saw The Prince? It certainly looked like him, but with the long hair and glasses, it was hard to know for sure.

"Looks like he's going to the pool level," Devon said into the radio.

"We've got him in sight," replied the voice of one of the officers. Devon wasn't sure who was talking, as there were so many on the team now. He watched on camera as the man walked off the escalators and through the beach entrance outside. There were people everywhere. Mandalay Bay was famous for their beach parties, and tonight they had live entertainment. The entire area, which included four pools, two Jacuzzis, a river, a wave pool and a stage on the sand beach were all packed for the season-opening bash. Just another over-the-top event on NASCAR weekend to grab tourist dollars and muddy the waters for a clean arrest.

"Arrest him when it's safe. Don't shoot. Too many people around."

"Roger that."

Devon watched the man as he snaked his way through the crowd. While he was the only one in a long coat, once he was in with the larger group, many of whom were wearing light coats to protect against the evening chill, he was getting harder to find.

"Fuck, I've lost him," Devon cursed quietly, as his eyes darted across multiple screens. "Anyone see him down there?"

Three voices came back, but no one could see him. Where the hell had he gone?

The stage lights lit up and the band started to play. The yells and screams from the beach area were deafening. Everyone was jumping up and down, dancing to the beat as the singer belted out his first song.

Ten police officers were already in the pool area when The Prince got to the beach level; now, less than ten minutes later, there were fifty officers and FBI scouring the crowd for the potential killer. They pushed their way through a thousand or more people, trying to find the man who had been terrorizing the Las Vegas Strip for the past week. Devon's heart was pounding so hard that he thought it might burst as he called Holland on his cell. "He's here. Get your team over here; we've had a sighting, but we've lost him in the crowd." It was a tough call; on the one hand, there was a chance, however slim, that this wasn't Warren Frank. On the other hand, if the team lost track of him, he might get away with another murder, and that wasn't a chance Devon was willing to take.

Holland could leave a few guys at the Hard Rock, and the rest could secure the area around Mandalay Bay. It was one of the largest properties on the Strip, and by the sounds of it, they needed all hands on deck. "We're on our way."

Devon paced back and forth, watching over a dozen screens in the control room, and could barely contain himself. "Get a perimeter set up around this entire property now!" he screamed into the radio. "I want a man every ten feet around the hotel. No one gets in or out from this point forward."

Ninety-Two

THE JEWELRY STORE ALARM went off at exactly 10 p.m. It was precisely ten minutes before the next murder was about to take place on the other side of the city. The thief flipped open a hidden panel by the front door, which housed the security panel, and punched in a six-digit sequence. The alarm went silent. The door was locked, and a small remote control explosive device was placed on the inside of the door frame.

The thief checked the time; the phone would ring in the next two minutes. The security company would be calling to check that everything was okay. If the phone was not answered and the proper verbal code wasn't spoken, they would send someone to check things out. Once dispatched, the security guard would be on site in about six minutes. Total time to complete the task; eight minutes, maybe ten if the thief could stall them on the phone. If by chance the security guard arrived before the thief was done, the explosive device could be detonated; but that assumed that the guard would come in through the front door and wouldn't come with backup. Not really a great Plan B.

Dressed as a security guard, the thief turned on the lights in the store. If anyone came by, they would never suspect a security guard of the crime. The fake guard smashed the backs of the display cases and grabbed handfuls of diamond necklaces, rings and bracelets. The phone started ringing.

"Hello?"

"This is Standards Security. Please identify yourself." The voice on the other end of the line was very serious.

"Sorry, damn it, you want my security code, right? Just let me find that for you." The thief continued to grab and stash items into a pillow case. "Damn it...I can't find the code. Please just give me a minute." The thief tried to sound panicked, which wasn't that much of a stretch, considering the circumstances. "I'm going to put the phone down for a minute and go into my desk in the back. I keep a copy of the verbal code in there. Okay?"

"You have one minute to give me the code, or I will dispatch the police."

"Sorry, I've never had this happen before in all the years I've worked here. I just can't remember the damn code. Please don't call police; I don't want to get fired. Two minutes, please?" the thief pleaded, and abruptly dropped the phone to the counter. It might have bought the extra time that was needed.

Then with a quick trip to the back, the fake security guard opened Grady's desk drawer with a crowbar and looked inside. As expected, there was a small, velour pouch. The thief opened up the drawstrings and took a quick glance inside. These diamonds didn't shine or sparkle, but they were the most valuable of all. Uncut and almost impossible to trace, they would get the best price on the black market.

A quick check of the time, and the thief knew that the security company would be sure to call the police in the next thirty seconds if they hadn't already. Knowing that the entire Las Vegas police force was in one of three places, the race track, Mandalay Bay or the Hard Rock, the thief was almost guaranteed a perfect getaway.

A voice was audible from the ear piece of the phone, "I'm calling the police."

The thief looked around the store and noticed a few last second must-have items, and stuffed them into the bag. Exiting through the back door, the security guard's jacket and pants were removed, but the blond wig was left in place. Underneath, the thief had on a pair of shorts and a T-shirt. After securing two rollerblades, the figure disappeared into the night. Another glance at the watch; it would only be about five minutes until the killer would be arrested.

Ninety-Three

THE COLLECTOR WAS PLEASED that there was such a big crowd gathered to see the live band on the beach. Everything was precisely as he had been promised. The long coat was a bit on the warm side, but he would be able to ditch it in a couple of minutes. He moved quickly into the large group of people in front of the stage and wormed his way up to the middle of the pack. He looked at his watch, 10:02. Ten seconds later, the band started a song, and the crowd erupted with cheers.

When everyone was looking toward the stage, he ducked down and removed both the wig and the long coat. Underneath, he wore a pair of casual pants and a golf shirt. No one even gave him a second glance as he undressed and dropped the items onto the sand, their attention one hundred percent on the electric personality of the singer.

He then worked his way toward the front of the stage, shrugging off a few angry glances and words with, "Sorry, my girlfriend is up there."

When he was just two rows of people from the front of the stage, he put his arm around the woman that he was here to see, and she turned to face him. "I thought you would never make it!" she yelled in his ear over the music.

She was dressed perfectly; beige Capri pants and a low cut T-shirt. It accentuated her cleavage so that when he looked down at her face, the swell of her breasts was easy to see. She was the final piece of the puzzle, and he was practically drooling looking at her. "Sorry, I had to take care of a few things for work." He pulled her close and rubbed her arm. Tonight was going to be the best night ever.

He just had one more thing to do, and he would be on his way to heaven.

At the end of the song, he spoke softly in her ear, "Reach into my pocket." He smiled at her when she looked confused by his request. "Just do it; it's not what you think."

The woman reached into his pocket and found a small velvet case. She looked up at him with her eyes wide. "What's this?"

The band started up again for another song number after thanking the crowd for coming out and celebrating the season opening of the beach and the pools. Warren didn't need to hear her words, her face said it all. She was pleased with the baubles that he had given her. They were high-end costume jewelry, but she wasn't smart enough to know that the earrings were fakes. In her mind, they were one carat diamond earrings that showed how much he cared.

She was the only one out of his uncommon collectables that he had wooed and who actually knew his real name. If it wasn't for her oversized nose, she could have been the one that tamed his evil ways. But just like the others, she was never going to be perfect. To top it off, the one time when he had suggested something a little kinky in the sack, she had responded with a disgusted grunt. No, she was better off as a puzzle piece instead of the whole enchilada.

"Let's go somewhere quieter," he said.

She nodded in agreement. He kissed her hard on the lips, and the two walked through the masses, over to the area of the pool that was flanked with cabanas. He had rented one earlier under a different name, and now he would have the privacy that he needed to finish his masterpiece.

Ninety-Four

SWEAT WAS POURING DOWN Devon's face. The stress was overwhelming — where the hell had Warren Frank gone? The ghostly way that the guy moved around the Las Vegas Strip was disconcerting. How could an ex-lawyer turned shoe mogul, who had never lived in the city, have such good instincts on how to get away with six murders? The answers would come in time; but first and foremost, they had to catch the bastard.

Holland's number came up on Devon's phone. "You here?"

"Yep, we've got a solid perimeter set up. He's not getting away this time. Guaranteed," Holland replied.

"I would love to believe you, but I'm not guaranteeing a damn thing at this point. He's in the crowd somewhere. We've got fifty-plus men down there, and no one can find him."

"We'll get him Devon, mark my words." Holland's confidence sounded real but Devon saw the glass as half-empty. The Lieutenant and the Mayor certainly wouldn't be patting anyone on the back at this point in time. Devon hit end, and scoured the screen for any sign of the ponytailed man.

Less than a minute later, he decided that watching from a computer control booth was no longer cutting the mustard. He was a hands-on kind of detective; staring at a series of monitors was doing nothing to improve his odds of catching their killer. He turned to Kincade. "Keep watching, and call me if you see anything. I'm heading down to the beach." As he ran toward the exit, he thought he might have heard the FBI agent trying to stop him, but he ignored the annoyance.

Two minutes later, Devon was walking from the hotel onto the man-made beach and pool area. The bright lights from the stage were pulsing with color across the writhing crowd. It was hard to distinguish faces from the back, and no one was pleased with letting him muscle his way toward the stage.

Three minutes later, trying to take the same path that he had seen Warren Frank take earlier, he got the break that he needed when he tripped over something in the sand. He radioed to the control booth. "He's not wearing the coat or the long hair anymore. Look for anyone who left the concert with a woman."

Devon stood in the middle of the beach party, wondering which way to turn. Did he go to the left? The right? Back into the casino or the hotel? He took a deep breath and let his instincts take over.

Ninety-Five

WARREN WALKED CASUALLY THROUGH the crowd with Whitney Harrison pulled close to him. To the hundreds of people who they passed on the way to the cabanas, they looked like a perfectly happy couple. She was smiling up at him, and he was looking down at her beautiful cleavage, trying to avoid getting a glimpse of her oversized nose.

When they got close to the poolside cabanas, he swept her into his arms, and carried her into the striped tent. The private space included a couch, a chair and a coffee table. All four sides were covered with privacy shades which could be lifted to allow more sun during the late afternoon, and less UV rays during the heat of the day. The Prince of Pumps had rented the space for the entire afternoon, and had hung out by the pool all day. Everything he needed was in place.

Warren placed his prey on the colorful, padded couch, and looked her over with long, slow motions. His eyes moved up and down her body, spending a considerable amount of time on her breasts. It almost brought him to tears. Tonight he would finally be able to fulfill his fantasy of having the perfect woman, and Whitney was going to be one of the key components.

Scarlett had come through for him in every way. From the very first kill a week ago when she had helped him to take the dark locks of hair through to today, everything had been perfectly timed and perfectly executed. Killing had become second nature. Not only had his confidence improved, but his skill had increased substantially as well. Scarlett was no longer his guide, but he thought that if he needed to repeat the process down the road, he was prepared both physically and mentally for the task.

He pulled his focus back to the beautiful breasts lying on the couch. They were full and round, but not too big. Maybe a 36C he guessed, and they were perfectly displayed in the low V-cut T-shirt. They were slightly tanned, but not dark and leathery. The cleavage was soft, and the skin looked silky and smooth. He felt himself getting excited as he shut the front screen to the cabana.

The mesh sides were not completely opaque; but if anyone looked over, they would simply see two lovers on the couch.

"Now, let me see you with those earrings," he whispered.

Whitney had already put them on, gathered her hair behind her neck, and was moving her head from side to side to allow him a better view.

"They're perfect. Thank you," she said.

"No. Your breasts are perfect."

He sat beside her and kissed her neck. He reached beside the cushion on the couch, and grabbed a small syringe that he had stashed earlier. He ran his free hand up from her leg to her waist, and just as he was about to touch her breast, he put the needle into her neck.

She looked at him with a mixture of shock and terror. He imagined that after receiving a pair of what she thought were large diamond earrings, the last thing she expected was a needle in the neck. She didn't even have a chance to scream before the drug took hold.

Ninety-Six

DEVON COULDN'T WAIT ANY longer; he had to make a move. Knowing that there were very few places private enough to take a life, he turned right at the stage, toward the more secluded South Lagoon Pool area. It was almost entirely deserted, with the exception of a few couples strolling around the property, lost in each other's eyes.

"Any sightings?" he asked over the radio.

Several voices responded with negative remarks.

Devon tried to get into the mind of the killer. Where would I take the woman? Somewhere close by, but not back into the hotel, because it's swarming with cops. He looked around the pool area, and was immediately struck by the sight of about a dozen cabanas. Most had the curtains pulled up, but there were three scattered around the pool deck with closed privacy screens. He un-holstered his gun.

Not wanting to alert Frank to his location, Devon chose not to call for backup. He didn't think there would be time. If the Prince had a woman in one of those tents, then moments, not minutes, were crucial.

Devon walked past the first two empty tents and tried to get an idea of what was in the third. The light of the day was gone, and it was hard for his eyes to adjust to the space beyond the dark meshed walls. He came around to the front, pushing the curtain back with his gun, ready for a confrontation with his killer.

The tent was empty.

The detective's heart was beating loudly in his ears. The next closed tent was three spaces down. If that one was empty, then the only other option was a cabana across from his current location. If he moved another five feet and the front door of the space was open, the occupants would be able to see him, and the element of surprise would be lost, not to mention that the chance of him being shot by one of the killer's hollow-point bullets increased tenfold.

He could hear that the band was announcing a twenty-minute break, and all of a sudden the Lagoon area was too quiet for his liking. The noise from the party had been covering his footsteps, and now he was exposed on so many levels...no noise, no light, and no backup. He decided to walk around to the back of the next few cabanas, to give himself a little more cover.

Devon walked behind the fourth cabana and the fifth, and was closing in on the sixth when he heard voices. There was definitely someone inside this one. Thinking that he was a little too vulnerable, he whispered into the radio, "South Lagoon Pool", and immediately turned the radio off. He didn't want any audible responses to the broadcast.

Devon doubled back to the far side of the fifth tent, and crept around toward the front. He wanted to keep his element of surprise, but needed to enter through the front opening in the curtains. With his adrenaline pumping at maximum velocity, he steadied his gun in a shooter's stance and burst through the curtain.

"Police! Get your hands in the air!"

Ninety-Seven

WARREN FRANK, AKA THE Prince, was leaning over top of an unconscious woman, with a gun held to her temple.

"Put the gun on the ground!" the detective yelled, as he came crashing into the cabana.

How the hell did they find me? The police should be everywhere but here.

"Warren, I won't tell you again — put the gun down." The cop had the muzzle of his weapon trained directly on his head.

The Prince, who had been holding the detective's stare, now looked away to Whitney's ample bosom. *Damn it.* His mind, that had been racing with lustful conjurings of the coming night's activities, was now taking stock of the reality that faced him at the other end of the gun. Where had he gone wrong? Scarlett had promised him that the police would be at the Hard Rock tonight. She was going to tip them off. He was supposed to have free reign in Mandalay Bay. What had happened?

Warren considered his options; give up the gun and his only means of defense? Or use the girl as cover to get his ass out of the casino and back on his private plane? If he could get to Mexico, he might have a fighting chance of evading arrest. He would have to give up his lucrative business either way; but he couldn't remember if Nevada had the death penalty or not, and based on his current situation, he didn't have time to Google it on his cell phone.

Warren decided to place his final bet in Las Vegas. "Stand back, or I'll put a bullet in her brain."

It was now the detective's turn — call or fold. Put a bullet in his chest and hope that he didn't pull the trigger in the meantime? Or try to bring in a negotiator? In the distance, he could hear heavy footsteps on either side of him. Backup had arrived.

"You don't want to kill her and make things worse, do you?" the cop asked.

"Hey, what's the difference at this point?" Warren replied, trying to look cocky, but feeling more scared than he was willing to admit.

"Let me have the girl, and we can talk."

"If I give you the girl, I have no bargaining power. Look, I was a lawyer for a lot of years. Let's not play games." He needed to stay calm, just like in the court room many years ago, and more recently in negotiations on hot-ticket shoe shipments. Talk slowly, and think quickly.

The cop spoke again "You're smart — sorry, I forgot your background. This entire hotel is a fortress. You can't get out. I just want to try to help you. I know you didn't do this on your own. Trust me — you have leverage. Just give up the girl, and we can talk more."

Warren thought about handing over the final parts of his masterpiece, and immediately hated the idea. Camilla was almost built. Tonight was the night that he had been waiting for. However, if he put his hands in the air, chances were that he would live to tell the tale. At least if he went to jail, he would most likely be left alone by the other inmates; a real-life lawyer was a hot commodity in lock-up, luckily wanted for his brain, and not his body.

"Just put the gun down, Warren. We can work this out."

The Prince kept thinking, but didn't move the gun away from the woman's head. He was starting to get a little pissed at Scarlett. If she hadn't encouraged him to live out his most wicked desires, then none of this would have happened. He would have been fine just buying the services of women who were willing to play dead. If it wasn't for the red-haired witch, he wouldn't be in this situation to begin with. Then he realized that if the cops were at Mandalay Bay, something bad must have happened to the one and only woman that ever really understood him. Scarlett was in trouble, too. That's when Warren Frank got mad.

The final deciding factor was the small red dot that all of a sudden showed up on his chest from the depths of the night. It was over. The Prince of Pumps pulled the gun away from his date, and swung his arms toward the detective at the front of the tent.

Ninety-Eight

EVERYTHING SEEMED TO HAPPEN all at once.

Devon pulled the trigger on his service weapon. At the same time, he heard a bullet rip by his ear. Then he felt a second bullet hit him in the arm. Then Warren Frank fell over, holding on to his leg.

But I wasn't aiming for his leg, Devon thought.

It seemed that in the same instant that Warren Frank was missing the detective with his first bullet, and hitting him with a second, another one was flying in the opposite direction toward the killer. The sharp-shooting sniper was a much better shot, and Frank screamed as two FBI agents got a direct hit.

Devon touched his arm and felt the warmth of his blood but didn't think it was a serious hit. He pushed Warren Frank off of the unconscious woman, and at the same time he kicked the man's gun outside the tent.

Devon yelled to everyone who was within ear shot, "Get an ambulance! This girl's dying!" He felt a faint pulse on the woman's neck but her eyes remained closed.

Three officers pulled Warren Frank's body from the cabana. He was still alive, but was losing quite a bit of blood. Devon heard someone radio for a second ambulance, but couldn't walk away from the woman. He held her hand and spoke quietly to her, telling her to hold on.

He couldn't help himself, and took a glance at the body parts that he knew Warren was after. The woman had beautiful breasts; but the thing that Devon found most attractive about her was her hands. Beautiful, slender hands, just like Mehgan's.

A voice interrupted his thoughts, "We'll take it from here."

Devon turned and moved away to let the paramedics do their job.

He watched as both the woman and The Prince were carried away on rolling beds to the waiting ambulances. The band had started up again, and Devon recognized the melody of a long-lost Beach Boys classic.

It was finally over. Warren Frank, the man who had been terrorizing the Las Vegas Strip for an entire week, was in custody. It was hard to believe that a man who had once been a successful lawyer, and then had parlayed his money into a multi-billion dollar Internet business, could be so sick and twisted. Proof positive that money can't buy happiness.

Ninety-Nine

"TELL ME EVERYTHING YOU can remember from today," the detective said to the owner of the store. After all of the excitement of the past seven days, the entire force was exhausted. Over ninety percent of all available officers were on the Strip. He was one of the few that were left to secure the remainder of the massive city. Overall, things had been pretty quiet; but there was still the odd domestic dispute or street fight that had to be dealt with. Everything else was being put on the back burner. The vandals, shoplifters, drug dealers and hookers were on ignore. However, the robbery of a high-profile jeweler like Grady Tellam still made the grade for an immediate response.

"There's nothing to tell. Business as usual. I just can't believe that this happened." Grady was almost in tears. Insurance would pay for the majority of the stolen inventory; but he hadn't signed up for the extra rider which would cover the uncut diamonds. He had been so caught up with Mehgan that his head had been in the clouds for most of the past month. He cursed himself for letting his little head do the thinking.

Mehgan stood by his side and squeezed his hand as he spoke to the police, and he cursed himself a second time for thinking that she was a mistake. As soon as the call came in, she had jumped off the couch and hurried him out the door, promising to stay by his side until everything was resolved. His only regret was that the robbery hadn't happened about twenty minutes later. They were in various states of undress when the call came in, and by all estimates, they would have completed the act less than a half-hour later. Now it would have to wait a few hours while he dealt with the police, the insurance company, and worst of all, the high-profile celebrity who owned the uncut diamonds. In actuality, he wondered if he could even focus on Mehgan long enough to get it up again after what had happened. The whole thing would have to wait until tomorrow.

"Did you have any unusual customers over the past few days? Anyone who looked suspicious?" The officer was taking notes.

"Really nothing strange. There was a man who was here late today. I had to hurry him out at about ten to six." He glanced at Mehgan. "We had a date." The security officer gave him a knowing nod.

Grady looked at Mehgan and smiled, wondering if he should tell the officer the rest of the story and risk making it look like he was blaming her for the night's events. He decided that he could save the details of his lax closing procedures for a later time.

"Do you have security tapes that we can look at?" The officer pointed toward the cameras mounted on the back wall above the display counter.

"Of course. I'll get you the tapes right now." Grady was walking toward the back of the store when Mehgan's cell phone rang.

She took the call and a minute later hit end. She yelled to Grady as she was running out the door, "I've got to go! They caught the sicko who's been killing the women on the Strip." She was gone before either he or the officer could comment.

One Hundred

WHEN DEVON WALKED INTO headquarters, he was met by a very upset Mehgan Bowman. "What happened? Are you okay? Someone told me you got shot?"

"I'll live. We caught him in the act. Lucky for our vic, we got there in time; and lucky for me, he had bad aim," Devon said. "The bullet just grazed my arm."

"Thank God." She shuffled from foot to foot. "Anyway, I just wanted to see you and make sure you were okay."

Devon thought that he saw the beginnings of a tear in her eye. "Thanks. I have a shitload of paperwork to do, but maybe later..." He hesitated for a moment wondering if he should ask her out for coffee.

Mehgan hugged him and gave him a brief kiss. It wasn't a long embrace, but Devon believed it to be heartfelt. "It's been nice working with you, detective. You take care of yourself." With that, she walked out the front door of the station house.

Devon was too tired to try to decipher what the hug and kiss meant. She hadn't even tried to get the inside scoop. Maybe she truly cared? He had too many other things to worry about. He told himself that he would think about the reporter...in a few days. Now was not the time to fall in love.

There were still so many strands of evidence to unravel. Warren Frank was the Strip Killer, but how did everyone else fall in?

Peter Tamis from the Hard Rock had an obvious motive. Word

on the street was that Tamis owed some money to the mob, and was desperate to pay it back. It wasn't just his hotel on the line, it was his life. The fight had been stopped in the middle of the sixth round because of the implications.

The Dedicated Defense employee, Lyle Hants, who was seen at each crime scene, seemed to be an innocent bystander, at least for now. He was a regular blackjack player who frequented most of the casinos on the strip on a weekly basis. There were no obvious ties to Warren Frank or Peter Tamis.

Paul Gregory was released once the owner of Siren's had confirmed that there were no dead bodies involved in any of his sessions. Apparently, the women were willing to spend some time in a freezer before giving themselves over to the wealthy businessman.

Reverend Clark had all but ruined his chances of redemption in the eyes of his parishioners. In the eyes of the law, he was a free man. The church wasn't quite so accepting of his pathetic attempt to regain the pulpit. Reverend Ralph Fortis had taken over the small church, and was very vocal about his contempt for Earl Wesley Clark... though he would leave the official judgment up to the Almighty.

Jackie Temple was going to be charged with the use of an unlicensed firearm, but Colin Young was apparently unwilling to press charges. He was still in the trauma unit of the hospital, but was recovering nicely.

In another trauma ward at Valley Medical, Barb Goldfinch, the woman who had lost her eyes at the Luxor, was in stable condition. The doctor's anticipated a slow, but complete, recovery. Psychologists were being brought in to deal with the mental wounds left by the killer's brutal attack.

Warren Frank had lawyered up and was secured safely in the jail's infirmary cell after a brief trip to the hospital to get patched up. Devon wanted to talk to him more than anything. If he could just get more information...who was the mystery woman who called Mehgan and led them to the house in Henderson? There were still so many details that they needed to know.

Devon met Holland and Kincade in the WAR room for their final wrap-up meeting. Their exhaustion showed in their bloodshot eyes and unshaven faces.

"I'm heading back to Quantico in the morning," Kincade said. "I'm happy that I got to work with you. You guys have a hell of a team."

"We couldn't have done it without you." Devon shook the agent's hand and smiled.

"I'll get my paperwork done from home, but I can be back on a plane in short order if you need me," Kincade added.

"Thanks for everything," Holland said.

Devon saw a look that passed between the two that was an unmistakable secret knowledge. He wondered what had happened when the two were working outside of the office. Had Holland told Kincade about his desire to leave homicide? Had Kincade encouraged him?

The three men sat together in silence for a minute before Kincade stood up to leave. Devon and Holland were finally going to spend some quality time at home for the first time in a week, and it felt good. The paperwork and the rest of the mystery could be solved after a good night's sleep.

MONDAY

One Hundred One

DEVON HAD SLEPT FOR a full fourteen hours before the nagging loose ends of the case wormed their way into his brain. Now that he had a clear head, he wanted to get back at it. There was nothing keeping him at home, no wife or children. Work was his passion, and it was time to finish putting the puzzle together.

He was met with well-wishers who congratulated him on the arrest of Warren Frank as he walked to his desk. When he got there, he immediately saw a huge note on his computer screen — "Call me ASAP". The note was signed by a fellow officer, and he wondered why the other man hadn't just called his cell. He tugged at his belt, and realized that he had forgotten it at home *again*. That was a bad habit that he was going to have to break.

Nathan Quince was a veteran on the force, and after he told Devon his suspicions, the two men were sitting in the WAR room five minutes later viewing a video.

Devon looked at the footage and was stunned by what he saw. "You sure on the dates and times here?"

"One hundred percent sure. This is the person who robbed the jewelry store. Got away with a stash that easily totaled twenty million, maybe more," Nathan said.

Quince was well-known on the force for being a straight shooter, but what Devon was seeing didn't make sense. "Holy shit. We got played." Devon's face was white as he called Holland from the conference room phone. He felt guilty disturbing him at home after only one day off, but didn't see any other choice.

"Hey partner, I think you'll want to come down to the office." Devon was pacing back and forth in the WAR room, and decided to make another call while he waited for his partner to arrive. It would take Holland forty minutes at least. If he played his cards right, they could go directly into the interrogation room when he walked through the doors.

One Hundred Two

GRADY STOOD IN HIS shop and surveyed the damage. There was broken glass everywhere. His whole life was in ruins. He had been cooperative, handing over the surveillance videos and the records of his inventory at the time of the robbery. Now he was in a state of flux. What am I supposed to do, he wondered. It was overwhelming.

While the diamond rings, necklaces and other sparkly items were fully detailed, the uncut diamonds weren't as easily identifiable. All diamonds have specific characteristics that make them special, but these small differences aren't noted and documented until their final polish. At that time, cut, color, clarity and carat are all described in minute detail and provided as proof of ownership to the lucky recipient of the new piece. It was akin to a fingerprint for the gem. The uncut stones were essentially undocumented illegal immigrants up to that point. They were a very marketable commodity, as they were virtually untraceable.

Grady had spoken to his celebrity client, and promised to replace the expensive baubles; but the damage to his reputation was done. The word on the street was that while Grady was one of the best, he could no longer be trusted. To make things worse, he hadn't seen Mehgan since she ran out the door when the Strip Killer was arrested. He had tried her cell phone a couple of times, but all he got was her voicemail. He just wanted to hear her voice; but he realized that she was equally busy getting the inside scoop on the biggest story in recent Nevada history, not to mention the scandal over the big fight — his robbery didn't even rate in the top ten items of the week.

The silence in the closed-up showroom was broken when the phone, making him jump a foot off his chair. He didn't even want to answer it. It would probably just be another customer phoning to cancel an order or get a deposit back. He glanced at the call display and his mood improved slightly. The caller ID said that the LVPD were calling. Grady took a deep breath, hoping that they were calling with good news.

"Grady here."

"Mr. Tellam, this is Detective Cartwright from the LVPD. Do you have a few moments to talk?"

Of course I have a few moments to talk, I have no goddamn business anymore—what else could possibly be taking up my time? His patience was at its breaking point, and then some. "Sure, sure. Have you found out who did this?" *Please let them have good news — please.*

"We've been reviewing your videotapes, and we're wondering if you can come down to the precinct to chat. We might have something."

Grady's heart skipped a beat with excitement. *They might have something. Please Lord, let it be true.* "I'll leave right now. It'll take me about a half-hour, but I'm on my way."

He hung up the phone and ran out the door. A tiny little part of his brain was hoping that he might run into Mehgan at the police headquarters. Maybe his luck was about to turn around.

One Hundred Three

DEVON ASKED GRADY TELLAM the first question after he showed the jewelry store owner the video from his store, "Do you know this woman?"

Grady stared at the screen and looked confused as to what his eyes were telling him. He watched the monitor as the woman smashed the displays and grabbed his stock of diamonds from the shattered cases. "She's the security woman who was in the store two weeks ago. She came in because there was a problem with the security panel. She asked me to punch in my code and…oh, shit." The video continued, and he saw the woman answer the phone, put it down, and move toward the back of the store toward his office. Tears were falling as he yelled at the screen, "Get out of my office! She's going to take the loose gems!"

Devon thought that if you could literally see the light bulb turn on in a person's head, that the picture of the three of them in the interrogation room would have been priceless. Just as the upset jeweler's light lit up, Devon had an epiphany of his own. Holland stayed to get more detail from Tellam while Devon made another phone call.

"Kincade? Yeah, I need your help. I'm going to send you two pictures, and I need you to use your special software to confirm that it's the same person."

It was a long fifteen minutes after he sent the photographs via email before he got the response. The hair was different and the clothing was different, but the two pictures were a match.

One more piece of the puzzle fell into place. One down and one to go.

Devon took the recording of the mystery woman's final call and downloaded it to his laptop. He grabbed Holland for a road trip, leaving Grady Tellam at the station house.

"I'll explain in the car!" Devon yelled.

Devon raced through the Aria's casino floor, searching everywhere for Cindy or one of the other waitresses that he had interviewed about Stacy Bailey. It was ten minutes before they found one of the women. The blond bombshell was serving drinks off of her tray in the high limit area. Red ropes blocked the detective's entrance to the space. A security guard tried to pull them back, but Devon pushed on while Holland fumbled for his badge.

Devon was standing beside the waitress as he opened up his laptop. He hit the enter key and said, "Listen." Two voices could be heard on the small speakers. "Do you recognize either of these women?" he asked.

The waitress looked confused, and was a little stunned with being ambushed in the middle of her shift; but she knew who was on the recording. "I don't know the second woman, but the first one is Stacy."

One Hundred Four

WARREN FRANK WAS BROUGHT from his cell in handcuffs and leg irons. His knee was in a brace, but the bullet had not shattered his knee cap. His arm was in a sling — the slug having just nicked the fatty part of his bicep. Devon was pleased that the man was hobbling into the room, and looked to be in a fair amount of pain; but he wished that the sniper had done a more thorough job. Unfortunately, the sharp shooter was worried about hitting the detective, and had opted for a more passive approach.

Frank had handpicked his lawyer, having had decades of experience with criminal cases himself. Mike Cross was well-known in the Phoenix area for being a ruthless negotiator, who had pulled a proverbial rabbit out of a hat on more than one occasion in a murder trial. His creative tactics that pushed the limits of the legal system had made him very unpopular with law enforcement, and well worth the exorbitant fees to his guilty clientele. Rumor had it that his last client, movie mogul Sean Kade, had paid close to ten million dollars for his freedom after he killed a woman during a session of rough sex. He had walked out a free man, despite the fact that he had come close to killing three other women in a similar fashion in the four years prior to his arrest. Mike Cross was a magician in the courtroom, and even the great Harry Houdini would be amazed at how he made evidence disappear.

Cross wasn't pleased to have to come back to the jailhouse after an already long day working with his new client, looking for legal loopholes in the case. The two men sat across the table from Devon and Holland in an interview room, not knowing why there was such an urgency to meet. "Okay boys, this better be good," Cross said.

Devon glanced at Holland, grinned, and turned back to the lawyer. "Oh, it's good." He stared at the Prince, and tried to get inside his head. He wanted the man to understand that what he was about to say was going to change the game. It was an interrogation tactic used by the best officers, and the best poker players.

"Get on with it, Detective. I've got better things to do than watch you try to intimidate my client."

Devon broke his stare with Warren, and opened his laptop on the desk. He made a few quick clicks on the keyboard, and turned the screen toward the two men. "This video was taken the same night that we arrested you, Mr. Frank. Do you want to explain it to me?"

Devon watched as Cross and his client processed what they were seeing. He wanted to see the reaction to what amounted to a good piece of evidence that would *help* their defense. Not something that the police would typically show a suspect; but under the strange circumstances, it was a fitting thing to do.

Frank's face went white. "I...I...why are you showing this to me?"

Mike Cross shook his head, unable to believe his luck. "You gentlemen just screwed your case against Mr. Frank. What's your angle?"

Holland spoke first. "We didn't screw our case, and you know it. Your client is guilty as sin of five murders and two attempted murders. We have a mountain of evidence against him — too much for even you, Mr. Cross. We caught him with a gun to a young woman's head. This video doesn't change a thing. What we want to know is, who the woman in the video is, and where we can find her now."

"Mr. Frank has nothing to say."

Devon looked at their suspect. He didn't seem quite as confident as his high-priced lawyer, but he wasn't looking like he wanted to talk. It was time to play his final card and go all in on their bet. "She's the one who gave you up, you know. She called us and told us exactly where you were going to be. That wasn't part of your deal, was it? I can't imagine that you agreed that she would rat you out on the very last day. Just as you were about to finish your statue, she told us to meet you at Mandalay Bay. Was that the deal? I guess she has the last laugh, huh? She gets the diamonds, and you get some silver bracelets." Devon chuckled and leaned back in his chair. By the look on Warren Frank's face, the message had hit its mark.

The Prince leaned in close to his lawyer and spoke in soft tones. Cross whispered in his client's ear and turned back toward the detectives. "What are you willing to do for us if Mr. Frank can help you?"

"We'll recommend life with a possibility of parole," Holland said.

Devon knew that there was still a chance he could get his client acquitted; but it was a really bad bet all around. In a city like Vegas, a smart man knew the odds.

Cross nodded to his client. "He'll tell you what he knows once we have your agreement in writing from the DA."

One Hundred Five

DEVON AND HOLLAND WALKED outside the interrogation room where the District Attorney was waiting behind the one-way glass. They exchanged nods. As soon as they had seen the jewelry store video, Holland and Devon had called Nathan Liam to the station house. The debate had already taken place long before Warren was put in the hot seat.

The conversation had been relatively short. "We have to find out who she is. There's something fucked up about what we're seeing here. This woman is behind one of the biggest robberies in our city, and there's no way she should be in this video at all. Warren's our tie to her. Plus, my instincts are telling me that this string of murders is not what we think it is."

Nathan Liam was all for solving a robbery; but the political backlash from giving this guy the potential for parole wasn't a heartwarming thought. A large percentage of the public wanted to see him fry. If the DA's office didn't live up to their end of the deal, the repercussions could be devastating. In the end he agreed to the terms of the deal.

"I want all of the details — everything that he knows," Liam called out, as the detectives walked back into the holding cell.

Devon pushed a signed agreement over to the other side of the desk, where the defense attorney read it over. The real agreement, the binding one, would come much later; but for the time being, Mike

Cross seemed happy with the two paragraphs written on the DA's letterhead.

"Mr. Frank, do you understand that as a part of this agreement, you are required to tell us the whole truth about the murders, your involvement in the robbery of the jewelry store, and your relationship with the woman on the videotape?" Devon asked.

Warren Frank glanced at his lawyer, who nodded his approval. "Yes."

"Do you also understand that if you are untruthful in any way, we will reinstate our original sentencing recommendations immediately?"

This time Frank didn't bother to look at his attorney before he spoke. "I used to be a lawyer, remember? I have Mike in the room as an advisor, and because he's the best in the business; but you can bet your badge on the fact that I understand what I'm agreeing to."

Holland, Devon and Cross all looked a little surprised by the outburst.

Devon placed the handheld recorder on the table and pressed the record button. "Well in that case, I will start the recorder, and you can start by telling us how you got involved with Stacy Bailey."

It was 10 p.m. when The Prince of Pumps started his story. No one knew that the discussion would last six hours. Even more surprising was what he said. No one in the room doubted that it was the truth, because no one could make up as story that crazy. Fact was, indeed, stranger than fiction.

One Hundred Six

"STACY BAILEY. I LOVED that woman. She was the most wonderful, amazing, sexy, woman to grace the Las Vegas Strip. She was all of those things and more; but she was also bad news, at least for me. I first met her when she was working at a club called Sirens. It's a special members-only social club that caters to people with very particular tastes." Warren was very relaxed and matter of fact about his story. It almost felt like he wanted to tell the details; that in some sick way, he was proud of what he had done.

The two detectives were taking a few notes as they listened, knowing that the in-room security was catching every facial expression and every word. A handheld recorder was just a backup to the in-house audio/video system.

"I guess you can say that I have special needs when it comes to sex." Warren paused, "How do I put this without sounding crude? I prefer my playmates cold. Not sure when that fantasy started for me. I remember being a teenager and thinking it would be cool to screw a dead woman. I wanted to play with their cold flesh. I would be able to do anything to them that I wanted without asking. It was quite the compelling thought. I even killed a couple of women in California so that I could test the theory — see if it was really as exciting as I imagined. It was."

Mike Cross grabbed his client's arm. "Stick to the facts of *this* case Warren, unless you want the death penalty on a different set of murders." He looked at Devon and added, "You have to agree that the last comment will be removed from the official transcript of this interview, or we won't be going any further."

The vein running down Devon's forehead grew enlarged and blue, but he said the word that the lawyer wanted to hear, "Agreed."

"So, as I was saying; I was interested in having sex with dead women. The fantasy was overwhelming, so to satisfy my cravings, I started to use the services of prostitutes when I came to Vegas. That was back when I was still a lawyer myself. Back then, in the early 90s, I was only here about once a month — came in to blow some of my hard-earned cash, have a few drinks, and take in a show, so to speak. I hired some girls who didn't mind lying perfectly still during the act...playing dead. As you can imagine, there weren't very many non-working girls who were lined up to get a piece of that action."

Devon didn't care about the man's sick fantasy. He wanted to get right to business. "Who is the woman in the security video?"

"It's Scarlett. But if you want me to tell you more, I would like to have a couple of little items. I'm damn hungry, and you know that the food in these places sucks. I'll keep going, but I remember a lot better if my stomach is full. I also need to hear a copy of the phone conversation you told me about. I assume that you still keep that type of thing. Two tiny items that are absolutely critical, or I'll walk back to my cell and you can go back home trying to figure out what happened this last week."

Devon jumped in before Holland went across the table and strangled their suspect. "Don't play games with us, Mr. Frank. Just get on with the story."

Warren ignored the detective. "Have you ever had the tapas at Julian Serrano's in the Aria? They are absolutely amazing. Little bites of mind-blowing flavor. I know that I could think a lot better, remember more, if you got me dinner from there. They should be able to accommodate a few plates for you if you call right away. Remember when you arrested me and you talked about leverage? I would like to use some of it now." Frank leaned back in his seat.

Holland jumped up from his chair and leaned over the table in a menacing stance, but Devon stuck his arm out to keep things under control. "We'll see what we can do for you."

The two detectives left the room.

Holland slammed the door behind them. "That motherfucker thinks that he can use us to order his dinner for him? I don't think so. What does he think; we're the concierge at the Bellagio, for fuck's sake?"

Devon looked at the Lieutenant and the DA who were behind the glass wall, and grimaced before turning to talk to his partner. "Holland, I hate this too, but he's right; he's holding all the cards right now, and we have to be smart about it. We need to know the details of the murders; we need to know about the jewelry store robbery, and most of all, we need to know if there are other people that we should arrest. Maybe the fact that he wants us to order tapas plays to our advantage. We can give him just a little bit at a time until we have the whole story."

Somehow that was the best argument that Devon Cartwright could come up with, but it seemed to resonate with the angry detective. "The balls on this guy amaze me. Asking for a snack in the middle of an interview?"

"There's a first time for everything. Hey, who knows; if I was to ever get arrested, I might ask for that too. He gets points for creativity. Let's go get a copy of that tape — the easy part. Getting the Lieutenant here to sign off on a bill from a high-end restaurant might be the tougher task. Right Lieu?"

One Hundred Seven

FORTY MINUTES LATER, THE room was filled with mouth-watering smells and sights. Holland set the dishes up along his side of the table. "Which one of these is your favorite?"

"Hard to say; they're all excellent. But if I had to choose...I guess the Brava potatoes."

"Excellent. Then we'll save those for last. You need to tell us something substantial, and we'll start to share some of this food... now GO!" Holland was in bad-cop mode. Devon wondered if part of it wasn't that his stomach was grumbling with hunger, sitting in front of a five star meal that they couldn't eat.

"Let me hear the tape first. Non-negotiable." Frank sat with his arms crossed and stared directly at Devon.

Devon took his laptop and hit play on the media player.

A woman's voice said, *"He's taking his last victim tonight. He's going to Mandalay Bay. He'll be there sometime between 8 and 10. He keeps changing his look. He'll be hard to find."*

Another woman's voice was recorded speaking next, *"Who is he going to kill? Did he tell you her name?"*

The first woman spoke again. *"I'm not sure, but I can tell you that she will be beautiful, just like the rest. Tell the police. Go get him. Please don't let him kill anyone else."*

The line went dead, and the recording ended.

Warren Frank's face gave little away as to how he was feeling. On the outside he looked calm and collected; but in the way that his eyes darted back and forth, it was obvious that he recognized the voice.

"Thank you detective. Give me a bite of that scallop, and I'm pretty sure that I'll remember a whole bunch about Scarlett."

Devon passed over a plastic fork and the takeout container filled with a perfectly seared sea scallop coated with Romesco sauce. Warren Frank cringed at using a plastic utensil, but managed to cut the chunk of seafood into two halves and quickly devoured one of the pieces.

"When I was using the services of the prostitutes, I found out another little quirky thing about my sexuality; I was getting turned off more easily in my old age. I found it hard to keep an erection if I noticed even the smallest imperfection on a woman. There are a ton of beautiful women in Vegas, and each one usually has a piece of their anatomy that draws me to them. In some cases it's their long, muscular legs, or their strong-but-lean arms. But I noticed really quickly that even if a particular woman has the most stunning eyes, chances are good that her legs might be too short, or her hair might be dried out and frizzy. Perfection was impossible to find. Imagine if this scallop was perfectly cooked and was beautifully displayed on the plate, and then you noticed a hair in the sauce. It'll turn you off your dinner, that's for sure. The same can be said for a beautiful woman.

"The harder I looked, the more that I realized that the only way to get a perfect woman was to make her myself. And based on the fact that warm wasn't a necessary critieria for me to find someone sexually attractive, it seemed possible. It was about that time that I decided to retire as a lawyer and start the online shoe company. There were so many good reasons to change professions: I had more flexibility in my schedule, I was making more money, and the women flocked to me like gamblers to Las Vegas Boulevard. As you know, I was very successful, which got me the nickname Prince of Pumps. With the money came some unexpected perks, like my membership to Sirens. That's where I met Scarlett, or as you know her, Stacy Bailey."

Everyone in the room sat in stunned silence. If there had been any doubt, it was now gone...Stacy Bailey was Scarlett.

"So you and Stacy planned to kill women so that you could have sex with dead bodies?"

Frank interrupted, "Not dead *bodies*. The perfect woman who happened to be dead. I named her Camilla...beautiful name for a very uncommon collection of perfect body parts."

"Who was the woman that you murdered in the Aria? For all intents and purposes, she was Stacy Bailey. Who is she really? And where is the woman who robbed the jewelry store?" There were so many questions that Devon wanted to ask. This was just the beginning.

"When I started going to Sirens, I requested women who would play dead. Once the management figured out what I liked, they took it to the next level, and the girls would spend a half-hour under an ice cold shower before my session with them. I started to tip really well, and the experience just got better and better. Eventually I found a favorite play toy...she called herself Scarlett. She wore a bright red wig that fell around her shoulders, and she always wore the most slutty clothes...exactly as I liked it. She did the shower thing for me so that I could have the thrill of the freezing skin in my hands. Then one day after a particularly long play session, she spoke to me. Whispered to me that she understood why it turned me on. She asked if I wanted to take it to the next level of real. She told me what she had in mind, and I agreed."

"That's when she helped you kill women?" Holland asked.

Even Cross, the defense lawyer, was sitting in stunned silence.

"Time for a trade. Did you get me the Chicken Croquetas?" The Prince held out his hand. "I'm ready for more leverage."

Reluctantly, Holland passed over the light-brown chicken-filled dumplings covered in Béchamel sauce. "Talk while you eat."

"It's not polite to talk with your mouth full, Detective. It won't take me long to eat these." He started to chew on his first croquetas as pleasured moans came out of him. Holland was getting visibly irritated, and Devon grabbed his partner's leg to calm him down. A few minutes later, Frank wiped his face on the sleeve of his prison jumpsuit, and continued on.

"Scarlett told me that she would arrange for a special treat for me the next time I came. I could hardly wait to see her that day. I was so nervous and excited. When I walked into the room, she was out cold. I mean, unconscious and freezing. She had handwritten a note that said she had taken a tranquilizer that would wear off in an hour, but that for the next sixty minutes she was mine to do whatever I wanted. I remember sitting there thinking that it must be a joke… had she actually knocked herself out so that she wouldn't move and ruin the experience? Did she really trust me that much? From that moment on, I was hooked. She was the perfect woman on the inside, even if her outsides were only perfect in some areas. She had great hands and a nice chest; but it was her willingness to do what I wanted that made her sexually attractive. Anyway, as my business became more and more successful, my visits to Sirens increased, and my sessions with Scarlett were two and three times a week. I practically started living in Vegas, and went back and forth to Phoenix when my General Manager needed me to sign paperwork; everything else I did online."

"So Scarlett gave you some pretty realistic morgue sessions. How did that progress to actual murder?" Devon asked.

"She gave me everything I needed to succeed. Not only was she a great play toy, she was a fantastic mentor as well."

One Hundred Eight

WARREN FRANK WAS EYEING up the next of the takeout containers on the other side of the table. "Not a chance. You can keep talking, or there won't be any more of these plates coming your way." Holland nipped the thought in the bud. They still didn't know anything other than the fact that Frank met Scarlett, aka Stacy Bailey, at the same private fetish club frequented by Paul Gregory. Was it a coincidence? It was time to get to the meat of the story.

"Like I said, I went to see her dozens of times over the next few months. Then one day, when I got into the room, she was sitting upright on the bed, awake and alert. I was disappointed. I was used to her being in a much more submissive position, and for a second I was pissed off that she wasn't ready for me like our other sessions. That's when she told me what she had in mind. How she would help me to get real dead bodies — all I had to do was pay her five million. A small price to pay for the real thing. That's where the conversation started; but eventually I confessed what I really wanted — not just a dead body, a perfect dead body. At first her eyes were wide, but then I think she got the master plan in place in her brain. She controlled me like I was her puppet; but at the time, I didn't care. If it wasn't for the fact that I know she was the one who ratted me out, I still wouldn't be talking to you. Once you played that tape, it all became clear; she set me up. The bitch is going to pay."

Holland and Devon glanced at each other. Things were about to get good. Finally, the truth was going to come out.

"A month ago, she told me to decide which women I wanted. The only criteria was that they had to be staff at the MGM hotels, and I couldn't pick two women from the same hotel. I blew hundreds of hours playing blackjack over the years; I already had a pretty good idea of some of the pieces that I wanted. For the rest, I went on a shopping spree. I handpicked each and every body part, and took pictures with a hidden camera. I spent hours picking just the right people to give me a perfectly shaped woman. I think you can agree that I did a good job getting each piece just right. Camilla is magnificent...just magnificent. My only real regret is that I didn't start using my play toy earlier. I kept thinking that I would wait until she was complete." Their suspect drifted off into his own thoughts.

Devon felt ill watching their killer get excited over the thoughts. "So you picked the women and made the patchwork printout. How did you get access to the women to kill them? How did you get into the hotels without being detected?"

"Scarlett gave me everything. I was given access cards, casino maps, everything that I needed to complete the murders; even instruction on the dissections and the disposal of the bodies. She planned it all out, every single detail, and it worked perfectly; until the last day. But I guess you know that, don't you detectives."

"We know about the house in Henderson. We've been there, so there's no need to pretend," Devon said.

Frank's face went white. "You didn't touch her did you?"

Devon's stomach churned with the visual the comment gave him and continued on, ignoring the question. "What's the meaning of Divinity's Desire?"

"Have you ever heard of something called the Divine Proportion or the Golden Ratio?" Met with blank stares, he continued. "Scientists have proven that the foundation of everything beautiful is the Divine Proportion, which is basically 1.6, give or take." More blank stares. "The ratio is found in everything, from nature to man-made art, and it's how the human brain judges beauty. It's hardwired into our subconscious. I wanted the perfect woman...Divinity's Desire."

No religious context whatsoever. They had been led astray by the note in Stacy's house. God had nothing to do with the killer's motivation...it was just a sick fantasy of perfection.

"Tell us about your first victim, Stacy Bailey."

This was the moment of truth for Warren Frank, and he looked around the room. Devon wondered how much was he actually going to tell. The whole truth, a partial truth omitting certain facts, or a completely fabricated fairytale? All of the men sat silently waiting for the information.

"The lobster and pineapple skewers, please."

One Hundred Nine

WARREN FINISHED THE THREE bites of the seafood. He had decided on his next move as he was savoring the small treat. After today, he would be forced to eat the slop that the prison system passed off as food. That was going to be the hardest part of the ordeal — the total lack of flavor and seasoning in his meals. With his money had come another benefit — world-class cuisine for every meal. Though he did enjoy a burger every once in a while, they were typically of the gourmet variety. No In and Out Burgers for the Prince of Pumps. That was all gone now; but for the next few hours, he could enjoy the delicate and delicious tapas one last time.

"Tell us how Stacy Bailey managed to be your first victim, but somehow robbed a jewelry store a week later."

Warren shrugged his shoulders, "It's pretty simple isn't it?...I didn't kill her."

"Then who did you kill?"

"Wow, you guys really aren't all that smart, are you? The woman looked *identical* to Stacy, but wasn't Stacy. Get it?"

"We couldn't find any evidence that she has a twin. Plus, why would she work with you to kill her twin sister?"

"All I know is that she hated the sister. She didn't get into the details, but I think the sister stole her fiancée or something — caused some crazy family rift. Not only did she help me plan the murder of her sister, she helped me do it." Warren kept thinking how the bitch deserved to go down for her betrayal of his trust. The words came so much easier when he could maintain the anger.

"What? She helped you do it?" Devon was the first one to speak, but the same words were on everyone's lips.

"It was her way of showing me that she could be trusted. We did it together. I wanted a brunette, and her sister was a brunette — it worked out perfectly. Stacy's hair is really brown, but she wears a red wig when she's working at Sirens. Once she showed me how easy it was to kill her sister and take her hair, I knew that the rest of the women would be a cinch."

Warren Frank watched the three men and gave them time to let the news sink it. Stacy Bailey wasn't dead; she was the ring leader in the murders. She had killed her own twin sister. It took almost a full minute before they asked their next question.

"So Stacy Bailey...Scarlett killed her sister; and then how did the next murders go down?"

"Like I said, Scarlett set it all up. She gave me the kit. Told me who to take on what nights and where to do it. Even gave me a suitcase for the body at the Mirage. Everything was planned to the last detail."

Holland and Devon excused themselves from the room.

One Hundred Ten

"GET MAUREEN LAMONT ON the phone. Doesn't she check fingerprints when the corpses come in to the morgue? Doesn't she need that for identification?"

Maureen picked up her home phone on the third ring. She didn't seem pleased to be woken up in the middle of the night.

Devon didn't wait for pleasantries; he got straight to the point. "Isn't it standard practice to fingerprint the victims for identification when the bodies come in to the morgue?"

"Of course. Why?" The ME sounded sleepy.

"Did you do that with Stacy Bailey, our first victim?"

"Of course. What's going on?" Maureen was slightly more alert with each question.

"We have reason to believe that Stacy Bailey is actually her own twin. Did you run her fingerprints against the database or the Aria's security logs?"

"Dammit," Maureen said, now fully awake and angry. "I took the prints, but we had so many victims piling up, and her face matched the Aria's security records. I haven't run them yet. If we get a positive ID from family or co-workers, and things are backing up like they were, I run them after the fact. I've been sorting through the rest when I can fit it in. I've been more worried about getting you ready for trial."

"Fuck, she got us good. Why would we suspect a dead woman of killing herself? She gave us the Pros and Cons list, she left the purse in her closet; she made all of the calls. She's one cold, calculating bitch," Devon said.

Holland was looking on and got the gist of the conversation. "Tell her to run the prints now. We need to know who's dead and who's alive."

Devon gave the ME some instructions as to next steps, and hung up the phone. "Where is our mystery woman now?" Devon asked.

"Let's go find out," Holland replied, as he opened the door to the interrogation room.

Devon realized that they were only scratching the surface of the story, and they were down to just two more dishes from the restaurant. This was a long night that was about to get even longer, and their leverage was being consumed at a rapid rate.

When they walked in, the two detectives could see that the defense lawyer, Mike Cross, was mortified with what was spewing from his client's lips. It didn't look like the two had conversed much on the truth prior to joining this meeting. Devon wondered if the legendary Mr. Cross was losing his edge, or his stomach, as he heard about the first murder and scalping.

"So, did you know the women personally? Or did you drug them to get them to go with you?" Devon was taking the lead again.

"Some I knew and some were strangers. I drugged most of them because it was easier to get them to stay still when I shot them. When you are harvesting body parts, you have to be careful where you put the bullet, or it ruins the parts that you want to save. Scarlett helped with that, too. She gave me a map of where to put the bullet, and where to make the cuts so that I could keep the right areas intact."

"So you just worked with Stacy? Anyone else?"

"Scarlett," Warren corrected. "She was the one who understood me best, and who explained the murder kit. She was the one I interacted with."

Mike Cross finally started to talk again. "Okay, you have proof that Stacy Bailey was the instigator in the murder plan. I think that we've fulfilled our end of the bargain. Mr. Frank will be returning to his cell now."

"Not yet," Devon growled. "What about the owner of the

Hard Rock. How was he involved? Who gave Scarlett the security access?"

Warren looked smug and bored. "Not so fast. I'll take some of those Brava Potatoes now."

One Hundred Eleven

MEHGAN BOWMAN WAS FINISHING up her piece on the infamous Strip Killer. It was due in just a couple of hours; but Devon Cartwright was on her mind. Despite everything that had happened over the past nine days, she found herself wondering, if the circumstances were different, if she would have dated the rugged homicide detective. He was everything that she liked in a man; tall, dark, handsome, smart, and he had a good job. Best of all, he was available — no ex-wives or children to cloud her relationship with him. She leaned back in her chair, took her fingers away from the keyboard, and picked up a glass of champagne.

She read the words on the screen, and wondered if anyone would be pissed at her after they read them. She was telling some truths that no one wanted to hear about Vegas and the people who called it home. She was detailing not only the story of Warren Frank, but also the story of so many people who came to Sin City looking to fulfill their deepest fantasies. Sure there was a great side to Vegas; that was what the tourism board wanted to show, and for the most part it was real. The origins of Las Vegas might have been to give couples a place to get divorced; but now it was better known as a place to get married, gamble, eat, drink, see world-class entertainment and to relax in an oasis in the dessert. It was all of those things and more. She was going to miss it when she left.

Mehgan read over what she considered to be some of the best work of her career. She felt like she had captured the true spirit of the Prince of Pumps, and how the brave detectives in the LVPD had brought him to his knees. She re-read her favorite paragraphs in the article a few more times.

Warren Frank is no different than the suburban housewife from Iowa who comes to Vegas looking to escape from her life as a soccer-mom. He is no different than the young groom who comes to town from Los Angeles looking to inject some excitement into his last few days as a bachelor. He is no different than the couple who comes from New York to blow off some steam and win a few bucks at the slot machines or tables. Warren Frank wanted what Las Vegas promises in every radio advertisement, in every TV commercial, with every blinking light and in every clang, click and clatter of the slot machines — he wanted to fulfill his fantasies. Most of all, he wanted the promise that Sin City keeps all her secrets safe for those who take advantage of her bounty.

Many readers will argue that comparing a serial killer to a housewife looking to have a few drinks and play blackjack is ludicrous. People come to Las Vegas for a dollar's worth of a dream. Maybe one day...(fill in your dream here). Some dreams will be ignored, and some will be fulfilled. We all want our chance to tug on the handle of the slot machine called life. Let's hope that the suburban housewives win more often than the Warren Frank's of the world.

Happy with the completed article, Mehgan hit send on the email which would whisk the Word document to her boss and the editing team. She glanced at her watch. She had an hour before she had to leave. One more quick email to write, and then it was time to catch her flight. The words were simple, short and to the point..."*Sorry — in another time and place, it probably would have worked.*" She set a delay on the email so that it wouldn't be sent for another twenty-four hours. Devon Cartwright deserved to know how she felt.

Mehgan grabbed her suitcase and took one last look around her apartment. For the past ten years it had been adequate for her basic needs; but it just never met the standards that she wanted for her life. She was just like Warren Frank and the millions of others who came to Vegas looking for an escape. But in just a few short hours, it was all going to be a distant memory of a life that was gambled for a chance on a better future....amazingly, it was a bet that had actually paid off.

Her only regret was that she wouldn't have time to say goodbye to the Prince of Pumps in person; after all, if it wasn't for his help, none of her dreams would be coming true.

One Hundred Twelve

"How did Stacy...Scarlett..."Devon corrected himself, "How did she get the security codes and pass keys that you needed? How did she know where and when you should kill the women without being caught? Did she have someone else on the inside?" Devon wanted everyone who had a hand in the murders behind bars. Holland was outside tracking down more detail with the ME.

Warren Frank was still eating the ample portion of potatoes, but managed to squeeze in the answer between bites, "Let's see...I think the answer would be — yes, the bitch had help. She probably fucked them over just like she screwed me. But I'm not sure that I want to talk about that just yet. These spicy potatoes are making me thirsty. I need a water. And not that tap water crap. I prefer sparkling water. Maybe a Pellegrino."

Timing couldn't have been better. A text from Holland popped up on his phone — *Come see me when you can.*

"Maybe your lawyer would like to get that for you. I'm really tired of being your personal assistant today. Mr. Cross, do you have a couple of dollars on you? There's an all-night bodega across the street. They should have what your client is asking for." Devon wanted a few minutes to check in with Holland and see if Lamont had any information.

Devon looked over at Mike Cross and saw fatigue in the man's eyes. He knew that no matter how many times you were involved in murder cases, it was never easy to sit and listen to a man confess to killing and mutilating women...especially when it was *your* client. Being on the prosecution's side of law enforcement, criminal defense lawyers were not some of his favorite people; but today, looking across the table, he actually had a twinge of sympathy for the profession. Cross really had nothing to do or say that would help the situation. At this point, his only role was to stop his client from confessing to other crimes that would result in more charges. He probably wanted a break from the cinderblock room himself. Devon thought that he might be doing him a favor.

Cross frowned at his client and the detective, but agreed to go across the street. "The interview will stop until I get back."

Devon wondered how much the killer would ultimately have to pay for that water. The five dollar bottle would probably cost close to a thousand by the time the padded hourly charge was included, along with taxes. It served him right...no sympathy for the devil.

One Hundred Thirteen

MEHGAN BOWMAN WENT THROUGH the security gates at McCarran International airport. She had packed light, and everything was stuffed into two carry-on bags. The circumstances forced her to leave everything of her prior life behind; but there hadn't been that much that she would miss anyway.

She sat at the gate and looked up at the clock. The plane would be boarding in about twenty minutes, and leaving within the hour. Just a few more hours after that, and she would be in paradise for the rest of her life.

She thought back to when she first met Stacy in the Luxor's LAX nightclub. They had become instant friends. Little did she know that the chance meeting would change her life forever. Stacy was so... alluring, and real. It was hard to describe how much she really cared for her new-found friend. The men in the clubs wanted to be with her, and the women wanted to be near her. She had a way of knowing just the right thing to say that would reel you in to her personality. The experts say that you don't remember what a person says to you, but you will always remember how they make you feel. Stacy Bailey had a way of making everyone feel like they were special, and therefore gained loyalty and trust.

Mehgan had started hanging out with the waitress several times a week, and as they became closer, Stacy had admitted to her involvement in Sirens. She said it was easy money, and unlike the prostitutes that did outcall services, the girls at Sirens were protected by security, and were able to keep the majority of their profits, minus a small cut for the house. At first the story was intriguing and appealed to the reporter in her blood. Then as time went on, Stacy pulled her further and further into the dark underworld, and finally told her the plan to rob one of her customers.

Grady was the jeweler to all of the most rich and famous citizens and visitors to the city. More importantly, he had told Stacy about all of his deepest darkest fantasies during romps at Sirens. He was a sitting duck. All Mehgan had to do was seduce him on a specific timeline, and Stacy would take care of the rest. Mehgan had never even considered stealing a pen from work up to that point; but the woman from Sirens was very convincing. Plus, her part of the deal never put her in the spotlight. Who would ever think that a reporter from the Las Vegas Sun would be part of the robbery? Stacy was so sure that she could get away with it, and the bonus at the end was worth the risk. Mehgan's cut would be three million of the total ten million dollars that Stacy estimated was available for the taking.

At first it seemed crazy, then it seemed plausible, then even probable. Within three months of the initial discussion, Mehgan was ready to go, and waiting on Stacy to pull the trigger. Then it all went so breakneck quick...Mehgan doing an article on the jewelry store, going on a date with Grady, another date, printing the article to scare people off of the Strip, another date, and finally the night in question. It had been her own idea to get in close with the cops on the case to "help" with the investigation. Being on the inside meant that she could intervene to move the investigation one way or another, and keep the cops on target for Stacy's timelines. It was her contribution to the overall plan, and it still didn't incur any additional risk.

Mehgan knew the exact moment that the robbery was going to take place, and the exact moment that Warren Frank was going to be arrested...give or take a few minutes. Her only job that night was to keep Grady hot and heavy so that his body was screaming for her and thinking with the wrong head. Stacy was responsible for everything else, including making sure that the young reporter never had to have sex with the old codger from the store. Money could buy a lot of things, but for Mehgan, it could never buy her ability to ignore the old man boobies and wrinkled butt that came along with dating someone twenty years older than her. Timing was critical, but Mehgan reasoned that giving the old fuck a blow job was well worth three million if the phone call didn't arrive at precisely the right moment. It would have been the most expensive orgasm in the history of the Strip.

Now here she was, waiting for the plane that would take her to Stacy and to her share of the loot. She looked at the clock on the terminal wall; two more minutes until they boarded. She glanced around the waiting area, and noticed a hottie sitting alone about three rows over. Early thirties, with a body to die for... she hoped that he was sitting next to her, instead of the big, fat, sweaty guy that she normally got. The hot guy made eye contact and she smiled...yes, this was going to be the beginning of something really good.

One Hundred Fourteen

OKAY, SO THE HOT guy hadn't been sitting close to her on the plane; but she had still managed to make eye contact again as she left the airport. Cancun wasn't all that big of a place. Maybe she would run into him again. For the umpteenth time that day, her thoughts went back to Devon Cartwright. He would have been an interesting man to get to know better. But, after today, she would no longer be Mehgan Bowman, and she would never be back in Las Vegas. On the upside, after today, she would be rich, and she could have any guy that she wanted.

She took a cab to the resort, and marveled at the beauty of the tropical paradise. Vegas had palm trees, but this was a luscious, green blanket dotted with colorful flowers in every direction. No dusty desert, no red rock landscaping — just unspoiled nature.

As she walked up to the check-in counter at the hotel, she could barely contain her excitement. "I'm meeting a friend. I think she's already checked us in."

"Yes ma'am. What is your friend's name?" The Mexican woman behind the counter had a smile that filled her face.

"Sandra Cayley." They had agreed that they would use each of their middle names as the alias for the Mexican hotel. It was the first of many stops they would be making. Just a day or two here, then off to the next location, until they finally reached their new home in Europe — Stacy had figured everything out to the last perfect detail.

The woman behind the counter clacked at the keys, hit enter, clacked some more, hit enter again. "Could your friend be under a different name?"

"Sorry? What did you say?" Mehgan was confused.

"Your friend, she has a different name? I not find her."

"Try Cayley Sandra. The other way around."

The front desk clerk's fingers worked the keyboard again. *Click, clack, enter, click, click, clack, enter.* "She not here. Are you at wrong hotel? Maybe she staying somewhere else?"

Mehgan grabbed the handles of her suitcases and looked behind her. There was a line. She needed to call Stacy to find out what was going on. She had called yesterday to confirm the name of the hotel and the flight schedule. Stacy had said it was beautiful in the hotel, and had described the lobby to a tee. "Sorry, I need to make a phone call. I'll be right back."

As Mehgan walked from the front desk to a sitting area a few feet off to the right, she noticed that her luck was improving. The hot guy from the plane was standing in the check in line at the same hotel. Unfortunately, she didn't have time to start flirting; first things first, find Stacy, and *then* try to meet the guy. If he was staying in the hotel, they would run into each other at the pool or the bar; there was plenty of time.

Mehgan looked at her phone, which had switched itself into roaming mode. The call would cost about ten bucks a minute, but it would be the last call that she would make on this phone, and she was never going to pay the bill, so it really didn't matter. She went to the phone log and retrieved the number that Stacy had called her from the day prior. After a few moments, a message broadcast that the number was no longer in service. A wave of panic swept over her as she considered that Stacy might have been picked up by the police, and might be sitting in a Mexican jail somewhere. Or maybe the cops were hot on her trail, and she had to take off and couldn't use her phone.

She went back to the front desk. "Did anyone leave a package or an envelope for me? My name is Mehgan Bowman."

The front desk clerk looked a bit irritated for the interruption, but took a moment to look on the back counter. "Mehgan...Mehgan," she said, as she thumbed through a stack of mail. "Here is the letter." The woman handed over the envelope without asking for ID.

Mehgan opened the envelope to find a room key for a suite on the third floor. Okay, Stacy had to change her code name at the last second, and had to ditch the cell phone. This cloak-and-dagger stuff was nerve-wracking, and the reporter couldn't wait to see her friend — everything would be better once she saw Stacy. The hot guy was almost to the front of the line and for a split second, Mehgan was tempted to go and chat him up. Oh well, like the old saying goes — there are plenty of fish in the sea.

One Hundred Fifteen

THE INTERVIEW WITH WARREN Frank continued for hours more. He had given up the details of each and every moment of his interactions with Stacy Bailey, aka Scarlett. The story seemed to be too strange to be true. A prominent businessman throws his whole life away for a collection of perfect body parts. Plus, he admitted that he paid her five million dollars for the instruction kit.

Frank seemed to be in the dark when it came to the robbery. If Stacy had planned it from the beginning, he had no knowledge of her escapades. He knew nothing about who else was involved in the making of his instruction sheets. He mused that she must have had at least a security guard or two on her payroll.

Frank had no details on the tie-in to Peter Tamis. According to Stacy, a friend had provided the home for his use for an indefinite term. Warren Frank seemed to be as much in the dark as everyone else involved in the case and also denied any knowledge of Bill Baxter and Stacy's previous work arrangements.

"I can't believe that she did this alone. Tamis has to be involved somehow. And at least one of the security companies is in on this," Holland said to his partner, just outside of the interrogation room.

"We've got Tamis in lock-up. He'll talk eventually. Frank said that he doesn't have an address for Stacy, and I believe it — he was just a pawn," Devon replied. "I'm going to talk to the Lieutenant to get permission to go after her. She's a murderer and a thief. I figure he'll approve the expenses."

Devon looked at his partner and wondered if he should ask the question that was on the top of his mind. It could backfire..."You thought any more about putting in for a transfer? Or are you gonna go and get this woman with me?"

Holland's mind seemed to drift away. Devon knew that he was probably thinking of his wife and daughter.

"I talked to Maggie yesterday. Even before she heard the latest developments, she told me to keep going...said that I would be a bear if I wasn't working homicide. Said she wanted our kids to grow up in a community that was protected by men like me. Said she felt safer...I guess I wanted her to make the choice. I didn't want to be my dad, you know."

Devon grabbed his partner's hand with a firm grip and shook it vigorously. "Maggie is a good woman. Glad to have you back, buddy."

One Hundred Sixteen

THE ELEVATORS IN THE hotel were as slow as the second coming, and Mehgan considered taking the stairs. The weight of two carry-on suitcases and her purse convinced her otherwise. Three flights was normally not an issue; but she was feeling the effects of the humidity, and it was making her feel sticky and tired. Her body was used to the dry desert heat, and a cold shower was going to feel like a million bucks. The elevator finally opened up with a sharp *bing* of a bell, and she got in. After pressing the button for the third floor, she leaned against the back wall of the enclosure, finally able to relax. The heavy doors pulled together, and she started the rise to her new life.

Mehgan knocked lightly on the door to announce herself as she put the key in the lock. The room's temperature was in stark contrast to the hot outdoor air, and she was thrilled to have air conditioning. "Stacy, you here?" she called out.

No one answered, so she dropped her bags at the front door, and after a quick glance in the room, headed to the washroom to throw some water on her face and empty her bladder. She was a little disappointed that her partner wasn't here to meet her, and that the instructions to get into the room were changed without her knowledge; but in a few days, none of that would matter. She just had to keep her focus on the big prize.

Just as the first droplets of cold water hit her face, she heard a key in the door. Yay, Stacy was finally here, and they could go and grab a drink at the bar. All would be forgiven once she had a vodka and coke in her system.

Mehgan was coming out of the bathroom at the same moment that the man was coming in. Both screamed like little girls as they ran into each other in the doorway.

"Get out of my room!" Mehgan yelled.

"You're wrong lady, this is *my* room!"

Mehgan was surprised that the man in front of her was the same hottie that she had seen on the plane and then again in the lobby. "Look, there must be a mistake. Just go back to the front desk and tell them that you were given the wrong room key."

"I can't do that, because a friend of mine checked me in already. This is *her* room and *her* room key. Take your own advice and *you* go to the hotel lobby," he said.

Mehgan looked at him again, and something clicked. It was an ah-ha moment that she hadn't even considered would be a possibility up until the exact second that she heard those words. "What's your friend's name?" It seemed that Stacy had more than one partner.

"Look lady; please just go back to the lobby. I'm sure they can get you another room A-sap."

Mehgan screamed at him, "What is your friend's name? Tell me what her name is!"

The man looked confused, but seemed to understood that there was only one way to get rid of the screaming lunatic in his hotel suite. "Stacy is her name. Now go back downstairs before I call security."

"Look, asshole. If you came here to meet Stacy Bailey, then we are *both* in the right room. I saw you on the plane from Vegas. Obviously, she wanted us to meet here. I wish she would have told me ahead of time; but I'm sure she'll be here soon to explain, so why don't you just sit and relax."

The strange man settled into a less-aggressive stance and stepped back from the doorway. "She didn't tell me that you would be here either. I'm sorry."

Her head was spinning...what part had the guy played in the overall plan? Had he been part of the inside team? Mehgan walked past him and grabbed her luggage from the hallway. "I'm going to go and sit on the balcony until she gets back." She walked into the main part of the suite and put her bags beside the farthest queen size bed. There was no way she was unpacking until Stacy showed up. She was about to walk out onto the outdoor balcony when something caught her eye. There were white envelopes on each of the beds. One was addressed to her, and the other was addressed to someone named Lyle, presumably the hot guy who was currently using the facilities.

Mehgan opened the envelope with her name on it, pulled out a single page and read the first few lines. The string of curses that came out of her mouth went on for a long time, and brought the strange man from the washroom running.

"I'm going to hunt that bitch down if it's the last thing I do."

One Hundred Seventeen

THE PLAN HAD GONE off without a hitch. Stacy Bailey ordered another drink from the bartender at Foxy's. The outdoor cantina in the Caribbean was known for its celebrity guest list at New Year's eve. Early spring was a perfect time to rest, relax and drink the house specialty — the Pain Killer. A mixture of local rum, pineapple juice and coconut milk, it was a deadly strong concoction. One could make you relax, two would numb your face and three could kill whatever pain you had, physical or mental. It was a favorite drink of the tourists and locals alike. Today, it was exactly what Stacy needed.

The islands were God's country, in her mind. They were the bluest water, coupled with the greenest grass, the tallest trees and the most fragrant flowers. Best of all, there were so many islands, that if you wanted to disappear for a few years, it was easy to do. The word paradise didn't even come close to describing the scenery, and the people were friendly and kind. She was pleased that she had chosen this place to spend a couple of years. Eventually she would move on, but for now, it was perfect.

She mentally gave herself a pat on the back. From her initial conversations with the Hard Rock's owner, to her manipulation of Griz Hanson, her rich Chinese customer, Stacy Bailey, Lyle Hants and her sister, not one thing had misfired the whole time.

By now Lyle and Mehgan would be at the hotel and would understand what had happened. They would know that they weren't going to get a cut of the diamonds, or anything else, for that matter.

Lyle would be back at work in a couple of weeks, developing the software that ran the hotel security systems. He was the one piece of the puzzle that she wished she could have brought along with her. He was a specimen for sure; and his need for a dominant woman, that had brought him into her life two years before, turned her on.

Mehgan Bowman was a patsy right from the start, but she had served a purpose. She wrote the articles that got the fight moved, which had paid out handsomely; and she had played the sexy lure for Grady Tellam. It was just dumb luck that she had weaseled her way into the police investigation. She had been an inside source that was worth three million dollars Stacy had promised her.

If not for Mehgan's insider knowledge, Bill Baxter might have blabbed too much. He was silenced as soon as Mehgan had told her the police were looking for his sorry-ass. It turned out his life was worth a grand total of ten thousand dollars.

In payment for Mehgan's loyalty, a two-week vacation with Lyle was all she was getting, but it was a generous offer, seeing as she would be able to go back to work, and her boss would be in the dark about her real involvement. Neither Lyle nor Mehgan would be implicated in the murders or the robbery. So, after they were done lounging in the sun, they could go back to their regular lives. Stacy thought that once they were over the initial shock of the situation, they might actually enjoy each other's company. Both of them were nice people. Maybe one day they might even fall in love.

Peter at the Hard Rock had paid her a half-million for getting the fight moved to his hotel, getting Chet to go down in the sixth, and getting the Chinese businessman, Bobby Fung, to stay at his hotel. She wondered if he had made the money he needed to pay the mobster who had financed his hotel. On the one hand, she kind of liked the man; but she hoped that the cops would put two and two together and arrest him — she thought that she had provided enough clues. He had been a generous customer over the years; but no matter what, he would always think of her as a whore.

The diamonds were safely tucked away, and wouldn't be sold for at least another five years. They were considered too hot for the time being, which was fine. The five million from Warren Frank, and five hundred thousand from Peter Tamis would tide her over until she could sell the rocks.

Over and above the thrill of the huge wad of money and diamonds, Stacy was even more excited about the other successful part of the operation. Her sister was finally out of her life. Over the years, she had heard many stories about identical twins that were bonded in special ways. Not so with her and Brandy. The bitch had done the ultimate in betrayals, and now she had paid the price.

From the moment that Stacy had first met Todd, she was head over heels in love. Everything he said and did was perfect. He sent flowers, he arranged for romantic dinners, he even gave her massages when she got home from work. Six months later, they were engaged. He was a stock broker, and he didn't want her working in the casinos anymore...he wanted her to stay at home and make babies. It was all perfect. Then, after leaving her shift early one night, she came home to find him in bed...with her. The only person that should have been by her side through thick and thin...her best friend...her damn twin! She had yelled, screamed and thrown a few things at the two of them; but nothing could take away the pain of what she had seen.

Brandy had tried to apologize and explain. But the final blow came when she said she can been a victim of love. *A fucking victim?* Unless Todd raped her, which it was obvious he didn't, Brandy was never a victim. She made the choice to sleep with Todd. She was a manipulative, lying cheat...but never a victim. Stacy never forgot the knife that her sister had twisted in her heart. The happy couple got married, and then it was Brandy, not Stacy, who was staying at home instead of serving drinks at the casino. The bitch had stolen everything away.

The plan came together quickly after that.

Brandy had been happy when Stacy called and suggested that she come to Vegas. They would spend two nights in the hotel, and then off to Paris for a girl's week to reconnect. Everything was forgiven...

"You look sad," the man behind the bar said. His head was covered in dreadlocks, and he was dressed in shorts and a multi-colored shirt.

"No, not sad. I'm happy to be here. I've been waiting a long time for this."

"Where you from?" he asked the blond with the bright-green eyes.

"Southern U.S. I'm supposed to be taking a vacation but I'm likin' it so much, I might stay for a while."

The man behind the counter grinned with a huge, gap-toothed smile. "A pretty lady like you would be missed if you never went back. There's no man who gonna miss you? No motha, brotha, or sista?"

"I lost my sister recently. Terrible accident. Guess you could say that I lost a piece of myself when she died." Stacy stirred the milky drink and took a big gulp. Her face was starting to feel the effects of the rum.

"Sorry ta' hear that. Well, you stay as long as you need to. The islands are great for losin' track of your problems. Sometimes people lose their old self and find someone new instead."

Stacy nodded and smiled. The Rasta bartender had no idea how close he was to the truth.

"So, what's your name pretty lady?"

The two people she admired most were Calamity Jane and Bonnie Parker, both top-notch thieves in their time. "Jane Parker. But everyone just calls me Ruby."

Acknowledgements

First and foremost, thank you to all of the wonderful readers who take the time to read my books. Your support is truly appreciated.

As always, I am indebted to my husband, Wayne, who makes me smile every day and encourages me to keep going even when times get tough.

A special thank you to Calgary Police homicide detective, Robin Greenwood (ret.), who took time out to read and critique my first draft.

As well, my appreciation goes out to the wonderful staff at Emeril's New Orleans Fish House in the MGM Las Vegas: Carie Baker (who gave me ideas for perfect kill sites); and Isaac and Arturo (bartenders supreme who are an endless source of entertainment).

Scott Bryan was irreplaceable; showing me how to shoot weapons at the Las Vegas Gun Store, and teaching me about ammunition (though any errors in the novel are completely my own).

Thank you to those who read my first draft of this story and helped me to make it better: Stacy Stevens, Ginny Hanes, Mike Gill, and my sister, Tania Werner.

Thanks once again to: Steven MacDonald for his creative cover design; the real Lee Fisher (LVA Fotos) for the author portrait; and to my editor Lee Ann, who provide invaluable input to the finished novel.

Finally, for all of the hardworking waitresses, waiters, and service staff who are the heart of every restaurant, bar, and hotel – I salute you!

LISA DEWAR HAS WORKED in the Information Technology industry for over twenty years. When she isn't working or writing fiction, she actively seeks out animal adventures around the globe. Lisa lives in Alberta, Canada with her husband, Wayne, and their two cats.

For more information on upcoming novels
or to contact Lisa, please visit
www.lisadewarbooks.com